W. D. CAMPBELL

INTO THE WRONG HANDS

This book is a work of realistic fiction. Names, Characters, Places, and Incidents have been changed or are products of the author's imagination. Any resemblance to actual events, or locales, or persons, living or dead is entirely coincidental.

KMP
KREEATIVEMINDS PUBLICATIONS
ATLANTA

INTO THE WRONG HANDS

Published By:
KREEATIVEMINDS PUBLICATIONS
Book cover designed by: Mike Marrone of Clash Graphics

This book is an original publication of
Library of congress Cataloging-in-Publication Data

ISBN:**978-0-692-89561-0**
First KreeativeMinds Publications paper edition
10 9 8 7 6 5 4 3 2 1

www.intothewronghands.com

Printed in the United States of America

W. D. CAMPBELL

INTO THE WRONG HANDS

KMP
KREEATIVEMINDS PUBLICATIONS
ATLANTA

"Author's Notes"

I felt it would be generous to provide validation to the readers, and unbelievers who surprise the hell out of me by detailing secrets of the underground world of Identity Theft.

I was taken on an uninvited trip through memory lane of rare footages, rare scenes, and the whereabouts of one man and his loyal associates.

Inside these pages, you're about to read about an unimaginable world, but beware, it happens in our day-to-day lives and right under our noses.

Governments around the world have tried to clamp down on the destruction of I.D.T., but one man's knowledge, one man's ability to share his experiences will change the minds of millions.

People beware or should I say to all of you who are reading this…always try to protect who you are and your credentials. Because if you don't, someone else may just try to use them and become you for as long as it is financially convenient to do so.

W.D. Campbell

Prologue

Somewhere in an undisclosed location...I could hear him say...

Alright people, I'm going to make this brief. Our operation has been compromised; they're on to us big time and it's just a matter of time before we get discovered, and we all know what that means.

His baritone voice broke through the silence in the room, commanding everyone's undivided attention. This was a very serious matter, he knew it, and he wanted to make sure they knew it too. There was no time for mistakes, no time for second-guessing. Every moment would count against the clock, so it was vital that every member of his team was on point in this situation.

"Because things just got real one of his team members blurted out. Is that what you were trying to say?"

"Everything must be cleaned up!" he bellowed, slamming his hand on the table for emphasis. "Credit cards need to be cut up in a million pieces, profiles, credit reports, and banking records all need to be shredded. And all hard drives on every computer we have must be wiped cleaned." Then as if it was an afterthought, he added, "oh, and your cell phones, lay them all on the table."

A couple of the men sitting to his left looked nervous. This made him a little agitated and struck a nerve. He had seemed really calm up until that point.

"Excuse me," he said, scowling at the two gentlemen. "Did I say something to offend you?"

The look of defeat was evident on their faces, they couldn't even look at their leader except out of the corner of their eyes.

"Look at me when I'm talking to you!" he ordered. Is there a problem here? Because if there is, I have absolutely no problem eliminating that problem, right here, right now!

“And believe me, I will not lose a wink of sleep over it. So, is everyone clear on what needs to be done?”

At that moment, a rat scurried across the floor --the only sound that was heard. Everyone at the table was still and quiet as scanned documents and items were sprawled across the top of the table. The leader focused on the four-legged critter that had quietly invaded this clandestine meeting.

“You guys see that rat over there in the corner?” As if the rodent knew they were looking; it suddenly paused in its tracks.

“It’s ironic that he would show up at a time like this. Because I believe he is not the only rat in the room.” His statement caused mouths to drop and shocked expressions came across all the faces in the room as he continued to speak.

“The only differences between that rat over there and the one I'm speaking of is, one has four legs, and the other has two. One can talk and that rat over there certainly isn’t talking!”

There was dead silence in the room as everyone glanced at each other. Yet no one moved or changed their original facial expression for fear of looking suspicious. Everyone present wondered who he was talking about. Who was the other rat in the room?

“Oh, don't worry, it will be revealed in due time he said with a smirk on his face. For now, the mission at hand is of the utmost importance. Learned a long time ago that every rat has its day. Well, I will make sure that the rat on this team is exterminated in due time. I am Averie Bod'e. My word is my bond and those that know me know that.”

“The world of Mr. AVERIE BOD`E”

There will be lots of unanswered questions as you read about the life of Averie Bod’e. Yet, the most raised question is, was he just a myth?

From one state to the next...

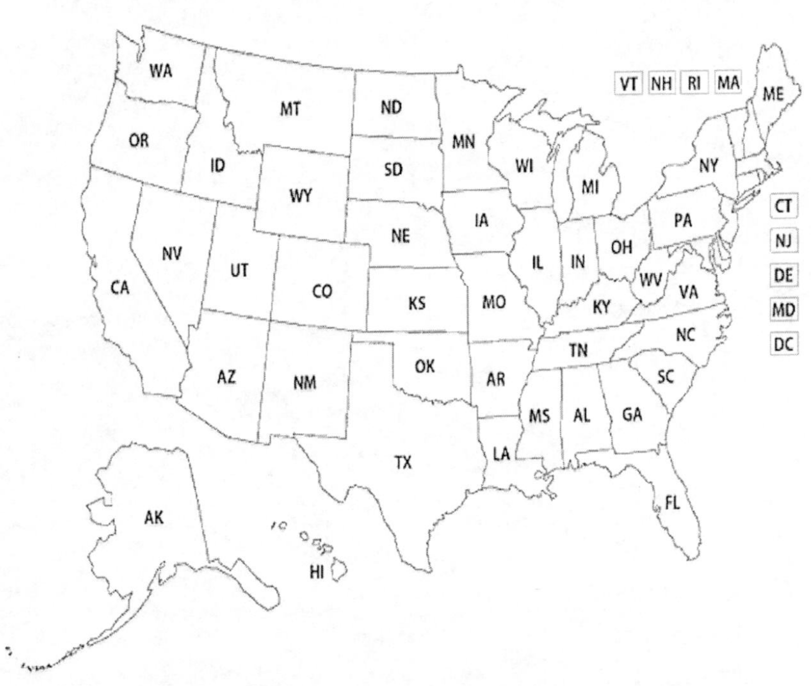

Millions will do anything to stop him... He on the other hand...will do whatever it takes from falling...

INTO THE WRONG HANDS

1

September 12, 2017
1:15 PM

The convoy of unmarked sedans sped down Interstate 20/75 South / 285 East

They were on their way to apprehend the nefarious Averie Bod'e. They had been secretly tipped off by an anonymous source. Using sophisticated tracking devices, the authorities were able to mount a special striking task force to go out and bring him in. Their motivation was simple: take down the head and the rest would fall.

F.B.I. special agent, Mark Bellows, Secret Service special agent, Darius Cornwall, and G.B.I. special agent, Melanie Perez, oversaw the entire operation. On several occasions, he had cleverly managed to talk and maneuver his way out of the hands of the force. It had taken nearly a year's worth of sleepless nights to even get this close to bringing down one of America's most wanted and feared men. So, their plan of action had to work perfectly. Failure was not an option; they could not let this man slip through their fingers again.

The image of each team member was displayed on the monitor mounted on the dashboard of the black SUV. Each vehicle knew the subject and all of them had a role to play in his capture.

"I still can't believe he made himself into all of those people. Did you read the file on this guy?"

"Did I? I couldn't put it down. It's amazing at how easily we all can fall victim to having our identities stolen or manipulated. If we can get him in custody, we will be doing the entire world a great service," Agent Cornwall stated emphatically as he swerved in and out of traffic with agent Perez.

"If? Oh, we will get him. There's no doubt in my mind. Too much time has been spent on this operation, not to mention the bonus Director Samuel Jackson talked about in the briefing."

Special agents Darius Cornwall and Melanie Perez were determined to make good on their word to Director Jackson. Nothing was going to get in the way of completing this mission.

Sirens blazed and filled the airspace of the city of Atlanta, echoing off the tall buildings as the cars roared through the Peachtree streets. Each agent, and the locals, had their assignment. They knew the danger involved, they just had to follow the directives to the letter to ensure success. In addition, backup was ready and brought in to give aerial support. With all the coverage and the latest technology, there was no chance of escape. The high-speed trail of federal and local police vehicles entered through a tunnel on 75 south exiting the city. Their destination was the secret meeting location of Mr. Averie Bod'e and his regime. The tracking device would lead them right to him, at least that was their hope. So far, every piece of information they had received seemed to be accurate. And now, after seeing the large storage units set off from the main road, they knew they had sniffed him out.

A few more miles later, they were there.

"Averie Bod`e, this is the F.B.I., come out with your hands in the air," then he paused for effect. This felt so good. "We have the whole place surrounded."

The voice coming through the bullhorn echoed against the metal walls of the warehouse. "We know you're armed, we want to take you peaceably, so don't force us to take you by force. It won't be pretty; cooperating is your best move!" The voice on the bullhorn shouted once again.

Inside, there was panic as the team scurried.

"Averie, come on, let's go! We must leave now. They're too close," Claude warned.

"I believe they have already gotten too close," Averie added calmly. He was obviously disturbed by something else. His peace had been disrupted by this intrusion and more so by the leak in the once-secure fortress of people he surrounded himself with. Thoughts ran through his head as sharp as lighting as to who would have and why?

"Frank, pull him out. You guys must get out of there now. They'll be coming in any second now." Frank called out through his earpiece. He was positioned at the rendezvous point and had a clear visual on the authorities posted out front.

"We'll make it."

"Is everything together Steve?" Mr. B. asked calmly, as if time were on their side.

"Yes, I have the plane tickets and all the passports. How long before you reach me?"

"What's with all the questions? You'll know when I get there; you need to get out of there first. Just be at the destination. Oh, and Steve, if I find out it was you who set us up, I'd sure hate to be you." Mr. B.'s tone was threatening enough for him to get the message.

"What! Why would you think I would do something like that?" Steve said defensively.

"Too many unanswered questions. Just remember what I said."

"Whatever, old man!" He hung up the phone with authority.

"Averie, we need to go now, Mr. B. is awaiting us."

Averie had known Mr. B. for a very long time and never questioned him. He had proven to be the most faithful member of his team and all Averie had to do was say the word and Mr. B. would act --one swing and darkness would fill his victim's world.

"Alex, what do you see?"

"A whole lot of feds, sir."

"What are they doing outside and how much time before they come in?"

"Swat team is in position, maybe three minutes tops, sir." Averie just nodded.

"Tom, you, Claude, and Alex, know what needs to be done here, right?"

"Yes, we're just waiting for everyone to clear out, sir."

"Remember, leave no evidence. The last thing we need is a paper trail."

"Gotcha, Boss."

"I'll see you guys in 30 minutes."

Outside there was activity, enough to draw the attention of those inside.

"Hey… I think they're coming in!"

This news did not sit well with Averie.

"I just asked you twenty seconds ago, how much time we had," Averie ran his palm over his face. How did they even find us -- on foot no less -- unless someone on my team provided them with our GPS tracking device."

No one spoke as he paced. And when he stopped pacing, the menace in his voice was unmistakable.

"When I find out who did this, they'll wish they were never born. I promise you!"

His threat was loud and clear. All the others knew what he was capable of doing. The room remained quiet.

"You have 60 seconds to come out or we'll smoke you out," came the voice over the bullhorn.

"What do we do now Boss?"

"Time for plan B. Everyone get your gear on. Thirty seconds."

"Twenty seconds, Averie, I'm giving you twenty seconds and counting."

"Is everybody ready?"

"Yes Boss. We're ready to make history again," said Tom who had always been the dramatic one. A loud boom came as the battering ram crumbled the steel door entrance to the warehouse.

"F.B.I. ---Get on your knees now! Hands up! Hands up!"

The shouts were coming from every angle. No one responded as more agents entered in a flurry.

"Boom–Boom–Boom. All agents take cover!"

"Frank, raise it up. Let's get a move on it, move it now." Averie instructed from his head piece to the earphones of his team.

"Yes sir."

"This pipeline was a splendid idea sir, the perfect escape," said Alex.

"Yes, now hurry your ass up and get in."

The F.B.I. agents searched around for traces of Averie and his team. When the dust cleared, they were nowhere to be found.

"Where did they go? I want answers and I want them now!" Special Agent Bellows, the lead agent in charge called out.

At the scheduled time, all of Averie's men were present and accounted for. The team was ready to split up and get prepared for the upcoming flight and Phase II of their operation. Averie felt relieved that he had once again eluded the authorities and had full confidence that his plans would succeed. There was a lot riding on the success of his new mission and so much at stake.

After Averie bid farewell to his comrades, his long-time journeyman, Mr. B., prepared for their trip ahead. Always close by, Mr. B was his right-hand man.

"Well, Mr. B., we should be getting out of here."

Right at that moment, a black helicopter hovered above them. Down below, an army of black Sedans screeched to a halt. Averie was surrounded on every side. There was no escaping this. Guns were drawn and pointed at both Averie and Mr. B. ordering them to exit from their vehicle. They could go nowhere; there was no means of escape. The end had come well before its time and Averie Bod`e was finally boxed in. "Damn it!" was all he said to Mr. B.

2

It was flashing on the news now…. the apprehension of an unknown perpetrator…finally caught.

The popular local news anchor was standing outside live at the Federal Courthouse in Atlanta for the arraignment of Averie Bod`e. As the other anchors positioned themselves around the podium back at the studio, I heard one of them say, "Vicki, can you tell us what's happening now at the courthouse?"

"As you can see behind me, there are many police officials from all agencies ready for the unexpected," Vicki said, looking directly into the TV camera, with the courthouse looming in the background.

No other story was more newsworthy that day and the media was out in full force. How did he do it and get away with it for so long? The word "Notorious" was an understatement when it came to describing this menacing figure. However, truth be told, he wasn't menacing to the naked eye. In fact, his appearance was quite alluring and that's exactly what allowed him to ease his way into the lives of thousands, making his actions the ire of many. One man and his team of devoted colleagues had put together an organization that was as tight knit as the mob. This team was tailored and orchestrated by the mind of a genius. The people who were victimized and those who were now witnessing this event, could hardly use the term 'genius' to boost this man's already bolstered ego, but the truth is the truth. Respect should be given on any level when it is due.

"Vicki, can you give us an account of what's actually going on inside?"

"Sharon, I've just been informed from inside sources that moments ago Mr. Averie Bod`e was transported by helicopter and then escorted through a secret tunnel in the building by his trial lawyers."

"What should we expect to take place next?"

"I was told that they would process this arraignment as quickly as possible. In fact, they have cancelled all court hearings this morning specifically for this case."

"Now, that's a first!" the corresponding reporter commented.

What was not expressed was just how detrimental it was to bring Averie Bod`e to justice. It was not just a case of bringing down a criminal; this was a matter of national security. His presence in society would impact as many as the AIDSs epidemic or a Natural Disaster. Why? Because Averie Bod`e was capable of taking down thousands of people with one sequence of events. The world didn't understand the magnitude of the damage that could be done by this one man.

"Vicki, let me get the facts straight. The United States government has built a case against Averie Bod`e, one of the most notorious identity fraud villains. A threat not only to our country but also to the world, hoping to convict him and put him away for how many years?"

"Wait! I'm hearing now that Mr. Averie Bod`e and the driver in the apprehension and their attorneys are in front of the judge for the arraignment to enter a plea?"

Vicki, can you go over the charges for us. Tell us exactly what Mr. Averie Bod`e has been charged with?

SUPERIOR COURTS
OF THE
UNITED STATES OF AMERICA
VS.
AVERIE BOD`E

January – December
Criminal No. 17CR17010-B
Defendant: Offense[s]
Counts: 1-40
Conspiracy to commit forgery-Felon
Counts: 41-400
Financial Identity Fraud –Felon

To all charges, how does your client wish to plea?
"Not Guilty"
"Bail?"

3

He just pleaded not guilty….

Pure pandemonium broke out inside the Federal Court house building in downtown Atlanta. The massive number of people there and their reaction to the news mirrored what it would have been if this were a high-profile murder trial. When news of the plea bargain leaked, some people cried, while most-- livid and irate -- yelled obscenities and threatened the officers guarding the court room.

"He just can't get away with this!" someone shouted.

This isn't justice! Someone else yelled out, "he's a thief", loud enough for the presiding judge to get an ear full.

"We will have order in this courtroom. Order I say!" The judge continually banged her gavel trying to regain control of the courtroom. The noise finally subsided, then ceased.

"There will be no more outbursts in my courtroom. None! Is that understood?"

"Silence filled the air."

"Anymore outbursts from this moment on and I will have those responsible held for contempt."

A low whisper came from the crowd, "I cannot believe what is happening here. Why is this person even given the opportunity to make a plea? He should be in chains with all the damage he's done to so many lives."

"Wait a minute. Didn't I say no more interruptions in my

courtroom? That does apply to you too young lady." A very famous female talk show host had blurted out. The judge politely told her, "You may be a star in T.V. land, but in this courtroom, I have star power, got it?"

Some found the judge's candor refreshing and stress relieving. A light chuckle circled the room. At that point, the TV star started to speak again, "Crystal clear, your honor. I do apologize for my comment."

"But your Honor, are you seriously allowing this enemy of the state and his associate back into society again. Not again please."

"Please refrain from anymore open statements or opinions young lady."

"Yes, Your Honor," she responded humbly.

"Mr. Bod`e, you do understand each of the charges that have been brought against you? Correct?"

"Yes Ma'am."

"No, you'll address me as Your Honor."

"*Yes, your honor, with your non-getting-laid ass*," was what Averie really wanted to say, but instead, with a smile, he said, "yes ma'am, Your Honor."

"Giving me the turtle eyes," the judge said, giving Averie a look. "Have there been any threats or promises made to you by this court or the prosecutor?"

"No ma'am, I mean Your Honor."

"People on bail?"

"Your honor the defendant is a flight risk and threat to society. The people ask that bail be denied, that the defendant be remanded."

"Your honor, my client is a model citizen and last time I checked innocent till guilty."

"If you make bond Mr. Bod'e, which I do know you will, you're not to travel outside the country or the confines of this state. If you need to travel outside the state, you may contact your lawyer and he will need to make a request. Do you understand Mr. Bod`e?"

"Yes, your honor."

"Bond is set at 4 million dollars cash. Court is dismissed."

There were celebrities present, as well as dignitaries and government officials. It appeared to be that Averie Bod'e had just as many friends as he did enemies. Or maybe no one wanted to miss the opportunity to be seen, since cameras were everywhere.

*****

The sound of cell doors closing vibrated throughout the narrow corridor. Officers with dull brown uniforms patrolled the hallway; one was in route delivering mail. She was a hefty girl, far from what the outside world would consider attractive, but for jail standards she was the cream of the crop.

She passed by cell 26 then backed up to the door, looked in her mail basket and began sifting through it, letter after letter. She handed me my mail through the opening of the door. The last thing she passed to me was the USA Today newspaper. Like every day, I flipped to the entertainment section first and began perusing the headlines.

One article caught my attention; the one about the new television shows, "Empire", and "Power." Featured in the article were the characters of the shows and their prowess in the music and nightlife scene. The way the writer described them was eye-opening and had me intrigued to say the least. I admired the main character for his ingenuity and *do whatever it takes to get to the top* and *keep his family fed and safe* attitude. Then the other character for his vision and zest to protect his family at all cost. Both had past experiences from the streets. One gave his all to leave, the other had obstacles that stood in his way. His past always drew him back in.

I had an immediate flashback of my life and the resemblance between the two was real for me. I could almost write the script for the show, since I knew what would happen next. I had lived a part of both of those characters' lives, but I had better things to focus on.

The next thing I did was check NASDAQ and monitored a few stocks I had invested in. Basically, keeping my mind on business while I pondered my next move. After a while of reading and thinking, I laid back on the hard mattress enveloped by a steel bunk frame and reflected on the times when things were better. I wondered how I got to this point. It's easy to ignore things when everything is going well. For some reason, we never see the end coming. We know that nothing lasts forever and that the end is inevitable. Yet it is always an afterthought. After things happens, we think about it.

My thoughts consumed me while I sat in the cold federal holding cell. The silence allowed me to meditate on what was ahead. The outside world was ready to judge me and the government wanted answers and its pound of flesh. They even sent a psychologist to try and pick my brain --that was real funny. When we finished the session, she wanted to pay me $1,000 an hour for counseling her.

Maybe counseling the counselor helped me. I had always justified what I did in my mind. It was about survival I had always told myself. I am a man who must provide for his family too. Yes, the things that I did were wrong but some good came out of it.

However, as I lay locked up in that cold jail cell my thoughts shifted. I knew I would have to find a way to make all this right. I had heard what those people said in the court room and even though I could care less about their opinion of me, there was no doubt that I was a devoted father and friend.

That's when I decided that I needed to fix this. I needed to find a way to redeem myself. It was ingenious, but it was a crime and a lot of people were affected. As part of my redemption I would share my story in an effort to help others avoid identity theft by sharing how it happens. They needed to know how their information can be used when it gets, "Into The Wrong Hands." I would Wake-Up America and possibly the world. This would not be easy to do; I would have to find the right person to share this kind of information with. It would have to be a special writer. He would need to experience the effects first hand to right the story. Yes, I would need to accomplish one final mission to clear all this up.

I knew how my mind operated. I knew what I was capable of and what I had done. I also knew if I needed to, I could hold a seminar on how to generate capital and charge an arm and a leg for the information that was housed inside the crevices of my brain. I had accumulated plenty of money during my successful run using a very simple plan. It was the most lucrative venture I'd ever put my mind to. I'm a risk taker by nature and this time, the risks had paid off -- in a major way. Of course, I must credit my team. I wouldn't have been able to do most of it without them. But that's why I had carefully selected them. They each brought a unique skillset to the team. However, with a group like them, you're always concerned about some of their intentions. When money is involved in anything, greed and envy always seem to somehow show up. It is part of the package.

That's why I had constantly tested my team. Those measures were necessary, especially since trust was required. The situation with Victoria had been one of those tests. I was constantly putting her in challenging situations to test her loyalty. Victoria was intelligent, determined, committed to the cause, and with the right grooming from the man in charge, she became as loyal as they come.

Victoria Cromwell had my attention from the first time she spoke. Once I got to know her, it threw me for a loop that she was so together. I knew she would be a challenge to me because I had trouble trusting a woman.

I wasn't really sure what to make of her at first. Maybe it was her beauty, maybe it was the professionalism she exuded. Either way, I stayed cautious until I was confident that she wasn't like the other women I'd encountered.

Little by little I began to share things with her, and soon she started to break me down and gain my trust. We were skeptical of each other at first, which was a good thing in my eyes.

As the only woman on my team, Victoria had to deal with

many challenges. In the beginning, the position of executive liaison seemed very appealing to her. However, when the plan began to unfold with all its clandestine activities, she realized that she wasn't part of an ordinary operation. I knew she was capable of doing what was necessary. Her credentials were second to none and, after I put her to the test, she made me a believer. She had proved herself worthy.

The rest of my team? Now that was another story. There were a couple members of the initial team who hadn't shown themselves to be as loyal as the others -- so I had to flush out the bad. Part of the process included the services of Victoria, Mr. B., Mr. Steve, and Mr. Matt. They would be needed for a much larger mission, so their skills at this level were vital.

Everything involving our escape had been planned perfectly. With the feds clamping down on us, we got away from them right under their nose. No one was the wiser and I had been set and ready to proceed with the next phase of the plan. That was until the boys in black had sniffed me out. Mr. B. and I were cornered while attempting to relocate to our safe house. Someone knew too much. Someone told too much. My capture seemed suspicious, leaving a nasty taste in my mouth. I closed my eyes, my hands clasped behind my head as I lay on the steel bed of the federal prison. Someone knew way too much.

It was TV time and I tuned into the news…

4

"For those just tuning in, I'm Sharon Seed of CSB 64 News in Atlanta bringing you an update this afternoon on what's leading up to be the Trial of the Century." Our own Vicki Hall is reporting from outside the Atlanta federal holding facility that houses the most notorious identity theft perpetrator of our generation.

"The arraignment itself this morning was something to behold. It could've easily been mistaken as a night at one of the award ceremonies, especially with all the paparazzi, media and celebrities in attendance, said Seed. Everyone wants to know how one man could so easily weave his way into the lives of so many people and easily take over the personal information of so many people within a five-year span and organize a multi-million-dollar enterprise right under our very noses."

"Vicki does anyone know the estimated value of those he's manipulated?"

"Sharon, it's said to be in the hundreds of millions, but there's no real way to determine an exact amount."

"I guess people feel a little safer now that he has been detained?"

"Well, Sharon for the time being, but it looks like only for a brief period. It's been rumored our government officials and Mr. Averie's legal team are working out a plea bargain deal." It looks like the Government wants information.

"Vicki, you really think they would rather know the secrets behind this madness than to prosecute him to the fullest?"

"Sharon, I don't know about them, but personally I'd like to find out what I can do to avoid becoming a victim. The information would be priceless to all of us. This is a movie."

"That's a bold statement, Vicki."

"Sharon to be brutally honest, people have worked hard to obtain the lifestyles they have and to see it all go down in shambles?" That's excruciating and heartbreaking. To know that this one man is the mastermind behind it is unbelievable.

"Well, I can see that this has really gotten to you."

"Yes, it has, Sharon. Do you know that there have already been over a total of one hundred-million people victimized in the United States by Identity Theft? Tens of billions of dollars per year have been taken from people like us, hardworking people."

Just look at the number of accounts he was charge with. This one man has a total of four-hundred counts, Ranging from forty counts of forgery to three-hundred and sixty counts of financial identity fraud.

"Wow! I don't think I've ever heard of any one person ever having that many charges."

"History was definitely made with this case."

"Surely they're not considering a bond in this situation?"

"Actually, Sharon I'm hearing that a bond has already been set."

"Wow! That is shocking, and for how much?"

"It was set at 4 million dollars."

"What, that's it? Only four million? He should've been looked at as a Madoff." Wow!

"Well he does have a great lawyer!"

"Actually, he's one of the best. Reports say at around 1pm, his trial attorney Mr. Mawuli Davis, posted bond for his client."

"Has there been a court date scheduled, Vicki?"

"Sharon he's set to go to preliminary hearing on October 25, 2017, which means that with the right resources, this man will be back on the streets in full operation until it's time for him to face trial. This is very scary."

"No one is safe!"

"Not while he's freed."

As I watched the news and checked my investments, my mind wandered back to, "Who set me up?"

I knew that in time, they would reveal themselves. I reminded myself that I needed to focus on the upcoming mission. The mission I had been planning prior to this minor setback. Yes, the court had an abundance of charges, and yes, they claimed to have overwhelming evidence against me, but I am no ordinary man. This was no ordinary case. I am the ultimate chess player, and moves like this were foreseen and had been replayed.

******

According to plan, Victoria was sent ahead to prepare. Steve accompanied her to make sure that everything was in order. While still in holding, I had to rely on my team members to make sure that business ran as usual and Mr. Frank was the main contact to this complex machine.

"Mr. Bod`e!" the voice came across loudly over the intercom. I definitely didn't appreciate being publicized; it irritated me to no end. You have a visitor.

This surprised me because I didn't anticipate anyone coming to see me, especially in this position. Then again, I figured if it was anyone it had to be the third I trusted most and it had to be about business.

I got dressed and made my way to the visitation area where a thick pane of glass separated me from my visitor. My every move was being monitored closely by cameras and armed guards. In their minds, they were fully aware of what I was capable of with just the right amount of contact.

"Keep it brief, Bod`e!" one of the guards ordered. I nodded to acknowledge who held the respect; in the back of my mind the truth was evident. I picked up the receiver as did my visitor.

"Mr. Frank., my friend, how is life treating you?"

"All is well, my friend, I am maintaining." This was code language explaining that things were still in order.

"It's only been two days, and the world is watching, they are all trying to figure me out."

"People don't understand or know who's really behind all this."

"Mr. Frank, I read an interesting article this morning on three fellas named Luscious Lyons, James "Ghost" St. Patrick and Todd Davis, you know of them?"

"Empire, Power, and Life Lock, Yes, sir. They all seem to be the talk of the town, other than you."

"These guys have quite a following, what do you think?"

"Sir, say no more. In time, it will be arranged."

"Frank, I love the way you think. And now how is the cupid?"

"Cupid is Cupid."

"Have we made contact with our writer?"

"The day is close at hand, sir. All the combinations are circling around."

"Excellent. What did you think about him? I'm sure you read the Intel?"

"Of course, I did. Very good choice, sir. Interesting to say the least, but excellent choice. I believe he's the right man for the job."

"Splendid! That only leaves one last order of business."

"Boss, that baby is in the hanger, ready for departure."

"So how is our friend, Attorney Mawuli, doing?"

"Handling business, as is to be expected. He has informed me that bond for both you and Mr. B. will be posted soon."

"As always, Mr. Frank, you've done well."

"See you on the other side, sir."

It made me feel good to know that the plan was moving forward in spite of my detainment. Soon the plans will be executed and move to the next phase, which will be to alert the nation as to exactly who I am and what I represent. It's so nice when plans fall into place.

5

My bond release was just as newsworthy as my capture. The media saw it as a miscarriage of justice and wondered if this is what they could expect from the trial. The public viewed the scene of me coming out of the holding facility and considered it a mockery of justice.

On the flipside of the coin, the team gleefully anticipated my arrival. Though I didn't show any displays of camaraderie, I did appreciate the efforts my team put forth to make sure I felt welcomed. Work had to be done, so all of that was short-lived.

Victoria was present and looking radiant as usual, far from how I left her when we escaped the fed infiltration. To carry out her role in our plan, she had to show a less than attractive appearance. I knew she'd recover just fine when this was all over. Now she was in her element, headlining a team of specialists. Her job was to organize and coordinate the other members, brief them on the itinerary, and keep everyone involved and focused on the importance of the project at hand. Being the only woman in a crew of men whose combined testosterone levels were higher than the altitude in Colorado was not easy. She had her work cut out for her and that was good since there was plenty of work to be done prior to my release.

Steve and Mr. B. were also very important pieces of the puzzle. They were as loyal as they come. Frank and the others had to play their roles and do their part in order for everything to come together and turn out successfully. And I too.

"One month, people," I barked like things had never changed. "Thirty days is what we have. I'm sure Mr. B. and

Victoria have discussed with you the seriousness of this time frame. The bond that allows me to be here speaking with you is only temporary. I still must stand trial and I will abide by the legal system set forth by this country's elite." I had everyone's attention. All were present, seated silently and listening intently to their leader's voice.

"But first, we've got a purpose, a responsibility I would say. It is part of our destiny to inform the people of this great country of the dangers that are present and await them. The enemy is closer than they realize. There is hope, however, and we are here to deliver the serum and the remedy. Now I ask of all of you, who is down with me and who's not?"

"Before I go any further, I must advise and warn each of you that there may be prison time involved for some of you. While we have been underground for many years, extremely careful in our pursuits and have managed to do what we do without a watchful eye; you all need to know that it is different now. We have been compromised. I looked at each member as I spoke and steadied my gaze upon Steve."

"Now, I'm going to address this issue once and once only. Within the next thirty days, there will be no one going home and no one will be late. No One! Everything has to be precise." I looked at Steve again. "Are we clear, Steve?"

"Yes, Boss."

"Excuses or tardiness will not be tolerated any longer. It is imperative that we're all on the same page here. Unknown whereabouts and tardiness raises red flags and we have no room for those. There's a lot at stake here, and there's very little margin for error. So, stay focused and keep your personal issues out of the building, is that clear?"

No one said a word which meant that everyone was in agreement, even if they weren't.

"Let's get down to business, shall we? Is everything ready with the Campbell subject?"

Frank took the lead and gave confirmation.

"Yes, everything is set up, Boss."

His role as head of security and surveillance was to make sure that there were eyes everywhere. Just as he finished with the security system at their headquarters, Frank installed a topnotch camera system undetectable by someone unaware of what was happening to them. Their subject would be none the wiser.

"Is everyone in their proper place?"

"Affirmative, sir," Alex spoke up.

"Wonderful. Today will be a momentous day in history." The team members looked at each other in agreement, knowing very well the magnitude of this project.

"Well now, I think it's time for us to meet our new comrade. Victoria, will you do the honors of passing out the file to everyone?"

Victoria stood up and slid a manila-colored folder across to each person seated at the conference table. I reached for the high-tech looking remote control and pressed a button and the wall behind them retracted. A projection screen came down, measuring 110" x 250." The team marveled at its size.

"Ah ha, Frank, I bet you didn't know about this," Claude joked.

"I had it installed while you guys were working in Aspen last month," I retorted proudly.

"It is a nice one, sir," Rick said, never one to miss an opportunity to brown-nose.

"It was only twelve-thousand and I purchased it legit. I didn't have time for anything else…"

"Um…can we get to the meeting," Victoria interjected.

"Yes, she's right. Lights off." The voice activated censor dimmed the lights and darkened the room just a little.

I clicked and a photograph appeared on the screen. My eyes locked in on the subject as I spoke.

"Today is like my birthday or anniversary of sorts." I was lost in my own thoughts.

"Uh… are you alright, Sir?" Mr. B. interrupted.

"Yes," I said, snapping out of it. "Yes, of course." I looked around the table at my team until my gaze circled back around to the screen. "If you'll turn to the first page; let's examine this together."

"SUBJECT FILE"

Name: Mr. William David Campbell
Age: 48 Height: 6'1" Weight: 220 lbs.
Race: N/A Eye Color? N/A
Place of Birth: New York
Education: University of California- Berkeley
MBA: Master's degree in Journalism
Marital Status: Divorced
Children: Two Beautiful Girls
Medical / Health: High blood pressure and Diabetic.
He was in an automobile accident, short-term coma,
Had extensive rehab and episodes of black-outs.
Ideal Mate: Educated, self-motivated, financially secure
Woman. Who knows what she wants in life.
Employment: 24-Year Journalist.
Bes: TIME MAGAZINE Best Writer in 2016
Finances: Stable
Credit Score? 820
Delinquent Accounts: None

"Mr. W.D. Campbell will be the subject today and for the next 30 days, beginning right now. With our help and influence, he will be dedicated to this project in its entirety.

"Mr. W.D. Campbell will undoubtedly be the perfect man for the job. He's the Best Writer in the nation right now. Today we begin what will become America's wake-up call courtesy of Mr. Campbell."

The room remained silent as orders were handed out to team members.

"Mr. Frank, attach the lines together to block any traces."

"It's done sir."

"Thank you. Victoria, make the call please."

"I'm wondering how long these pleasantries will last," she said while dialing the number in the file.

"The 'please' and 'thank you' remarks will be provided

when I see fit, Ms. Victoria."

"It's ringing, sir."

I then placed an earpiece in my ear as we tied the conversation to two lines. My team and I listened in intently as the subject's phone rang.

"THE SETTING"

The Boss: Mr. Averie Bod`e
The Subject: Mr. William D. Campbell
Date: August 3, 2017
Time: 5:50 A.M.
Site: Condo in Harlem, New York
Arrangement: Averie`s Meeting Room
Contract: Two Million Dollars
Time Frame: 30 Days

Life from now on will never be the same…

6

Day One… Back In Time "The Awakening"

My alarm clock woke me earlier than usual this morning. I thought I set it for 6:00 A.M., but instead it blared in my ears at approximately ten minutes till. With my breath kicking like Van Dame's round house. Lying on the pillow top mattress, I slid from beneath my 1,000 thread count 100% cotton sheets.

You sleep like a king when you sleep on the best.

I entered the bathroom nearly burning my toes on the heated blue tiled porcelain flooring. I turned on just the right mixture of hot and cold water and let it run. Soon the steam filled the glassed-in chamber, letting me know that the temperature was right. As soon as I began removing my paisley print silk pajamas, my home and cell phones rang simultaneously. I wondered how was that possible when my home line was disconnected.

Just to be sure, I went over to check my cordless which was still on the base. The light flashed when it rang, again telling me it was in perfect working condition. A few feet away, I heard the familiar yet distinct ring tone coming from my cellular phone. I was dumbfounded, staring at one phone and then the other. On the fifth ring, I went and answered the cell.

"Hello," my voice had not awakened yet.

A deep, smooth voice caressed my ear, "Good morning, Mr. W. D. Campbell."

"Who is this?"

"Someone, who has been investigating and observing your

every move for a while," It took a few seconds for me to register what this stranger was saying. Unconsciously I looked around to see if there were any signs of cameras or bugs in plain view. Maybe I had overlooked something somewhere.

"Look, whoever this is, I just got up and I really don't have time for games. I'm late as it is."

"Games!" the voice bellowed. "This is far from a game, Mr. Campbell. Or maybe you didn't hear both your house phone and cell phone ringing at the same time, wasn't that a bit odd to you?"

"Well, if this isn't some sort of prank, why are you calling me this time of the morning? And what's this business about you observing me? What are you F.B.I., C.I.A., I.R.S., or any other letters I forgot?"

"No Mr. Campbell," he answered bluntly. "How is it possible that both your phones rang at the same time when one of them has been disconnected for the past two months?" I was still pondering that one, but figured something would give. "Yesterday afternoon, at about 5:00 P.M., posing as yourself, I, or should I say you, contacted your phone company, New York Bell and had your services reconnected." I just listened intently.

"All of your home phone calls have been forwarded to my cell phone so you wouldn't have any reason to be suspicious or alarmed in any way."

My heart raced at the events taking place. It was like I was in a bad dream or twilight zone or something.

"In addition, I also opened an account with New York Bell yesterday, so that all creditors' questions will be forwarded from your home phone to the cell phone. I was very adamant, making sure we're not disturbed. Wasn't that nice of me?" His calm tone was eerie.

He snickered with a hint of sarcasm. "W.D. Campbell, another satisfied customer."

"Who the hell is this?"

"Who am I? Why I'm Mr. Averie Bod`e of course."

"He still maintained a coolness that rendered me helpless. Everybody wants to know who I really am, Mr. Campbell, everybody!"

For the life of me I couldn't understand what was going on and why it was happening to me. Had I pissed someone off and not known it?

"Really, Mr. Campbell, I'm you."

"You're me, but how?"

"Actually, I've been you for some time now, Mr. Campbell."

"No, I don't believe you're me, I think you're a lunatic," I yelled angrily into the receiver.

"A lunatic, no, I beg to differ. I've been William David Campbell, for at least two months now. In fact, I'm any and everyone I need to be. I'll be explaining all of this to you later, Mr. Campbell, however right now, the water in your shower is getting cold, and you need to get a move on."

Nothing was as it seemed. I didn't even want to question him anymore for fear of discovering something more shocking.

"Today, I will need your undivided attention and cooperation. Trust me, in due time, I will have it. So, Mr. Campbell, you need to cancel all your appointments for today."

"What about my job? I…,"

"Don't concern yourself with that. Posing as you, I've already called them and explained that I, you, will be taking a leave of absence. Now, pay close attention because what I'm going to tell you will affect you for the rest of your life."

"Okay, Mr. Everybody, you have my attention… you have it for right now."

"Do I detect sarcasm in your tone, Campbell? I am not to be fucked with." Now, go have a nice shower and in approximately 30 minutes, I will be contacting you again. "Don't try to call anyone because I'll know. Just remember as you're showering, I'm you." The phone clicked in my ear and for a moment I stood motionless. Suddenly, my home didn't feel as safe as it once did.

Before I put my cell phone down, I looked at the caller I.D. to see if there was a number; of course, it was blank. I tried 'Star 69' but that failed too. I've had my share of prank calls, living in New York, but this one was hardly the same.

7

Victoria, I need a word with you and Steve, the rest of you excuse us, please. It was more of a command than a request from Averie. Both Steve and Victoria looked at each other like two students being sent to the principal's office.

"Look, I don't have time for any differences between the two of you. Is there any reason for me to take one of you off this project?"

"No sir," they replied in unison."

"Well then, I want you two to hug, kiss, shake hands, or whatever it is you need to do to get along so we can get on with business."

Steve spoke first, looking her in the eye. "Victoria, you are my girl, I'm sorry for being short with you on the phone."

"Mr. Shorty," she smiled, "I mean, Steve, I'm sorry for the things I said, will you forgive me?"

They hugged genuinely, putting their issues in the ground. Walking out of the meeting room, Averie whispered in Steve's ear.

"And Steve, no more tardiness, this is your first and last warning."

"Yes sir, I'm very sorry."

"Victoria, can you follow me please? Steve, tell everyone to study our primary, because he means everything to me right now. Let Mr. B. know that he'll be needed at the address in the file. Instruct Frank to go ahead and contact our personnel at the airport and have all the first-class seats available for departure this afternoon around 4 p.m. One way direct to Atlanta, Georgia."

Steve pulled out a miniature pad and started jotting down Averie's instructions.

"Have Tom and Claude pull the cars out of the underground parking and bring them around to the back door. I'll contact the others after I meet with Mr. Campbell."

"Anything else, Sir?"

"Call up Mr. Whon and tell him to have our usual tables reserved for breakfast. Also, make sure he keeps an eye on the usual perps lurking around the restaurant."

"Check."

"Lastly, in the event no one noticed this in the file, today is Mr. Campbell's birthday. Always greet him as Mr. Campbell and everyone must acknowledge his birthday. Let Mr. B. know that pickup will be set for 7a.m. Tom and Claude will be secondary in the escort."

"Got you, boss," Steve confirmed while exiting the room.

"Thank you, thank you all, now let's make it happen." Averie excused himself. They were halfway out the back door when he stopped them. "Oh, one more thing. From this day forward, and for the next 12 months, everyone will address each other with Mr. or Ms. and their first names. For instance: Mr. Steve, Mr. Frank, Ms. Victoria…got it?"

"Yes sir," they answered as they exited and the door closed.

"Very good, very good, Victoria, I need to go over a few things with you for the next couple of minutes."

"What, about Mr. Campbell?"

"We'll contact him shortly. Let him turn into a raisin in the shower while he tries to figure out what's coming next. Right now, I need to show you…and only you…this. This will not leave this room, comprendé?"

"I got you sir,"

"A knock interrupted the progress."

"Yes, what is it?" Frank entered, holding his cellphone to his ear.

"Sir, all travel arrangements have been made and

confirmed."

"Good. Are you taking care of ground transportation for when we arrive at PDK?"

"Will you be flying the helicopter to the mountain or will you be driving? There's a lot of construction in the path, so if you're planning on driving, you might consider one of the trucks, sir."

"No, I think I'll take the helicopter, but only our guest and Mr. B. will be traveling alongside me. The rest of you I want on the ground so the area and perimeter will be monitored."

"Not a problem. Sorry for the interruption sir,"

"You're alright, good day."

"Good day to you, sir. See you at the mountains."

"See you then Mr. Franklin."

It was the first-time Averie had used Mr. Frank's name openly. However, his closeness to Frank couldn't be seen by their business practices. They had been together for a long time, but always kept things professional in order to keep the secrecy of each project they were working on. They never crossed the line; personal dealings had the tendency to jeopardize the outcome of projects, and they decided that they would never compromise business. Once Frank was on his way, Averie resumed his conversation with Victoria who was ending a phone call with a contact on her end.

"Before I contact Mr. Campbell again, I want to show you this." They both approached the red velvet case he had pulled from the safe. Victoria's eyes were filled with curiosity as Averie opened the latch. She knew whatever she saw had to be kept with her to her grave.

8

William David Campbell had led a pretty boring life. Besides the birth of his daughters and having won the Pulitzer Prize, his life's highlights were few and far in between. He had missed the birth of his youngest daughter because he was snowed in while on assignment in the Midwest. He spent a countless number of years attempting to make up for it with his now ex-wife, Olivia.

William had treated April and Alexis with extra special care ever since they were young. They were his angels and, everywhere he went, he bragged about them. When April performed in her first dance recital, William called everyone he knew and invited them to the show, completely embarrassing her. When Alexis was in the city-wide Science Fair and won first place for her solar display, her proud papa took out space in the newspaper and entered her picture with the first-place trophy and ribbon.

That's just the kind of father he was, fully dedicated. If only he had been as dedicated to his marriage as he was to his daughters and his job, maybe it could have lasted longer. Instead he spent more time writing for the ***New York Times*** which received rave reviews. It was as a financial matter of necessity that he penned his first novel, "The Unforgiven of God's People." Without much marketing, the novel flew off the shelves of bookstores and newsstands. He was advised by his agent to self-publish and that took his sales to unimaginable levels. Best seller status was unavoidable and soon W.D. Campbell became a household name and was a sought-after author for interviews.

However, at home, his wife came in a distant third to his daughters and career.

Olivia stood strong by her husband, despite her constant pleas for attention, or at least, some acknowledgement of her existence in his world.

However, William continued to neglect her, always promising to take her places he never made time for. Something was always more important than his wife.

After a while, the only thing keeping their marriage together were their daughters. April and Alexis were excelling in school and were maturing into beautiful young women. Both were straight 'A' students throughout high school. April had plans to follow in her daddy's footsteps and attend college to study mass media journalism. This pleased William to his core.

Alexis, on the other hand, chose another route. She wanted to delve into the medical field just like her mother. She felt that becoming a physician would make a difference in the world. Olivia worked with children, developing ways to keep them from diseases. This type of humanitarian work made Olivia very compassionate, increasing her need for attention when she came home. She expelled in so much; she felt she deserved something in return.

Eventually, the girls graduated from high school and were off to college, leaving William and Olivia alone in the house for the first time in several years. Olivia had hoped that this was finally their time together as a couple. Their time to reconnect and pick up where they had left off over a decade ago. To her dismay, William fell into a depression instead and grew even more distant. No matter what his wife did, it wasn't enough to bring him around. So as a last plea, she decided to seduce him, hoping that good sex would revive their marriage.

So, one evening, she dressed provocatively wearing her favorite perfume attempting to lure William into the bedroom. He was engulfed in an article when she found him, scrolling on the computer screen in his office. Though she quietly walked up behind him, he felt her presence instantly. Without warning, she caressed his neck and then his face from behind. This only annoyed William.

He shoved her away, but she was persistent. William's eyes remained glued to the screen like she didn't even exist. Olivia had enough. She stormed out of the office, went into their once cozy bedroom and locked the door. A few moments later, she came out fully dressed, stomping down the stairs to make sure William heard her. The next thing that was heard was the front door slamming shut.

William didn't even realize she was gone until the next morning when he discovered that her side of the bed was untouched. He had been so consumed with his work, that he had fallen asleep right there at his desk.

A few days later, Olivia returned to pick up some more of her things, then she was off again. When he asked where she'd been, she offered "a friend's place," and that was it.

At first, the reality of Olivia being gone didn't really hit him, and then the loneliness set in. His precious daughters were off at school becoming women and his wife had departed, leaving him in an environment that was getting emptier by the second.

When he didn't hear from Alexis for months, it began to affect his health. The stress caused by the worry nearly overwhelmed him. William sought a diagnosis from his physician who diagnosed William with hypertension and high blood pressure. He instructed William to restructure his diet, exercise more, and more importantly, stop worrying. That was easy for him to say, as if he didn't just have his wife walk out on him, turning his world upside down.

One afternoon, while typing an article, he received a brown certified envelope at his downtown office. He opened it, read the contents, and then rested his head in his hands, trying to regain whatever sanity he had left. Quietly, William got up from his station and exited the building without a word to anyone. He hopped into his '79 classic Mercedes Benz, placed the envelope on the passenger seat, and pulled off in no particular direction.

William traveled through the busy New York streets with reckless abandonment. He swerved in and out of traffic trying to get nowhere fast. All he could think about was how his life was slowly heading south and he could do nothing to stop it.

"Divorce? How could she want a divorce?" he thought out loud, zooming past cars. Even though he had caused the situation, he never fathomed that Olivia would leave him.

William was exceeding speeds well over 60 mph when a car backed out of a parking lot and into his path. William jammed on his brakes, but that didn't do anything to soften the impact. The Mercedes skidded into the back end of the sports car tearing off the bumper. The collision sent William's car into a spin, smashing it into another car which was trying to avoid the scene unfolding before it.

William came out as the worst of all the parties involved. Because he hadn't remembered to put on his seat belt, his head slammed against the steering wheel knocking him unconscious. The second blow sent his body flying to the passenger side, pinning him against the door. He was pried out of his car and sent to the hospital by helicopter where he stayed for weeks. His Mercedes, a 1995 CS-350was not equipped with any air bag so had taken a severe blow to his head when he hit it against the steering wheel. As a result, he suffered head trauma. While the doctors surveyed his injuries, William slipped into a coma, alarming everyone.

The hospital tried to alert his next of kin about William's condition, but Olivia could not be reached. So, the hospital called April, who was the next on the list. She flew out from Berkeley, California immediately, catching the first available flight back east. April called her sister, Alexis, at a seminar in Virginia; she too dropped everything and made her way back home.

Once they arrived, they were able to contact Olivia on her cellphone, on the new number she had only given to them. As it turned out, Olivia was dating someone new, an old friend. Even though she was happier, she hid the sorrow that filled her when she saw William lying motionless on that gurney.

Weeks went by with William in a coma. When he finally showed signs of coming through, his fingers were the first to move. Later, he responded in mumbles when April spoke to him. Then finally, his eyes opened, but couldn't really focus. It was going to take some time for him to regain all of his faculties, but to them this was a wonderful start.

They all knew that recovery was going to be an uphill battle, but one thing was for sure, he was glad that his family was there to support him through it all. As far as his marriage went, they were still on a rocky foundation. The accident didn't help Olivia with any of her feelings. She still felt William was incapable of change. She decided to work with him to get him back to full strength, and then deal with their future when they got past this challenge.

9

Averie had six cameras secretly installed inside Mr. Campbell's penthouse; the bedroom, kitchen, office, library, fitness room, and living room. He'd been spying on Campbell's every move. Across the wall panel, behind Averie's sliding wall, there were video and audio tapes lined up, organized by date and time.

"Averie, how and when did you hook all this up?" Victoria asked, amazed at all of the surveillance equipment. "You never had a free minute to do all of this," she pondered.

"I did it two months ago, while you were on one of your shopping sprees."

Victoria had a worried look on her face.

"Don't you go there, Victoria, I wouldn't think of bugging your place."

"Well, that's good to know, because I have nothing to hide."

"And if you did, would you tell me?"

"You know we don't have any secrets, Averie."

"None that I know of, but everyone has skeletons in their closet, even me."

Just then, Victoria noticed a shadow move on one of the screens. "Averie, I think our subject is moving about."

"Where?"

"Right there, on the third monitor."

"Good. I believe it's time to give him his next set of instructions, shall we?"

"You know, this is some really creepy stuff, but it's kind of fun wondering how Mr. Campbell will react to what you tell him next. I know one thing, I wish he'd put a shirt on, that's an ugly scar on his left shoulder."

"Yes, he got that from a car accident a while back. The scar should be the least of his worries."

******

As I dried off, I went over to the mirror and looked at my reflection. I looked at the wrinkles on my face caused by years of stress, and then I turned and viewed the scar on my right side bringing back some painful memories.

The haunting sound of my two phones ringing broke me out of my trance. Funny thing it wasn't as frightening as it was earlier, partly because I already knew who it was. When I picked up, the same distinct sounding voice was on the other end.

"Hello, Mr. Campbell, are you ready?"

"It's only 6:26 am, you said 30 minutes, Mr. Everybody a/k/a Mr. I'm you."

"With the rate at which you're moving, you're going to make us late. You're not even dressed yet."

"How'd you know?" I asked in amazement.

"You need not worry about that. I know things about you that you probably thought were sacred. Remember, I am you. Oh, by the way, how's your wife, I mean ex-wife? I think that it is awful how she left you in your time of need."

"Look, whoever you are, that doesn't concern you."

"Oh, but it does, everything about you concerns me; but for now, hurry up and get dressed, "he said in a commanding tone. "We're on a very strict time schedule. A car will be there to pick you up precisely at 7:00 a.m."

"A car, what for?"

"We're heading to a meeting with someone to speak about some issues of national security."

"National Security!" I exclaimed.

"That doesn't sound like something I can handle; maybe you should be contacting the Secretary of Defense at the White House." I don't think my humor amused him.

"You're wasting time with this banter, Mr. Campbell; we

have a long day planned. Its 6:29 am and you have exactly thirty minutes to get dressed and be downstairs."

"But, I still must _________,"

"Seven o'clock. Downstairs, Mr. Campbell."

The phone clicked in my ear abruptly. I hurried to my closet and pulled out the only thing that didn't require preparation, a nice linen T-shirt and a pair of blue jeans pants that I had just gotten from the cleaners. I quickly put them on, splashed on a little Victoire Intense cologne, and brushed my teeth and head at the same time. This left only a couple of minutes to get downstairs. I grabbed my keys and elevator key card and dashed out.

I swiped the card in the slot to enter the elevator. The 14th floor is a keyed entry, custom made for me. Once I reached the lobby, I stormed pass the front desk.

"Mr. Campbell, sir, there's a call for you." Mr. Williams was waving his hand motioning me over to him. Who in the heck could be trying to reach me at the desk? I almost waved it off because of the rush I was in.

I took the call -- against my better judgment.

"Very good Mr. Campbell, I'm impressed."

"What now? I'm looking and you're not even outside."

"On the contrary, a car has been outside waiting for you for five minutes."

I looked down at my watch and sure enough, it was five minutes after seven.

"Are you coming out or what? I'd hate for us to be late for our appointment."

"I'm on my way." I left the concierge desk and headed for the door.

"Is everything alright, Mr. Campbell?" Mr. Williams asked.

"Yes, yes, everything's fine. Thank you for asking."

"Have a good day and a Happy Birthday."

10

I smiled, completely forgetting about today being my fiftieth birthday. I'm going to have to tip Mr. Williams, just for remembering.

Out front, a black Mercedes Benz MLC Class with tinted windows pulled up and a window came down. A voice different than the one I had heard earlier, said my name, "Mr. Campbell."

"Yes, that's me."

"Get in sir."

Without a second thought, I entered the vehicle. Once in the back seat, I surveyed my surroundings and noticed that the only other person in the car; was the driver and me. Now, my nerves began to get on edge. Was the driver the man behind the voice or someone else entirely? When he spoke, the voice didn't match the one I had heard or was he the same man?

"We'll be joining the others shortly," he said curtly.

Right then, another vehicle, a black Mercedes Benz GLS pulled up to my left side and one of its windows rolled down. I was hoping this wasn't a set-up because I was unarmed and unprotected.

"Good morning and Happy Birthday, Mr. Campbell." How did he know that?

"Good morning to you. Where is Mr. I'm everybody?"

"We're all having breakfast together this morning."

"All… who is this all he was referring to?"

"I hope you 'all' are paying."

"Yes, Mr. Campbell. We will be taking care of all

expenses, now what will be your pleasure?"

"I can have anything I want?"

"Yes Mr. Campbell, anything!"

"Well, in that case, I'll have 3 eggs, scrambled, three slices of wheat toast with a spoon of grape jelly, some turkey bacon, one glass of freshly squeezed orange juice, and a hot cup of decaffeinated coffee with 3 teaspoons of sugar."

"Are you sure that's all you want, Mr. Campbell?"

"Yes, thank you."

We rode a few miles in silence before the driver handed me a cellphone. "He wants to speak with you."

"Who?"

"Mr. A.B."

"I was really confused now, Mr. Who?"

"Mr. A.B. Mr. Averie Bod`e." All these code names and secrecies; who are these people and more importantly, who is Mr. Averie Bod`e? Before I took the phone, I asked the driver, "Am I in some kind of trouble with the law or something?"

"No, not at all, Mr. Campbell. In fact, you're about to have an unusual and profitable experience today. Right now, you need to get on the phone."

I placed the receiver to my ear and listened.

"Good morning again, Mr. Campbell. I understand you have a lot of questions about what's about to take place. Just sit back and relax. In twenty minutes or so we will be formally introduced."

"Good," I thought. That would at least erase some of the mystery of this guy.

"Trust me, Mr. Campbell, we mean you no harm, sir."

"You have yet to give me any information concerning our meeting," I said.

"You will have all the answers to all of your questions soon. In the meantime, try to calm down. Have my driver hand you today's newspaper, maybe reading will relax your mood."

"Maybe you're right," I replied. I handed the phone back

to the driver as he slid me the morning paper, still wrapped in plastic. I unraveled it and read across some of the headlines. One in particular stood out like a sore thumb.

I noticed the acronym F.I.F. printed in bold letters across the top of the lead article. It gave details on America's No. 1 crime of the century: Identity-Theft. I read the article not realizing the impact it would have on me. Certain lines were highlighted for emphasis. One line that caught my attention was this one: *"The U.S. and virtually all nations are in desperate need of specialized taskforces, investigation teams and other resources to put a stop to Financial Identity Fraud."* It went on to read, *"This crime has stricken businesses and consumers in all nations. Approximately 15 million United States residents have had their identities compromised each year with financial losses totaling upwards of $50 billion. Millions of victims hit by F.I.F., Financial Identity Fraud, in the past 15 years. The crime is like no other; identity-thieves actually transform themselves into their victims and then begin to destroy their entire financial livelihood, sometimes in a matter of minutes, leaving them, excuse my language, but leaving their finances all f....d up. No money in the bank, fraudulent transactions, delinquent accounts, bad credit, and now they have the hassle of going through their banks, credit unions and the labyrinthian dispute process with all 3 credit agencies." This very story aired on one of the major networks not too long ago, but of course many didn't pay much attention to it. Governments of lesser technical advancements are hard-pressed and desperate to gain control, even the least amount over F.I.F.*

"Approximately 108 million citizens of the United States have been victimized in a record-setting fifteen years; more than any other single crime. That's about one-third of the U.S. population; and that number, if not brought to a halt in the very near future, could climb as much as 50% by the middle of 2020; that's staggering. More than 15 million consumers and businesses become prime victims of this

heinous crime each year. The government states that proper resources will be delegated to prevent and eliminate the perpetrators of ID Theft."

"Still, till this day, it hasn't happened."

I thought about some of the things Mr. Bod`e had said to me earlier – "I can be anyone and everyone." His statement, though haunting, had not registered. Not even when he said, "I've been you for a while, until now."

Being a veteran journalist and a best-selling author, I admired the complexity of this whole situation. He says that he wants to share some vital information on past and present events. Maybe I'll give this little meeting a chance after all. What didn't make sense was, why me? Out of over 326 million people here in the United States; what does he want me to do with the information?

I looked up as we approached a stop light. The second car in our motorcade pulled in front of us, as a sign for us to follow. We made a right, drove for a few miles, made another right, and pulled into the parking lot of a breakfast restaurant.

We parked beside the lead car, about twenty feet from the entrance. I noticed that the driver of the other car got out first, then my driver followed suit. They met at the hood of the vehicle and began to talk. A third vehicle pulled up, a brand new all black colored H2 Hummer with sparkling chrome 30 inch rims; its brilliance blinded me. I was amazed at the newness of all three vehicles, all black, and all brand-new models.

For some odd reason the driver of my car got in the Hummer. I could tell that something important was being discussed, but what? My instincts told me they were discussing me. I couldn't see who was inside the Hummer because of the dark tint on the windows.

A few short minutes later, the doors of the second car flew open and both occupants stepped out. They were both dressed in black suits. They surveyed the parking lot before the driver of the car came back and asked me to step out, which I did immediately. I exited without resistance.

The men in the Hummer got out and approached me like I was Jason Bourne. Each took up a position around me, forming a protective circle; they were better than Secret Service. Each person spoke to me saying, "Good morning, Mr. Campbell" and "Happy Birthday." As hard as their features were, their manners and open greetings softened their appearances. My driver instructed me to follow them. I became part of an entourage heading into the restaurant.

We walked right past the dining area and went into the kitchen where two other black-suited men were waiting for us.

They ordered me to turn in any metal items I had in my possession. I did as I was told and offered up my watch, a Mont Blanc writing pen, my condo keys, and the Polo framed glasses I wore.

One of the suits said "Do you mind if I search you, Mr. Campbell?"

"Do I have a choice?" I asked, knowing fully well what the answer would be.

"Not really."

"In that case get your search on. I have nothing to hide. Just don't touch the goods." He couldn't help but crack a smile on his stone face.

I proceeded to lift my arms above my head and spread my legs. I placed my hands on an open wall in front of me and allowed them to frisk me.

The second of the suits asked me to remove my shoes and belt and place them on the table top. They thoroughly checked me and my items as if I were an inmate entering a maximum-security prison. After the shakedown, my shoes were the only things that were returned to me.

"Your watch, pen, glasses, belt and keys will not be in your possession during the meeting, Mr. Campbell."

"And what shall I do when my pants fall, get an exposure charge? I won't have to worry about that; I'll be too busy bumping into innocent people eating because I won't be able to see anyway."

Chuckling to himself, one of the other suits stated, "Go ahead and give him his belt and glasses, Mr. Bod`e will understand."

"I'm just following orders," my driver said. "You can explain."

"Fine, here you go, Mr. Campbell."

After I got dressed, as best as they would allow me to, we re-entered the seating area; we were ushered to a table that was obviously reserved for us. Upon sitting, I was served a cup of decaffeinated coffee with a teaspoon of sugar, just the way I like it.

As I enjoyed my first cup of coffee of the day, my driver's cell phone rang. He answered it on the first ring and after a minute or two I heard, "yeah boss," then he hung up.

"Mr. Averie Bod`e will be here shortly," he stated to no one in particular."

The manager, an Asian man, came over to our table and whispered something inaudible in my driver's ear. His response to whatever was said was "three." I was curious to know what 'three' meant. It must've been visible on my face, because my driver turned to me and explained that the manager wanted to know how many pieces of toast I had ordered earlier. Everyone seemed to laugh at the silly look I gave them.

My driver's phone chirped again, interrupting my embarrassing moment. "Okay," was his reply; "Mr. Bod`e is here."

Without warning, all the men in black suits began to move about, and in unison towards the entrance.

I took a sip of my coffee and looked out the window at all the commotion in the parking lot. I watched as the men formed a perimeter ushering in a green sports car. Its dual exhaust purred like a satisfied kitten, and moved with the smoothness of a feline.

The driver found an open space near the other three vehicles and parked in front of the other black cars. They immediately secured the front and back of the car. The lead man opened the door and made way for a debonair looking man; I presume this to be the big man himself, Mr. Averie Bod`e.

My driver confirms it by saying, “there, Mr. Campbell, is your early wake-up call.”

“So, that’s him, huh?”

“Yes.”

“So, I finally get to meet the new me, Mr. W.D. Averie Bod`e.” My driver smiled. The other gentlemen in black suits escorted the one they call “Boss” inside the restaurant and approached our table.

“When he comes over to the table, don’t say anything; just listen,” one of the men said to me. “Afterwards, you’ll be able to ask questions.” I responded with a nod.

The men accompanying Averie, stopped before me, allowing him to emerge from the center. It was all such a spectacle!

“Mr. W.D. Campbell.”

The voice was one I recognized. He nodded, motioning two of the men to close the heavy velvet curtains around our table.

“Good morning, and Happy Birthday, sir.”

“Thank you,” I said, smiling at the strange man in the brown suit.

I knew there was some sort of reason for all the privacy. It was a security matter for them, as well and for myself. Once the blinds were shut, Mr. Bod`e felt a bit more comfortable.

“Hello, my friend,” he said cordially.

Looking at him it was easy to believe we were really friends. I reached out to shake his hand and returned his greeting. He asked if he could join me at the table for breakfast.

“Sure,” I answered, as if I really had any choice I motioned to an empty chair opposite me and he sat down with his back to the wall, facing the door; it seemed, exactly the way he wanted it.

My driver was waving, trying to flag down the middle-aged Asian man, obviously, the manager we had seen earlier. He came over to our table and began to speak in his native language to Mr. Bod`e. To my surprise, Mr. Bod`e responded in the same language. A man fluent in Chinese is not something you see every day.

After their conversation, they both said 'Hoy,' and bowed to one another. The manager turned on his heels and walked back to the kitchen as fast as he could.

"Where did you learn to speak such perfect Chinese?"

"Here and there" he replied.

My driver had told me the manager was a very dear friend of Mr. Bod`e's. Not only was he the manager, but he was also the owner. I thought to myself, this guy must have connections. He also mentioned that even though this was an ordinary breakfast spot, it was also one of Mr. A.B.'s safety zones. The little Asian man was summoned once again, this time for a formal introduction. "Mr. Campbell, this is Mr. Whon."

He nodded and took my hand at the same time.

"Mr. Whon, W.D. Campbell."

Mr. Whon greeted me in perfect English, no accent apparent at all.

"Good morning, Mr. Campbell. It's a pleasure to meet you. Would you like another cup of coffee? Decaf, isn't it?"

"Why, yes, thank you."

Mr. Bod`e informed Mr. Whon that we were ready for breakfast. Be easy on the salt when preparing Mr. Campbell's meal; we're trying to watch his blood pressure.

I was truly astonished at how much he actually knew about me. That made me think back to the article I read on the way over. Things were getting more and more interesting by the minute.

11

There are some things in life that just don't make any sense. And then there are the things that, if you wait long enough, will begin to pan out or become clearer with time. I chose to wait out this situation with Mr. Averie Bod`e and let him tell his own story.

Over breakfast, his team said very little.

Mr. Bod`e did most of the talking. And he was about to say something to me at the moment when his cellphone rang. He answered it without saying a word, his eyes on me the whole time. It was apparent that whoever was on the other end of the line was doing all the talking. I tried my best to make out what they were saying, but the only thing I heard was the high-pitch tone of a female's voice.

When he finished, he placed the phone on the table as if to say that it was on display. I thought back to earlier, when he had mentioned to me that he'd opened an AT&T account in my name. Studying the phone closely, it signified style and grace, sort of like the man sitting before me. I could tell that he had a certain style of living that he had to maintain.

"Excuse me, if you don't mind, I need to wash my hands before I eat."

"Of course, Mr. Campbell."

As I rose, a black suit rose with me.

"Ahh…Thank you for the sitter, but I think I'm a big boy now."

Mr. Bod`e laughed, and then responded.

"It's for your own protection, Mr. Campbell. For you and for us. Accept my offer, please."

I looked at my escort in jest. "Hold my hand tightly so I don't get lost on the way."

Everyone at the table chuckled; however, my escort didn't think it was funny at all. I don't think he enjoyed this part of his job any more than I did. While in the bathroom, I thought about how much class Mr. Bod`e displayed. Every step was planned precisely, no detail overlooked. Overall, he was as smooth as black ice on asphalt; unnoticed it could be very dangerous.

I returned to the table and saw everyone sharing a box of handy-wipes. I was glad to see that sanitizing was important to them as well.

"You do things the way you want, I'll do things effective and simple," Mr. Averie Bod`e said, wiping his hands free of germs.

"Mr. Campbell, I'd like to introduce you to some of my team while we eat."

My food had arrived on time and I sat down to enjoy it.

"Your sitter, you should know, is Mr. Steve. Mr. B. is the name of your alert chauffer, who is also my second in command."

I kind of figured that out by how much respect was given to him.

"The nine security men, starting at my left are, Mr. Alex, Mr. Claude, Mr. Tom, Mr. Matt, Mr. Steve, Mr. Isaiah, Mr. Tim, Mr. Rick and last, but surely not least, is Mr. Frank, who plays more roles than one. I noticed that he was the only one wearing glasses. "He's next in line to Mr. B." They all nodded at me in greeting.

"What does the 'B.' stand for?" I asked. Everyone fell silent as if I had asked something forbidden.

"What would make you ask that?" Mr. B. inquired with a stern look. "If I told you, I'd have to kill you."

"Damn, I guess I don't need to know that badly."

"I'll tell you this much, the 'B.' stands for business, because that's all I'm about. Enough said."

He smiled, finalizing the conversation.

I looked to Mr. Bod`e who appeared impatient.

"Please forgive me for the interruption." My voice quivered and I didn't have a clue as to why.

"Are you alright, Mr. Campbell? Be at ease, we are here to service and protect you. No harm in questioning something you're unsure of."

His tone was so calm it was almost frightening. If I wasn't careful I could easily see my feet planted in cement and being thrown into the river to sleep with the fishes. Mr. B. kept urging me to relax; all questions will be addressed in due time. They would be discussing the reason why I had been called to this meeting. Attorneys and their assistants would be introduced later. I turned to face Mr. B. and spoke, probably a little more aggressively than I had intended.

"What the hell are you talking about? I guess I'm supposed to just sit here in the company of a bunch of strangers I don't even know and not say shit? You all might be involved in some sort of criminal activity. All I have to go on is that he says he's me and you all don't mean me no harm."

"Please settle down Mr. Campbell, your voice has raised some attention so you must settle down."

Mr. Bod`e spoke with smoothness. I tried to look at the attention I had attracted, but could not see the other side of the thick curtain covering our table.

"Please, be patient, Mr. Campbell," Mr. Bod`e continued, "All, or at least most of the things you want to know, will be revealed to you before the sun sets. Now, enjoy your breakfast."

A million thoughts raced through my head as I put the finishing touches on my plate. I had long lost my appetite, but ate only as a courtesy. I was still filled with an uncontrollable rage. I hated to be left hanging. Maybe if I showed that I wasn't scared of these dudes, they might give me some answers.

Everyone sat silently, like they were waiting for the next man to speak. Finally, I jumped out of my seat, nuts in my palm.

"Look, all morning long I've been held captive like a prisoner. Now, I don't know what's going on, but 'I'm tired of all of this." I was trying my best to put my "Scare" game down, hoping it worked.

"I'm out of here!" I started toward the door before I noticed a burley, physically imposing security figure.

"Who the fuck are you talking to like that? Don't get your scrawny ass whipped in here!"

Who's scrawny? I thought; I'm almost 200 pounds, but in relation to the incredible hulks stunt doubles, I paled in comparison. I quickly walked back toward the table and sat down abruptly, acting like I was delirious.

"Is something wrong Mr. Campbell?" Mr. Bod`e asked.

"I'm just feeling a little dizzy; it happens sometimes when I don't have my glasses on." Mr. Bod`e gave me a look of disbelief. I think I just cost myself a strike in his book for that outburst. I could tell something was bothering him by his disposition as he continued to eat. He kept looking around nervously, watching whoever came through the doors. He even had an eye on his own men. I'd better watch my step and stay on my P's and Q's with these guys.

A few moments later, Mr. Whon approached our table and asked Mr. Bod`e for a word or two alone. Averie excused himself from the table and wandered over to a secluded area with Mr. Whon. The conversation wasn't long and in a matter of minutes, he returned and instructed everyone to meet outside in the parking lot. He told Mr. B. to stay with me; then he gave him what looked to be a credit card.

Mr. Whon came back after all the others had left, and dropped the breakfast tab on the table. Mr. B. didn't even look at it; he just gave Mr. Whon the credit card and told him to handle it and to do it quickly because we had business to handle. I tried to figure out what kind of business would have these guys so paranoid.

As a veteran journalist, I'd planned to find out. My instinct told me that beneath the surface I could smell a life changing, bestselling story coming out of all this.

I went to take my last swallow of coffee, when Mr. Frank, next in command under Mr. B. scampered in and yelled, "Let's go! Code Green! Eight minutes!"

"Mr. Whon," Mr. B. called out. The older Asian was already on his way, receipt in hand. As he signed for the men, I peeped through the blinds and saw Mr. Bod`e climbing into the driver's seat of the sports car.

The security men were in their vehicles on either side and in the back of Mr. Bod`e's car, engines ready.

A pang hit the pit of my stomach. I felt like I was in the company of the secret service or KGB.

Being my nosey ass, I glanced at the bill before he gave it to Mr. Whon. The total came to $141.33 but there was a tip of two-hundred dollars.

"Damn!" I voiced without realizing. Mr. B. smiled seeing my eyes bulge at the number.

"The tip is larger than the meal itself," I stated the obvious.

"Trust me; Money is nothing to us. You'll understand later."

"I know everything is always later with these guys."

12

Frank yelled again, "Three minutes, move it, B! We have to go now!" In a flash, I was ushered out the door. Mr. Bod`e was waiting but on the brink of impatience.

"Mr. B., what took you so long?" he asked pointing to his Cartier diamond encrusted timepiece.

Mr. B. nodded in my direction. "He had questions."

"No more questions, Mr. Campbell!" His voice came through clenched teeth.

"One minute!" Mr. Frank called out.

With all of the madness going on around me, I temporarily blanked out. Moments later, I came to. I don't remember how I got there, but I was riding comfortably in the passenger seat of the 2017 Chevy Corvette Stingray Coupe. It looked like a Robot from the movie "Power Rangers." As I tried to find my bearings, I couldn't help but notice the fine black leather interior with yellow trim matching the flawless paint job. The wood grain on the dashboard and steering wheel was immaculate. I thought to myself, "These people are living the good life."

When he shifted into another gear, I had to struggle to fasten my seatbelt. The V-8 came to life and I heard the exhaust spit out from the dual pipes. The other security was in tow; although I couldn't turn around to see them, I could only trust they were there. Even though I was told not to ask any more questions, the journalist in me wouldn't allow me not to.

"Where are we going?"

He never took his eyes off the road. Mr. Bod`e zigzagged through traffic like a skilled NASCAR driver.

"To my office in Manhattan," he replied.

"Are we running from someone?"

He simply answered, "Yes." He sensed the next question about to roll off my lips. "The Feds."

"Ah…Man!" Please Lord; watch over me through all of this. I'm way too sexy to go to prison. Don't let your favorite son…okay, second favorite son, go out like that.

Mr. Bod`e saw me mumbling my prayer out of the corner of his eye.

"Be easy, Mr. Campbell. They don't know it's me. This is merely a precaution."

I breathed a momentary sigh of relief.

"We will be safer on the other side of the city, my side."

"His side?"

"I own Manhattan."

Who did he think he was Rockefeller, Michael Bloomberg, David K., George S., or Bill G.?

"So, how long have you been on the run?"

"I've been ducking and dodging incarceration for over 15 years, Mr. Campbell. And for the greater portion of that time, I've amassed a fortune and built an empire in the process."

He spoke so nonchalantly you would never know we were traveling at over 80 mph. I thought maybe he was just trying to impress me with a tall tale.

"You see, when you are running or hiding yourself, your true self, you really don't care about certain things; your attitude changes drastically."

"I see."

"It's all about taking big steps and profiting greatly. Producing challenges and finding a way to win. I go all out. I don't sit around waiting to be caught. Bottom line, I make moves, Mr. Campbell."

"I can roll with that. In fact, it sounds like a rush."

"You have no idea how true you are."

I wallowed in the moment as we blew by buildings that appeared as blurs.

"They're not after you for murder, are they?" I had to ask.

"No, Mr. Campbell, not at all. Do I look like I could kill someone?"

"Hell, you don't look like me but you say that you are, so anything is possible." He produced a laugh at my statement, even though I was dead serious.

"Mr. Campbell, the members of the justice system are looking for me for a crime; more widespread and potentially lethal than murder. What I'm wanted for spans forty-one states and three foreign countries. And, before you ask me, I'm not a bank robber, drug trafficker, or weapons dealer."

That pretty much covers everything I could think of.

"Later at my office, you'll be given some of the details concerning all of this."

He was still swerving in and out of traffic.

"So, why did you pick me for your little whatever?"

"Isn't that clear? You're the best man for the job, Mr. Campbell."

What the heck is this guy talking about? "Hold up. I'm not a criminal and I don't intend to be involved in any of your criminal activity." He laughed again, although I didn't see the humor in this situation.

"No, No, Mr. Campbell. I would never involve you in any dealings of the underworld. You're not suited for it. However, you can use your considerable skills and resourceful connections to tell the world about it."

I had a few more questions, but I was distracted by our increase in speed and the approaching of the on-ramp merging onto the interstate. We were traveling over 100 mph and just as quickly as we got on, we shot off and were headed towards a stop light at the same speed. The light was still red with us seconds away from the intersection. The 6.2L LT1 V-8 force had me glued to the seat. I closed my eyes and said a silent prayer. Since meeting these guys, I seemed to have developed a closer relationship with God.

My prayer, for him to stop, went unanswered because he never slowed down. The threshold of the intersection was at hand and as the light magically turned green, we zoomed right through it. I held onto the seat for dear life.

He downshifted, dropping the speed to about half of what it had been before. I breathed a sigh of relief. Suddenly, I looked to my left and then to my right, and it seemed like out of nowhere, the whole security team had shown up, forming a diamond perimeter around us. I finally knew what it felt like to be royalty. I was really rolling with some top dogs.

"This is like traveling with the President of the United States," I said, watching our escorts keeping pace with us.

"In my world, Mr. Campbell, I *am* the President."

"Is that so?"

"That it is. You'll soon become a believer."

We were entering Manhattan when Mr. Bod`e turned his questions to me. "Why haven't you taken a vacation since you and your wife separated four years ago?"

That brought up some haunting memories. What was more frightening was his knowledge of my past. Who was this man?

"How do you know about my wife?"

"Don't you mean your ex-wife, Mr. Campbell?"

"Whatever. How did you get such personal information about me?" Silence filled the car, causing my blood to boil. "Look! I want to know right now!" I shouted. His calmness irritated me.

"It's what I do, Mr. Campbell," he stated flatly. "That's my line of work; to become anybody and receive huge profits in return for my troubles." The fact that he could justify it so casually infuriated me.

"You won't' get a damn thing pretending to be me!"

"What makes you so different?" He laughed to himself as if the joke was on me.

"Just who do you think you are? You think you're untouchable?"

He didn't respond to my idiotic statement. His faced

turned to stone as he continued to drive. I thought for a second and realized there was a lot at stake here.

First of all, a lot of planning had gone into today's meeting and the events that were sure to follow. So, in a sense, I was valuable to him; he couldn't harm me without taking a loss. My best bet was to calm down and watch my surroundings; there was still much to learn. I had to remember that there were many things he knew about me.

I watched him attach some sort of device to his cellphone before he hit a button and the phone sounded off in a strange and irritating tone. The party on the other line picked up on the first ring.

"I'm here," Mr. Bod`e spoke and then hung up.

We turned right at the next corner, then, not even a block down we hit a left into the lot of an immaculate office building.

"Not bad on the eyes," I said, obviously impressed.

"If you think this is something, wait until you see the inside."

My stomach knotted up with anxiety and I couldn't wait.

13

Observe Mr. Campbell, Perimeter four, Mr. Bod`e ordered through a walkie-talkie he had on the inside of the lapel of his jacket. His men broke off in a coordinated ground check. Others poured out of parked cars and from the building to do walking checks. They were so meticulous with their surveillance that Special Forces couldn't have done a better job. Mr. Bod`e noticed the expression on my face.

"We have to make sure no unwanted guests are watching our movements."

"The Feds?" I said bluntly.

"Very good, Sherlock."

Then I noticed her! Coming out of the building, sauntering towards us, was one of the most captivating women I've ever seen. She walked as if she had a heavenly hue around her. She looked, from my vantage point, to be about 5'5", but her posture made her appear taller. Her gait was steady, allowing whoever may have been watching to study every curve on her body.

The mystery woman had on a form-fitting body dress in an elegant gray. It had to be highly inappropriate for any business setting, with her golden legs showing, as well as a hint of cleavage up top, but who was I to argue with such beauty? From my estimate, she had to be in her early forties, however, her smooth complexion could've easily knocked off ten years. My mouth wanted to scream out…"Cookie."

By the time, she made it to the car, which seemed like an eternity, I was totally in awe of her aura.

She was the type of woman you see in your dreams or in some of those music videos the young guys watch nowadays.

As Mr. Bod`e let down his window, she bent down giving us a full view of her mountainous peaks.

She tossed him a key box the size of a remote control. Out of the blue, she said, "Nice color."

"Thanks."

"Tight Rims."

"Thank you, again."

"How much it set you back?"

"At Seventy-Five Grand."

"That isn't too bad, but you should have gotten the Maserati, maybe you could have taken me for a ride if you know what I mean." He smiled. The conversation sounded rehearsed.

She strolled off with just as much sex appeal as she had appeared with. I got caught up in the moment, focusing on her curvy-shaped butt. She looked better leaving than coming. Lust controlled my thoughts; I had to snap out of it. It was too late; a brick had formed in my crotch. As I looked conspicuously down at my pants, I noticed Averie watching me in the visor. He smiled. I pretended not to know what he was smiling at. Damn, I had to hurry up and get right. I counted backward from 10. That didn't work. I tried another tactic. I had to think unattractive, Grace Jones, Tammy Faye Baker in makeup, England's Susan Boyle; seeing someone's toothless midget grandma naked. That did it! I smiled at my accomplished mission. Averie noticed too.

"What!"

"Victoria does that to all the men. Don't be ashamed."

"My embarrassment was evident, but I kept it quiet."

"Damn, Mr. Lot of Questions has nothing to say. I see what keeps you quiet."

We began to move toward a gate leading to an underground parking garage. The other cars moved slowly behind us. Oddly, there wasn't an attendant at the gate. I assumed Averie wouldn't have overlooked such a detail.

Then, mysteriously, right before my eyes, Mr. Frank appeared. One second not there, the next, there.

He opened the gate and all five vehicles proceeded down the ramp to park. Once the opening widened, a few of the cars passed us blowing their horns as some sort of a signal. They then split up, going to the first and third levels to park.

There was an elevator entrance from each level; we remained on the ground floor and parked in front of the entrance doors.

Mr. Bod`e and I got in the elevator; joining us was Mr. B. He pulled out a plastic key card, like the one I had for my penthouse, and automatically ascended to the 20th floor. Before we knew it, the door dinged; we had arrived.

I couldn't believe my eyes when the doors parted. I thought heaven had opened its pearly gates and welcomed me in. Beautiful women with dream bodies were everywhere, covering the room like wall to wall carpet. They were from every nation, long hair, short hair; sexy and exotic ones as well.

"We must focus, W.D." Mr. A. B.'s voice snapped me back to reality.

We continued to walk past the sea of goddesses, following Mr. Bod`e down a hallway. At the end was an etched glass double doorway *with Mr. Averie Bod'e Meeting and Planning Room* engraved in it. There were probably a lot of sensitive things discussed in that room.

A key card was needed to enter this room as well.

Mr. Frank met us at the door, using his key card this time. It was as if each man had a door he was responsible for. When we stepped in, a security man already posted on the inside, asked me to stand in front of a transparent panel on the side wall. There was a red line, something like a laser, and it slowly scanned me from head to toe. I was cleared after the process was complete.

We moved further into the warehouse office where the

walls were adorned with the finest paintings, artwork from Monet to Picasso, plus others I couldn't even pronounce. They looked to be one of a kind.

Later I found out that this was just the tip of the iceberg.

Four big screen TVs filled the empty space on each of the walls in the massive office.

I turned to Mr. Frank and whispered, "Either your boss is extremely wealthy or he has one heck of a deal on this stuff."

"Mr. A.B. got the deal of the century, Mr. Campbell, it was a steal.

"I can imagine."

"No, you can't, but you will."

I didn't understand what he meant, but I didn't press the issue.

Walking in as if on cue, Mr. Bod`e and Ms. Sexy seemed to appear out of nowhere.

"The things you see in this room are gifts from someone very dear to me."

I naturally assumed that he was speaking of a woman.

"Wow!" You must really put your 'Hammer' down. This is a lot of love." They giggled at my innocence.

"Love has nothing to do with it, my friend. The plasma screens over there, they total at $24,381.48."

His mention of the cents did not escape me.

"The oil paintings over there, this one in particular," he said, turning to the replica Picasso, "$20,000. It was just purchased within the last 48 hours and had been shipped over from France."

"I thought you said they were gifts?"

"Oh, but they are, Mr. Campbell. They're from a friend, a mutual friend of ours."

"Wait a minute. I don't know anyone with this kind of money. Well, I know you now, but that's it," I said, obviously confused.

Averie winked at me and then showed me the waiting area.

"You see this sofa? It's one hundred percent genuine ostrich skin. Go ahead, touch it, feel how soft it is." I ran my fingers across the material. "It cost $12,000, Mr. Campbell."

I pulled my hand away like it was electricity.

"I really need to meet this mutual friend. I might have to put my 'Hammer' down to get some of these things." They all burst out laughing.

"Let's take a walk to the mini-kitchen, Mr. Campbell."

We entered a small room adjacent to the meeting room.

I was taken aback by the time that was taken to decorate the small place. Fine marble laced the floors and countertops.

The refrigerator and freezer combination was see-through and customized to fit in the wall space. It was fully stocked with gold wrapped bottles of Crystal.

"Wait. Wait. Wait." All of this is very impressive, to say the least, but what is this really about?"

"When our project is complete, I will allow you to crack open the huge collector's bottle. I have ice in my master suite. I keep it for major accomplishments."

"I'm not on any project. What are you talking about?"

I was confused.

"Believe me, Mr. Campbell; soon you will be very committed to our little project. Just wait and see."

14

Sometimes, when I blackout, things aren't what they appear to be. I've been like that ever since the accident. However, today is different. I keep pinching myself, hoping to wake up and start this day over. Back in the meeting room, I whispered to Mr. B.

"Do you know anything about this project?"

"Don't trip on what Mr. A.B. says sometimes. He likes confusion; it makes him feel in control. I assure you; he'll sit you down and give you all the information you need."

"Mr. B., can you come and hit the button on the remote?" Mr. Bod`e asked his assistant to get the remote from the stand. The button triggered the wall to rotate displaying 25 monitors, each one showing a different angle inside and outside of the building. You could see the buildings entire perimeter, even across the street.

"Goodness! doesn't anything get past you?"

"Just the way I like it," Mr. Bod`e replied. "Just the way I like it."

Mr. B. handed him the remote. He touched another button and the screens changed. All 25 screens had my face on them. Another touch and all of them fit together to make one huge picture of me. It was so large and clear you could see the pores on my face.

"I got my eye on you, Mr. Campbell," he said with a menacing laugh. "Sit down, Mr. Campbell, up here by me." I walked up to the chair on his right and pulled it out to sit down.

"Not there, sit here," he pointed to the one on his left.

"What's the difference?"

"You're not my right-hand man. That's Mr. B.'s position."

I followed my last instruction, taking the seat that faced the eerie picture of me.

"If I haven't gotten your attention yet, maybe I'll get it now." The vision of sexiness handed him a black pouch. He reached inside and pulled out a stack of bills wrapped with a gold clip. He slipped me the whole wad. On the money band, $25,000 was etched in. I flipped through and noticed they were big-faced hundreds.

"What's this for? I haven't done anything to earn this."

Averie clasped his hands together as a sign of total control.

"Consider this the initial payment on the project. Your time is very valuable to me. I know you'll be without work for a spell. Please accept this payment for starters. There's more to come if you make the choice to work for me."

Work for him? Shoot, from what I've seen, that's a no-brainer. But I couldn't rush it.

"I don't know. I'll have to think about it."

Mr. Bod`e didn't respond.

"You still haven't told me what this profit entails?"

"I was just about to get into all of that. Your patience is a must in all of this." He reached under the table and pulled out a copy of my autobiography and sat it on the table.

"Mr. Campbell, I've read your book in its entirety and studied every letter of it, I've tested you against your writings and I've evaluated you from afar. And I must say, thus far, you are who you say you are."

"Thanks…I guess. Wait a minute; I'm not the one pretending to be someone else."

He didn't respond to that.

"But, what I want to know now is this, if you are still as ambitious as you were when you wrote this book? And whether you are legal and trustworthy enough to go through with this project?"

"Of course, I am, as long as it doesn't hurt anyone, endanger me, or land me in prison," I said.

"None of that, Mr. Campbell."

"Well then, tell me more about this project."

"My cadre of intellects and I procure and re-develop standard personal profiles to gain the identity and portray the life of each person we become. I'll speak more on that in a minute."

For the first time today, I just listened.

"The reason why I chose you personally for this project, Mr. Campbell, is because you are a genius. Your book was an inspiration in my decision to start this project; to exploit my world. To let the world, know about the fastest growing, number one crime, worldwide, surpassing the lady of crime herself, Ann Rice."

"Financial Identity Fraud." He paused for emphasis.

"I would like to provide the world with the *ins and outs* and the *do's and don'ts* of F.I.F. Not to glorify it, but to explain it in its entirety."

"Is this a very lucrative business?"

"Yes, very much so."

"Then why choose to put it out?"

He looked deep into my eyes.

"Let's just say I've had a change of heart. Furthermore, I became you to get your full attention; so we could work together. I had to become you in order to amaze you and to entice you. I had to take your life, live it, play with it, and manipulate it into something useful for this cause. I had to put you, Mr. Campbell, in a compromising position. It's the only way I knew how to get you to work with me."

"You could've just asked straight up, without all that hassle."

"And what would you have said, Mr. Campbell?"

"Okay, you got me there."

"Now, let's see if we can clarify some things for you. First and foremost, this will be highly beneficial for you in the long run. You'll have all your prior engagements canceled for the next sixty days."

My eyes nearly popped out of my head. "Sixty days?"

"Mr. Campbell, you will be very well compensated for your troubles, if you choose to take on this project. I noticed you liked the Corvette."

"And… what if I do?"

"Just drop everything else and I'll give it to you. Let's call it a secondary down payment."

"How can you prove all of this is on the up and up?"

"I felt you might ask that question. I can provide you with personal information that only you should know. Afterward, I'll present to you our mutual friend."

Now that's what I've been waiting for.

All the morning's events have led up to this moment. Mr. Bod`e handed me a file containing several personal documents detailed in full. I was astonished at the collection of facts from my life which I thought was personal. I felt sheer violation resting on my conscious, but I held my emotions together for fear that I might give him one more advantage over me. Instead, I just read on in silence.

15

I flipped from page to page, perusing line for line the specifics of my personal and financial history. I could tell he had a copy by the way he followed along, pleased with his findings.

Your Full Name: William D. Campbell

Social Security Number: 323-91-0411

Birthdate: August 3, 1969

Age: Today you made the big '48'

Parents' Names: George and Louise, divorced, both residing in Terrell, Texas

Sister: Jada, who I'm sure is currently employed

Your two daughters: April and Alexis, both in college

Ex-Girlfriend: Angela Jones of Virginia

Lady Friend: Nicole of Atlanta, Ga.

And of course, your wife, oops…ex-wife, I should say, Ms. Olivia Walker. You both met in 1988 and married in 1995 in her hometown of Chicago, wasn't that nice."

Your auto loans were 1987, 1995, 2001, 2007, 2010, 2013 and lastly, this delightful year of 2017. I didn't forget the cash purchase of one 1979 Mercedes.

You do your banking in Atlanta and New York at JP where, I, too, do my banking.

You also have active accounts at Dells Argo and Fourth Federal.

Your checking account number: 1200115512
Your savings account number: 0111321097
Business account number: 9876543200
Credit Cards and Cid's Numbers are:
V-Card 4117 5213 0001 1233 / EXP. 07/18 (153)
M-Card 5114 4321 0014 1111 / EXP. 12/18 (404)
Black Express-Card 3311 550122 12435 / EXP. 08/20 (409)
And by the way, "I, never leave home without it."

Your PIN numbers are all displayed on the documents as you can see. Your last credit card transaction was this morning at approximately 9:04 am. It was also used yesterday at 5:26 pm; both your V-Card and Black Express card were very useful Mr. Campbell. Not to leave out your most precious asset – the company you own.

Medical Profile: High blood pressure, Diabetes and occasional blackouts.

"It also states that you had surgery done on your right shoulder due to an awful auto accident a few years ago, how is it now?"

"It gets a bit stiff when the weather chills, but other than that, I'll live."

"Good. Well since you have two of the deadliest health conditions, hypertension, and diabetes, that throwing arm of yours should be the least of your worries."

Medications: Hydrochlorothiazide 25 mg tablets
Metoprolol 50 mg tablets and your Levemir Insulin.

"That reminds me," Averie looked up from the file. "Have you taken your shot this morning, Mr. Campbell? I hate to sound patronizing but you know how you get."

"I did, right before we left."

"Well, there's a prescription for you in the refrigerator in case you forget."

"You know what? You never cease to amaze me."

"Why thank you. I do my best. Now let me continue. You have an existing passport that you received back in September.

You've done quite a bit of traveling this year, Mr. Campbell. London, Germany, Canada, Business, I suppose?"

"You should know. You know everything else."

"Are you trying to be a smart-ass?"

"No, but apparently, you are. However, you're not as smart as you appear. Some of your information is incorrect."

"Oh yeah, Like what?"

"Like the credit card transaction this morning at 9:04 a.m., and the one yesterday at 5:26 p.m., both of those are inaccurate. My Black Express card and V-Card balances are fine."

"Are you sure about that?" His smile left me with a twinge of doubt, but I brushed it off.

"As sure as I can be. Also, the auto loan… bogus.

I haven't so much as attempted to purchase a new vehicle. And speaking of the passports, well, you said yourself earlier, while endangering my life, why I haven't taken a vacation in the past four years. You know about the split with my wife, how come you are so misinformed about these other facts? And how come you're trying to deceive me with all the riffraff? First, you send a driver to pick me up, then you strip search me, cut into my phone lines, drive me frantically from one end of New York City to the other, then sit me in here and place my whole life story in front of me, telling me what I'm reading is true. I know what I'm reading isn't true and you can't trick me into believing so.

Furthermore, Mr. Averie Bod`e, you need to tighten up your C.I.A. skills. Instead of trying to be somebody, you need to try being yourself. Maybe you're lonely and need to get your rocks off or something so you chose innocent old me to be your guinea pig in some experiment you and your phony baloney staff cooked up. Well, I'm not buying it. You need _____."

Before I could get another word out, he stood up abruptly, screeching the chair from up under him, and slamming his fist on the table with the force of Serena Williams. I was stunned. I thought he was close to having me disappear.

While smiling at me, he responded in a raspy tone.

"Listen to me, Mr. Campbell, when was the last time you

checked your credit report? I'll tell you when, three months ago."

I was dumbfounded by his bluntness. It had been about 90 days; I remembered it distinctly because I was arguing on the phone with the extremely rude customer service representative.

"You know the 500 series Mercedes Benz in your parking garage, the loan dates back to 2010. It seems that you have a fetish for Mercedes Benzes."

My mouth dropped open with his next statement.

"The rims on our Stingray you rode here in were purchased by your 820-credit score and your signature. The breakfast this morning, your V-Card. Ooh, Mr. Whon sends his appreciation for the generous tip. All of this you see around you, furniture, TV's, paintings, all compliments of Mr. W.D. Campbell. And since we're speaking of your fortunes, why don't we celebrate by popping a four-hundred-dollar bottle of Crystal. The case only cost four grand, but hey, who's counting figures, right Mr. Campbell? Oh, by the way, thank you for this nice jewelry, blue and canary diamonds, they make a nice couple, don't you agree?"

His sarcasm was making my blood boil. He hummed a tune as he nonchalantly placed a black eel-skin briefcase on the table. He began to sequence the three-digit combination and then unlatched the hooks with a subtle pop. Mr. Bod`e shuffled around inside the case, making the sheets of paper rattle for my entertainment.

"Mr. Campbell, take a gander at these." He slid another bound folder full of documents. This time they were itemized transactions made in the last 59 days with not only my name but with my exact signature on them. This day was too overwhelming. I had to take a deep breath and count to ten before I digested what was in front of me.

16

The first document in the stack contained the stamped logo of the Manhattan Chevy Car Emporium. Everything from the bank lender, tax papers, license fee receipts, to the actual contract, was included. The license photo, which was a copy, matched mine. At the bottom, he continued by showing me a purchase of one brand new 2017 Canary Yellow Chevy Corvette Stingray, price totaling at $75,000.00. I nearly lost my breath after seeing that figure, but I read on.

Passports in my name and the receipts from airline and hotel stays, plus auto rentals, department stores credit of clothing sprees filled the next page. The total was over $12,000.

The next page showed a lease agreement in my name for a residence in the Atlanta-Buckhead area. My V-Credit card account was bumped up to $25,000 with an approval back in June of this year. The form also showed a duplicate of my card obtained from a possible fraudulent service. It looked authentic. There were also receipts from extensive shopping sprees. There were bank checks in my name.

I came across a listing for a Big Box store loan and credit line for $25,000. If I didn't see it for myself, I would've never thought my status was this good.

Loans credited for Electronics: $10,000 Appliances: $15,000, Jewelry: $10,000 for three pieces from Friedman's; credit line for furniture registered $7,500. After totaling the damages from all the fraudulent purchases, not to mention the $341.00 tab from breakfast, which counts too totaling a bit under$180,000 plus.

How could I have belittled this man? I deserved to be slapped. I was questioning the mind of a genius. He obviously had a wealth of resources and used them wisely. Although it was cleverly arranged, the intent could be considered malicious. My tongue was caught in knots, full of questions with no clue of how to ask them.

I really felt like I'd been tricked by the most heinous scam ever. The most unimaginable things had happened right under my nose. My whole life had been stolen as I was living it. To put it mildly, he just took a 20-inch poll, ungreased, and shoved it directly up my ass-hole, because I've been severely victimized!

Over and over, my mind kept flashing back to the ad on Identity Theft Protection, ID Patrol offered by a company called Equifax. They served as a constant reminder that I was not exempt to becoming a victim. I didn't pay the ad too much attention, but I do remember them guaranteeing safetyof up to a million dollars. In fact, I flipped the channel as fast as it took for me to land in this predicament.

Trying to regain some sort of composure, my mind reeled hastily for facts. I needed clarity. Mr. Averie Bod`e calmly stepped out of the room sensing that I needed some time to think. He was right in one regard, he had my undivided attention. But what exactly did he want from me? All the illegal transactions and sordid details, he could've skipped me with it.

Mr. Bod`e re-entered the room whistling yet another tune as if he didn't have a care in the world. He smiled while taking a seat at the head of the table; I guess you could say "my table," since I purchased it.

"Well, judging by that disheveled look on your face, I can tell you have a lot of questions. So, what's on your mind?"

"For starters, how many others like me, innocent working-class men and women, who have slaved hard to establish decent credit, how many of those lives have you destroyed?"

"You mean filing for bankruptcy, repaying the banks and credit lenders, doctoring paperwork and legal fees, things of that nature? Are you asking for a certain number of people?

I can't or should I say I'm not at liberty to disclose that information." His tone became real professional.

"That's rather evasive of you."

"Here are a few other inquiries that come to mind…."

"Okay, I'll try to answer as best as I can."

1.) How could someone have all this personal information provided to them, and then turn themselves into that someone?

2.) How do you get access to our information; are they inside sources?

3.) How long have you been in this business?

4.) How much money does it take to keep your business afloat?

5.) How much income have you produced from ripping peoples' livelihood away from them? It must be way in the millions!

6.) Have you ever been betrayed?

7.) Have you ever been caught while doing this?

8.) Do you ever plan, if not already today, to stop doing what you do?

9.) Have you ever thought of the serious damages you have afflicted on so many people's lives by damaging their livelihood?

10.) Have you ever once thought to repay any of the victims back? I, personally, really feel you need to do that, starting with me!

"Wow, that's quite a list. All of that was swimming around in that head of yours?"

"I just don't want any more surprises."

"Trust me, W.D. everything from this point on will be on the up and up." He pressed a button silently summoning one of his staff. Ms. Victoria sashayed into the room, taking up all the excess air out of the room. She definitely made it hard for any man or woman to breathe.

"Ms. Victoria, you are my witness that W.D. Campbell here has read over the various documents." She nodded.

"Ms. Victoria?" I asked curiously.

"Yes, I understand your inquisitiveness. It is coincidental that she shares the same name as your mother." We locked eyes. He smiled as if he knew something I didn't.

"Are we now on the same page, Mr. Campbell?"

"Excuse me?"

"Are you with us?"

"I must first know what 'with us' means?"

"All in due time, my friend."

"Tell me more."

17

It was time that I just listened; maybe some things would just reveal themselves in time. I wondered how he could become someone else so easily. Everything had to be precise, birth certificates, social security numbers, drivers' license numbers, expiration dates, even photos with weight, height, and eye and hair color. His resources must be endless and more ingenious than he is. I didn't know what I was up against, but I was sure that he would give me an idea.

"The reason I picked you is because you're a splendid author. The only way I could get your full undivided attention and gain your confidence was to achieve the one thing that would amaze and devastate you at the same time; taking your life and living it. I wanted to see us working together, you know, a compromised situation."

"A compromised situation? You mean by stealing my identity and putting me in a debt of up to two hundred-thousand-dollars? You call that a compromising situation? I call it Black Mail!" I shouted.

"Rest assured, Mr. Campbell, everything will be back as it was at the conclusion of our project. You must trust me."

"Just what do you mean by 'project'?"

"Ms. Victoria, the papers please."

She placed before me a clipboard with what looked to be a contract. I didn't even begin to read it, I was furious at the predicament I was in. If I had a gun, there probably would have been a few dead people to be cleaned up. Mr. A.B. sensed my change in attitude.

"You must not look at me with such disdain. Doing something crazy will not help you in this matter. Your cooperation will be beneficial in the long run. Just remember this, in my line of work, there is never a positive response for doing dirt in the world." He paused for emphasis. "I'm really not the bad guy here. In a sense, I'm a humanitarian, exploiting the #1 crime in America today. Think, before me, there were thousands of others and there had to be someone to teach me."

"Okay, okay, I get the picture. So, what's the plan?"

"Please read the contract, Mr. Campbell." Ms. Victoria's voice floated through the air like a satin-lined cloud.

I observed the bold lettering, highlighted with all the stipulations. There would be no information provided about the narrator or members of staff. Locations will also be omitted. As I read on, there was also a timeframe in which the story was to be completed.

All information will be provided by Mr. A.B., the narrator. The stories, ***"INTO THE WRONG HANDS"*** *and the sequel,* ***"INTO THE RIGHT HANDS*** "as well as all its expenses will be provided by Mr. A.B. The line that stuck out to me was, 'All relief from prior accounts, including existing charges, loans, and any other punitive damages will be reimbursed. Now that showed good faith. Maybe it was just a payoff to keep me quiet. Then I thought, I could still do the story and end up executed, so I quickly disregarded those notions.

"So, what would be my restitution for this project?"

"You will be paid in the amount of $2,000,000 for your services."

"Two Million Dollars?"

"Fifty percent as an advance after the contract is signed, then the balance at the completion of the project. There will be a working period of twelve months to complete the project."

He said he would provide all the necessary information to make the book realistic, intriguing, and most of all, accurate. From locations, dates, license makers, credit report providers, contractors, check makers, investors, inside corporate providers, credit card makers, birth certificates and social security providers, postal deliveries, real estate companies, vehicle purchases, mortgage buys, lines of credit and bank lenders; all this information is vital to legitimacy.

He would disclose how he defrauded millions of dollars from multi-million dollar businesses with only a signature. How he obtained and purchased an unlimited amount of identities in the past years. He's defrauded companies in over 37 states and used countless fraudulent identities in air flight travel and airline ticket purchases he's flown on, in which 40% were in First Class with purchases by someone else's credit cards. Corporations were the ones he mainly targeted. How women were vulnerable and most likely to be persuaded by the sight of money, his personality, and sex. Profitable gains 10,000% from what he put into the operation which was virtually an overnight success.

Mr. A.B. paused to catch his thoughts.

"Are you alright?" Ms. Victoria asked.

"Yes. Just reminding myself, that the past was daring… tricky even. There were many close calls with the law. I'll detail more during our interview. You'll need to record notes based on my recollections."

For the first time, I witnessed Mr. A.B. speak on a personal matter. Seeing this enigma of a man split into a multitude of personalities only excited me more. Writing his story may very well be worth the trouble and debts he ran up in my name. Two million dollars sure wouldn't hurt either.

"Where do I sign?"

"The Contract Agreement"

I agree to all stipulations and terms of the following written contract agreement dated on August 3, 2017 between both parties: Mr. Averie Bod`e and Mr. William D. Campbell for the stories "INTO THE WRONG HANDS" and the sequel "INTO THE RIGHT HANDS."

Both parties understand all terms contained in this contract.

Writers Fee/Payment: TWO MILLION DOLLARS.

First payment of $1 Million will be deposited on August 3, 2017 by bank wire only.

Balance of $1 Million balance will be provided at the completion of the story on the agreed date September 2, 2017.

All stipulations of this contract have been read and with the full knowledge in its entirety. Both parties will comply with all terms and successfully complete its session.

The Signatures below grants/confirms that this agreement will be non-voided in its session.

Signature of Parties:

______________________	______________________
Mr. Averie Bod`e	August 3, 2017
______________________	______________________
William D. Campbell	August 3, 2017
______________________	______________________
Attorney	August 3, 2017

18

Averie Bod`e incessant cough was a cause for alarm. It was an odd abnormality to a usually calm disposition. I had hardly noticed it when he first had a spell. Ms. Victoria offered him some water and he seemed to be fine. But his cough was more like a cross between tuberculosis and flu-like symptoms.

We had just shaken hands, solidifying our agreement to work together. I couldn't wait to wash my hand. His demeanor was all business.

"Are you taking something for that cough?" I asked, obviously concerned about his well-being.

"No, I'm not. It'll go away soon enough. I've been a little under the weather the last few days, but I'm fine. Do you understand what's about to take place?"

I said, let me go over this, "Basically, you want a book detailing the life you're leading. You want this book to be a warning to those not aware of the ever-present fraudulent crimes of identity theft"

"Very good, I believe you've grasped the concept."

"Now, you understand I'll need solitude, a place where I can work undisturbed. Frankly, I don't feel comfortable writing at my place anymore. I'll always feel like someone's watching me."

"I get your drift and I completely understand. I've

arranged a place for you to have all the peace and quiet you'll need to complete this project. We'll be doing a little traveling today. I have a quiet retreat right outside Atlanta, Georgia, actually."

"I chuckled."

"What's so funny?"

"It's just when you said you had a place, my mind thought back to my book where I described Atlanta as the ideal locale to do work. Now, you coincidentally mention this is where you reside."

"Well, I give you credit for painting such a vivid picture for me. You definitely influenced my decision to buy out there. I think you'll be pleased with the accommodations I have prepared for you. Once we arrive in Georgia, you'll receive the first half of your payment as promised. You really won't need any of it for the next 180 days because I'm taking care of everything for you."

That was rather nice of him I thought, considering that he had virtually stripped me of any financial security I once had and had worked so hard to get.

"It's approximately 12:14 in the afternoon; Mr. B. will drive you back to your condo to gather your things. Make sure you take your insulin shot while you're there… and, oh yeah don't forget that nice Norelco shaver that you use to shave your head. You know the one in the top left-hand drawer in your bathroom."

I shook my head. At this point, nothing else he said or did really surprised me. I was finally convinced that this man knew everything about me. Well, maybe not everything.

"We have a direct flight scheduled for 4:00 p.m., leaving LaGuardia heading to Atlanta Hartsfield."

"Who is we?"

"Oh, the team will be accompanying us. I'll meet you on the plane, but I'll see you before you see me."

"How so?" I asked, not sure what he meant.

"Let's just say that I'll be where you least expect me to be."

I took him at face value and didn't ask any more questions. He had one for me, "Do you prefer a window or aisle seat?"

"Window, I guess. I'd like to look out at the clouds and let my imagination take flight. Did you know that it's always sunny above the clouds?"

"I never paid any attention to that Mr. Campbell, I don't mean to cut this short, but we are on a strict timetable as I mentioned before. So, to ensure that we stay on track, Mr. B. will be advising you with time checks." Every second is important; as they say, 'time is money'.

There are specific things you'll need for the trip: your laptop, writing materials, and toiletries; all the rest will be provided. "So, I'll allow you ten minutes to get it all together."

"Ten minutes?" I inquired. "Can I use the bathroom or what?"

"Do what you must, just remember, ten minutes is all you have. And don't forget to take your insulin shot, sir."

I only stared, not saying a word.

19

Mr. B. and I were enroute back to my place down in Harlem. The day was halfway gone and it seemed like so much had already happened. I looked out the backseat window and tried to collect my thoughts as we rode along. As the hours progressed, I felt like I was losing control of my life. Who is the guy and why me Lord?

The driver was silent for most of the trip. He was one to follow orders; Mr. Bod`e certainly kept disciplined workers around him I thought. I wondered how much he was paying them. I decided to break the ice and try to strike up some kind of conversation. With all the riding we had done thus far, I felt we had developed some sort of a kinship.

"Do you enjoy what you do, Mr. B?"

"You mean working for Mr. A.B.? Sure. It has some definite benefits; besides we go way back which makes it sort of like an honor to serve him."

That's the most I ever heard him speak casually. General conversations from these mysterious guys; it was refreshing to hear. So, I guess that means you like working for him. "You make it seem as if he's a dictator and you're a faithful supporter."

"I don't know about the dictator part, but, I'm extremely faithful to him. Loyalty is a priority in my book."

We finally arrived at my place after some unexpected afternoon traffic. The talk I had with Mr. B. kept the trip from being a bore, but as soon as we stepped out of the car it was back to business as usual for him.

"Good day, Mr. Campbell," Mr. Williams greeted me from behind his post at the counter. I greeted him back and told him it was okay when he suspiciously eyed my escort.

Before we stepped into the elevator, Mr. B. returned my key card and keys. On the way up, I kept thinking how different my life was compared to the past four hours. The inside of my condo was even foreign to me now. I mean, everything was still in the same place; however, there was an air of invasion present.

Mr. B, the driver interrupted me by saying, "Remember, Mr. Campbell, ten minutes starting now."

I went through my bedroom grabbing necessary items for the journey. I put everything in my Louis Vuitton duffel. I purposely went to my bookshelf and removed a copy of my book as a reference for my next project. *"I always like to look back for inspiration."* Next, I went to the kitchen, snatching my insulin pills and started putting together a quick snack since I had a few minutes to spare.

Time, Mr. Campbell." Mr. B. was looking at his watch as I came from the kitchen with my bag over my shoulder and a sandwich in my hand.

Before we walked out the door, Mr. B. stopped me in my tracks.

"Mr. Campbell, I need you to put this on." He handed me a satchel with a curly wig, sunglasses, and a black trench coat.

Laughing, I said, "What's all this for?"

"Look!" he barked, startling me, "you ask too many damn questions. There are certain precautions we must take for your safety. Now, from this point on, you must start doing as I say without question, do you hear me? Our objective is not to raise any unnecessary suspicions about what we're doing; this project means too much to Mr. A.B."

I put the items on as ordered. Once I signed that contract, I knew I was at their mercy; everything I did from now on would be watched closely for any signs of disloyalty. However, humbling myself to do their will would be something new for me, I had always been my own man. Of course, thinking about the money helped me stay focused. What would you do for 2 million dollars?

We stepped into the elevator with me looking like a Halloween character. When I checked the mirror before we left, I couldn't believe how ridiculous I looked. I could've passed for one of those 'B' list actors in those soft porn movies. The elevator stopped on the second floor. I wanted to say something but I was already warned not to question anything. We got off in a rush and ran down the hallway to the fire exit. From there, we walked down the two remaining flights of stairs to the ground floor.

"You did grab your medicine, correct?"

"Yes, I did, sir. And thanks for being so concerned," I said, sarcastically.

Mr. B. kept looking at his watch as we pushed quickly through a side street door. As soon as the door swung open, a Black GMC van pulled up on cue. It barely stopped when a sliding side door opened and two sets of hands emerged from the darkness.

"In here, Mr. Campbell," a voice signaled.

Both Mr. B. and I climbed in as we pulled off all in one motion. I sat down and secured myself with a seat belt; I had learned from the ride earlier that these guys had no regard for speed. Mr. B. was next to me. One of my handlers returned to his passenger seat, the other sat behind us in the back of the van.

All of them were dressed in black just like before and I think I even recognized a couple of them from the restaurant. These were all Mr. Bod`e's men; and there was no way I could remember their names.

The driver, who Mr. B. later referred to as Alex, made a few calls on his cell and confirmed that we were on schedule.

Each man on this team had a responsibility and relied on the other for the plans to work. The whole scene was like an updated version of the A-Team television show.

I took in all the side conversations. When I heard Mr. Alex tell someone named Claude we'd be meeting Mr. A.B. at 4:00 p.m. it sounded strange since we were supposed to be taking off at that time. Mr. B. could see the anxious look on my face and knew I wanted to ask something.

"What, Mr. Campbell? What's on your mind?" he asked, winking at Claude.

"It's just…well; I thought we were…How can we? Oh, never mind, I'll find out when I find out."

"Damn! I almost had him," Claude said, while the others roared with laughter. Obviously, the joke was on me, but I didn't want to feed into it.

"Mr. Campbell, you almost cost that man $1,000. We bet that you would ask a question before the ride began. Now he owes me a grand. And I want my money when we get to Atlanta." Mr. Alex was holding out his hand for payment and smiling.

All the events of the morning had finally caught up with me. I leaned my head back and couldn't resist the urge to nod off. Before I knew it, I was knocked out cold, entering dreamland.

20

The sound of doors slamming woke me from my brief slumber. I wiped the saliva from my chin and looked around, still groggy from sleep. I was the only one left in the van. I quickly checked my surroundings to make sure that I wasn't being left for dead. We had arrived at LaGuardia International Airport.

The others had vacated the area; I assumed they had gone inside. Mr. B. was opening the back door to retrieve the bags and said, "We're running a bit late so you need to fix yourself up so we can get a move on."

I felt like I'd been sleeping for 5 hours but it had only been a little over 20 minutes. My disguise had shifted during my nap with my glasses nearly falling off my face. "How long do I have to wear this get-up?" I asked before I realized what I was doing. To my surprise, Mr. B. didn't snap.

"Once we get past the ticket counter and the first wave of security inside, you can return to your old self."

That was a relief even though I hadn't felt like myself all morning. I stepped out of the van and walked towards the back where Mr. B. was getting my belongings. Just as I did so, I observed an unidentified gentleman climbing into the driver's seat and speed off in the van.

"Why? What the…?" Mr. B. waved that off and motioned for me to follow him.

Inside the terminal it was so crowded it literally looked like a circus. There were people everywhere in search of their intended direction. All saw signs of all the major airlines represented at the long ticket counter in front of us. Delta, American, and United were side by side. I was quickly pushed into the Delta first class check-in line which wasn't as long as all the others.

There was a lady, who appeared to be in her mid-40, standing erect with one of those practiced smiles. Mr. B. was ahead of me and he gave her his I.D. and she typed in his information and pulled up his reservation.

"Is Mr. W.D. Campbell still traveling with you today, Mr. B?"

"Yes, Tammy." He slid to the side allowing me to be seen. I was embarrassed to be seen in the disguise, but hey, she didn't know me from Adam anyway. I happened to notice that this Tammy person and Mr. B. shared glances which led me to believe that they knew each other. I couldn't believe the extent they went to enlist an airline personnel as one of theirs.

She took Mr. B.'s word for it and cleared me based on a visual. She then handed him back his I.D. card and his two first-class E-tickets. Tammy explained the new electronic system before we left.

"Have a nice flight to Atlanta, Mr. Oliver Stenson, and Mr. Campbell."

"You take care, Tammy."

Oliver Stenson. That had to be an assumed name.

He smiled as to confirm my thought.

Because of the 9/11 attacks, air travel had become a tedious process. New York was especially concerned with safety, for fear of being placed under a microscope once again. We ventured towards one of the security areas where an attendant asked for our tickets.

We were screened with metal detecting wands and then had to go through a mild strip search. This was twice today that I'd been searched; I wished they would've been this cautious prior to the terrorist attacks.

Mr. B. looked at the time on the huge clock in the baggage claim area. "Come on, we've lost a lot of time with that search."

"Can I get out of this now?"

"There's a restroom over there, make it quick, Mr. Campbell."

I came out as quickly as I went in, and we were on our way, hustling through the terminal like O.J. Simpson in a Hertz commercial. We finally made it to Gate 33 and had to check in again. The line was extra-long. Mr. B. and I were both becoming impatient. All I wanted to do was sit down on the plane and collect my thoughts.

The sign behind the clerk said that the flight to Atlanta would be leaving on time. On time was music to my ears. If we were any later, we would've missed the flight, and who knows how Mr. Bod`e would've reacted to that? He's like Bruce Banner-The Hulk; I wouldn't want to see him when he's mad.

When boarding was announced, I finally settled down, knowing peace of mind was real. Mr. B. and I chose to board first, which was our privilege for being first class passengers. We passed by a suspicious looking British man walking with a cane. Mr. B. and I looked at each other, then to him and shook our heads. If it's going down, let's get it over with because it's too late to turn back now.

21

Entering the terminal's electronic doors stood a tall distinguished looking gentleman. He, too, was disguised elaborately wearing a London Fog coat. He was well aware of all of the onlookers and understood how many federal agents were eager to stumble upon him.

* * * * *

Today, I felt as if I turned myself into a 60-year-old British Counselor, accent and all. I knew that it was their custom to bypass any sort of strip searching, and airport security respected my wishes. I would have volunteered to the wand search and continued to the designated gate for departure. I would have sauntered through the crowded terminal unscathed, undisturbed and most important, under the radar.

* * * * *

There were 12 seats in the first-class section of the aircraft. I took my seat by the window in row 2, seat C. Mr. B. sat next to me in seat B. I guess that was appropriate to match his name. As I got comfortable, I saw some familiar faces entering the cabin. Matt and Tom came in and sat on the opposite side from us. A few minutes later, Rick, Greg, Alex, David, Claude and Mr. Frank all came in and started filling in the section.

An older British man walked in cautiously and sat in the row behind us. At first, I thought the whole first class was ours until he showed up. I guess I wasn't as special as I thought. My mind was distracted by the sheer sexiness of Ms. Victoria, who was the last to board along with three flight attendants who closed the door behind her. She winked at me then took a seat next to the older British man.

"Mr. B., would you mind if we switched seats?" Ms. Victoria's voice sounded heavenly over my shoulder. She smelled equally as divine the closer she got. I saw her in full view with her short tan linen skirt with matching jacket. Her white rayon blouse left little to the imagination. When she took the seat that Mr. B. had occupied, her skirt rose revealing a pair of golden legs so tantalizing I had to shift in my seat in order to keep from exposing my already growing erection.

My eyes locked in on her cleavage spilling out of her low-cut blouse.

"Am I bothering you by sitting here, Mr. Campbell?"

Hell yes! I wanted to say. "No, not at all." I couldn't hide the tent that formed in my pants. She noticed when I kept fidgeting.

"Mr. Campbell, you don't have to be ashamed. I don't want you to be nervous around me, I won't hurt you. My job is to help you stay calm and focused and I'm willing to take whatever measures are necessary."

I couldn't resist asking. "Ms. Victoria, are you flirting with me?"

"I'm just stating my responsibilities. You are one of my responsibilities, Mr. Campbell."

She still had certain seductiveness in her tone. Luckily for me, the flight attendant came around to take our drink and food orders while we taxied out. Once we hit the air, we would receive it. To tell the truth, I was glad she came when she did. Her interruption broke the awkward feeling I was developing inside.

I barely knew this Victoria woman, yet her sudden flirtatiousness stirred up some buried emotions. It had been so long since I'd experienced such emotion. My ex-wife had tried, unsuccessfully, to spark those feelings, but I was too drawn to my work to even notice. I guess that was what drove her away. One thing remained clear, though; a man will always be a man, and right now, this mystery woman was testing the restraints of my manhood.

"I'd like a Club Sandwich and a Cranberry juice with a splash of Vodka."

A much too familiar voice spoke from behind me to the attendant, "Absolutely no alcohol." The stewardess was caught off guard as well.

"Excuse me?" she directed to the unknown man.

"That's right, Mr. Campbell, you are restricted from consuming any alcoholic beverages for the duration of this project; only soda or water." It was stipulated in your contract.

"I don't remember seeing that."

"Well, it's in there; soda, water or nothing."

"It's my birthday! I can't have one drink?"

"Ma'am we'll have 2 colas and some ice water, thank you." The attendant moved on to the next row of seats to get their orders. As the others told her what they wanted, I asked Victoria where Mr. Bod`e was. "I thought we were to meet on the plane, but I didn't see him board."

"He's not far. In fact, he's enroute."

"What, he's taking another flight?"

"No, actually he's closer than you think." I wondered what was with all the riddles, but I let it pass. I looked out the window as we were lifting off. I always found that to be the most exhilarating part of the flight. It was like leaving all your cares on the ground.

Once we ascended to our flying altitude, I contemplated

whether I should get some rest or pull out my laptop and begin outlining. Another flight attendant came through our cabin with some magazines and newspapers.

"Is that U.S.A. Today current?" I asked.

"This morning's," she replied, showing me the date.

"I'll take it, thank you."

"Anything for you, ma'am?" Victoria was already starting to fade out.

"No thank you," she answered, her voice trailing off.

"You look tired."

"I am, Mr. Campbell. I'll be fine once we get to Atlanta."

I watched her drift off into a quiet snore. Even in sleep, she was stunning. The ocean of clouds drew my attention as we flew through them. Flying always created a certain calm within me.

22

One hour into my nap, I felt a hand shaking my shoulder. It was Mr. Frank letting me know that the flight attendant was coming around to start food service. In fact, I wasn't even hungry until he mentioned it.

"Here's your sandwich, Sir." The petite stewardess handed me a tray.

"Hold on a minute while I put my tray table down." When I reached for the tray, I expected to have to reach over Ms. Victoria, but she was no longer sitting next to me. I looked around without giving myself away. Mr. B. caught my eyes and chuckled to himself like he knew something I didn't.

"She parachuted out, Mr. Campbell," he said with the straightest expression.

"She jumped!" I took him seriously because he didn't seem like the type to joke. Besides, I wouldn't put anything past these 007 kinds of folk.

"She said she couldn't deal with your snoring one more minute." Just as dejection set in, I heard the locks on the lavatory door click and Ms. Victoria re-entered the cabin. Everyone burst out laughing, even the flight attendant and the British guy sitting behind me.

"Jokes on me, huh?"

"Happy Birthday, Sir," the petite one remarked, still giggling.

"What's your name, if I may ask?"

"It's Tia. Why?"

"I just thought a woman with such a lovely face had to have a lovely name to match. I was right."

"Well, thank you, Sir."

Ms. Victoria took the seat Mr. Frank had occupied and he came to sit by me with his food. Ms. Victoria gave me a look of disdain, watching me converse with Tia, the stewardess. She didn't strike me as the jealous type with all her confidence, but nothing was what it seemed.

"She's been hurt before; you have to excuse her. Going into a shell is her way of dealing with problems," Mr. Frank explained.

"I didn't know there was a problem. She flirted with me, I responded, that's it."

"Yeah, but you showed interest in the attendant."

"So!"

"These women, they can't be explained that simply."

"Sometimes their changing emotions are too much to deal with."

"There's something there with you two, I see the way you look at her."

"Who hurt her?"

"Averie."

"Everybody is a lot of people. Could you be more specific?"

"I was specific. Averie Bod`e hurt her. Ruined her life like he's done so many others."

It took me a second to catch on that he was talking about Mr. A.B., his boss. My question was what kind of relationship did they really have for her to be so scorned?

"He took her life to get her undivided attention. But by the time he gave it back to her, she wasn't able to recover. She's not happy, but she is content. So, my advice to you is to back off. Don't get too close to her for the rest of the day. She is very important to this project."

I turned to see her engaged in conversation with the British fella from across the aisle. I studied her pretty face which appeared a little more worn from the flawless beauty I had seen before. Frank was right, she looked like a woman who'd lost who she was inside by having the outside damaged. Now I understood how beautiful women and healthy spirits could turn cold. I just hoped that after this project I'd be able to return to some sort of normal life. One thing was for sure; I'd be two million dollars richer.

The food caused me to drift off again when they started showing the in-flight movie. It was one of those movies made for children, but funny enough for the adults to enjoy. I remembered seeing it advertised on T.V. but I didn't last long enough to watch it.

I was awakened abruptly by the sudden up and down motion of the plane. The pilot came on the intercom and announced that we had hit a patch of turbulence. Of all the times, I'd flown; this was probably the scariest part. No one, including the pilot, had control over what the change in wind pattern could do to a plane. That's why I always made sure to say my prayers hoping that God would see me through.

There had been too many events in the past where planes had gone down unexpectedly, killing hundreds of people onboard.

My stomach instantly became queasy and the sandwich that I'd stuffed down a little while ago was tossing around inside. The 'fasten seatbelt' sign was illuminated, halting my trip to the restroom.

"Are you feeling alright, Sir?" Tia looked genuinely concerned, noticing the flushed appearance on my face."

"The turbulence… it's messing my stomach up something awful."

"I'm sorry but you can't get up right now," she said, pointing to the sign.

"Aren't you supposed to be seated too?"

"Well, if I sit, who's going to take care of you?"

"Good point."

"Now, if you want I can bring you a warm compress to soothe your uneasiness."

"That would be great."

She tended to a couple of other passengers before she returned. With a pair of tongs, she handed me the steaming cloth, smiling in the process. I remembered what Frank had told me about Ms. Victoria and decided against flirting with Tia. The heat from the face towel was just what I needed. I thanked her graciously and leaned back against the comfortable seats.

I was finally able to relax while focusing my thoughts on something more pleasant. Tia was the first thing to come to mind. I wondered what her life was like, always being on the road, from this state to that. She probably came in contact with so many different people, especially men.

Can you imagine how often she got propositions and proposals during her trips? Dates probably came as numerous as the zip codes she touches. This guy I met at a fictional writing conference told me that he used to use his frequent flier miles to see how many conquests he could encounter. His target was primarily flight attendants. It was a challenge, somewhat of a sport for him to see which one and how many of these lonely, vulnerable women would fall victim to his predatory ways.

And if Tia did have a man, how committed could she be on the road like she was? I hated to be a black cloud on the institution of monogamy, but we were on the other side of the millennium where spontaneity ruled over old-fashioned relationships. Her man, if any, was probably at home wondering the same thing; lonely nights and cold sheets don't make good bedfellows.

I let the scenery outside my window become my pacifier through all the conflicting thoughts in my head. I didn't see any more of Tia until we were ready to land.

The heatwaves from the sun were our guide into Georgia.

The captain came on the intercom, once again announcing our arrival.

"We will be landing in Hot-Atlanta in approximately 10 minutes. The weather today is in the high 70's. Those of you connecting to Orlando, Florida will have an opportunity to make it to your gate in ample time. The flight doesn't leave for another 45 minutes. I'd like to thank you for flying Southwest Airlines. We hope that when you choose to see our beautiful country or abroad you choose Southwest Airlines as your carrier."

As much as I enjoyed flying, I was sort of glad to get off the flight. I'd already had my fill of drama for one day, and it wasn't even over yet. I had just lost two hours.

23

By the time we made it to Atlanta, it was about 7:00 p.m. We walked through the airport. The air was a bit unusual down south only 83 degrees in the summer, but I assumed it was just for the day.

I heard a voice come from the crowd of people in transit. "Mr. Campbell! W.D. Campbell." Hearing my name made me look in every direction to see where it was coming from. Finally, she made her presence known. I recognized her instantly as she approached. My escorts saw her rapid approach and made a make-shift perimeter around me.

"Mr. Campbell, it's me, Lisa Jones. You remember, from the Writer's Convention in Chicago?" I knew the face, just not the name.

"Ah yes, Lisa; it's been a few months, how have you been?"

"I'm fine," she said looking around at Mr. Frank and Alex just to get eye contact with me. "Who are these guys?"

"They're some business associates of mine."

"Business associates? They look more like security. What type of business brings you to Atlanta?"

"Actually, I'm here doing some research for the next thirty

days. I'll be north of here in the mountains, doing my research." I said this to keep her informed of my whereabouts, just in case something unexpected happened.

"I remember you telling me about a special friend who resides here, Stone Mountain I think?"

"Yes, she does."

"You plan on seeing her while you're here?"

"Hopefully, if my work doesn't keep me busy."

"Mr. William Campbell, a man who stays busy. Well when you're not too busy, maybe we can get together for dinner. Here's my card, call me when you get settled."

After she was out of sight, Mr. B. played twenty questions, trying to find out about her whereabouts and who she might know, while Victoria only stared. I told him, I didn't know that much about her. We had a couple of conversations, but nothing serious. When he saw I really didn't know anything, he left it alone.

We took the escalator down to the baggage claim area where the entrance to the terminal was.

"There's a car out front waiting for us." Mr. B. said. I noticed our split from the others. "Are we leaving them?" I asked pointing.

"No, they're going in another direction."

We exited the airport and walked towards a polished black Lincoln SUV limousine where a very attractive light-brown woman, who appeared to be in her late thirties, was waiting for us. She walked to the back door and opened it for us. She was quite beautiful to be a limo driver, even her smile was pleasant.

"How was your flight, Mr. Campbell?"

"Fine, just fine, Ms.…" I paused in order for her to fill in the rest.

"Belinda…Oh, and happy birthday" …I gave her a puzzled look.

"Thank you."

"Mr. B., are there any other bags?" she asked, motioning to the ones on the ground next to us.

"No, this is it."

We pulled away from the crowded Hartsfield-Jackson airport, leaving the confusion behind. The tranquil sky above was visible through the sunroof in the back. Since we'd landed, the temperature had inched up a bit more, not surprisingly being that it's August.

Ms. Belinda let down the privacy window that separated us from the driver's section.

"Are we going straight there, Sir?" she asked.

"Yes," he replied. "And no stops please."

While on our way, Mr. B. made a series of calls on his pocket-sized cell phone. I rested my head against the headrest to collect my thoughts. We seemed to be moving on highway 75 and then 85 at a gradual pace and I felt myself feeling a bit queasy. Mr. B. put his hand over the receiver and asked, "Are you alright?"

"I don't' know why, but I still feel tired."

He closed his cell and said that we should be arriving shortly. "When we get there, you'll be briefed on the conditions of your stay as well as the project." At that point, Mr. Campbell, you'll be able to relax for the rest of the evening. "Well, after we eat, that is."

"And when is that?"

"8:30 p.m."

"I might just sleep through it."

"Well, that's up to you, or depending on what Mr. A.B. has planned."

"Are you still nervous, Mr. Campbell?"

"Oh no, now I'm just curious."

"The air is cleaner here, unlike the smog in New York. Plus, it's been a rainy summer which reduced all the pollen. It should help relieve some of your stress considering your high blood pressure. Each time we come here, I feel a sense of freedom."

"How often do you all travel here?"

"We come when needed."

"I wish I could come out here more often," I said.

"After this, you'll have the time and money to do so."

Mr. Frank had an incredulous look on his face.

I wondered if the look was intended for me or whether there was something else on his mind.

"What's wrong, Mr. Frank?" I asked him. "You look disturbed."

"Nothing for you to worry yourself with, Mr. Campbell. You'll soon come to find out all about my facial expressions and the changes in my voice by the end of our business relationship."

"I'll keep my eyes and ears open."

"I promised you before and I promise you now; you're in good hands. Just stay focused, sir."

A few minutes later, we came upon a gated area. There was an armed security guard manning a booth when he saw us, he got out of the booth and headed in our direction. Ms. Belinda let down her window to hear what he had to say. While she answered him, Mr. B. stepped out without warning and began speaking on his cell phone.

Ms. Belinda exited upon the guard's request and moved to the hood of the car. She popped the hood before she got out and opened it when he told her to. He looked under it, inspecting for anything suspicious. They proceeded to the trunk and did the same. After everything passed his inspection, he permitted us to move forward.

Mr. B. stayed on foot and moved to the booth, still talking on his cell phone. Ms. Belinda drove me and Mr. Frank to the other side of the electronically operated gate. I watched as Mr. B. held a white document which he signed and gave to the guard before re-entering the limo.

"How do you feel about a helicopter ride?"

"I've been on plenty in my day, but not recently."

"Well, we're about to change that."

When we passed by the guard shack and made a right, the area beyond that point opened into a huge airstrip. There were various hangars and runways. Private jets were parked everywhere along with helipads that held helicopters of different sizes.

One particular jet caught my attention and I was completely in awe of its size and beauty. It had six windows on each side and a Canadian flag on its tail. It had to have been recently washed because the black and gold paint sparkled.

"Now this is living!" I thought out loud. Mr. B. just looked at the amazement on my face and smiled. We stopped at one of the last helipads. "We're here, Mr. Campbell," Mr. B. stated. We were parked in front of a black Scorpion Turbojet helicopter.

"Is this Mr. Everybody's or Averie Bod`e?"

"Maybe," he replied."

"One of his toys, I presume."

"Something like that."

Ms. Belinda opened the door for us to exit. The heat wave hit my face like we had just walked into a hot oven. The cool air conditioning inside the truck may have given me the chills, but a sudden anxiousness put my body right back in the right condition.

24

We approached the large bird and Mr. B. opened the side passenger door. I was surprised to see a chopper in such immaculate condition. Inside were four leather seats facing each other. I also noticed there was a pilot already on board.

The engine started up and the rotors began to turn as we strapped ourselves in.

"Fasten your seatbelts, gentlemen." We'd already done that. "We're going for a short and speedy ride."

I couldn't place it, but there was something familiar about the voice coming from the cockpit.

The pilot turned to speak, but I interrupted him before he could get a word out. "Excuse me, sir, but do I know you from somewhere?"

"Should you?" he asked.

"I don't know. It seems like we've met somewhere before."

He turned to face us, wearing a Cheshire grin. I now knew the face that fit the voice.

"It's you! You're the guy who was sitting behind me on the plane, the one with the British accent." But what was he doing piloting this chopper and what relationship did he have to Mr. Bod`e?

"Is there something wrong, Mr. Campbell? You haven't put it together yet?"

What happened next rendered me speechless. I watched in

stunned silence as he began to peel the skin from his nose. Well, what I thought was skin, until the whole nose piece came off, along with the rest of his facial disguise, and the hair piece. I could only look in disbelief. Mr. Averie Bod`e had his identity concealed the whole time.

"Are you still with us, Mr. Campbell?" Frank asked. I couldn't even find my voice. I didn't know what was real and what wasn't.

"I don't get it. Why did you have to hide your identity from me?" I directed my question at Mr. Averie Bod`e. And that's when he went into detail about the news articles I had read in the newspaper that morning. The front page had read: "Mr. Averie Bod'e, Trial of the Century."

"You needed to have a full understanding of what has been done to me. The feds are on high alert, and so are we. I've done my homework so that I can remain anonymous."

"That still doesn't answer my question, why did you feel the need to deceive me? You could've told me in private that you had to do this. I knew there was something odd going on when Mr. B. looked behind us on the plane, asking Mr. Bod`e permission to use my laptop. It's all making sense now."

"You're right, Mr. Campbell. I should've told you, my apologies."

With that said, we lifted off. We traveled about forty-five minutes sightseeing the beautiful city of Atlanta before heading northbound towards the blue-sky mountains. In the distance, there were several large retreats. Mr. Frank pointed to one in particular with some security guards posted at the gate.

"That's Mr. Averie Bod`e retreat; and yours for the next six months."

I had butterflies fluttering in my stomach thinking about the new career and the new life I was about to be starting.

Mr. Averie Bod`e instructed Mr. Frank to gather the things and prepare for landing. We entered the property's perimeter and I noticed a cadre of cars in front. The home was enormous on the ranch outside and from our viewpoint, I could see a horse ranch, a private ski slope, a wood shed the size of a high school gymnasium, and another small house adjacent to the main home.

"Hold on, Mr. Campbell, we're about to land."

Mr. Averie Bod`e touched down smoothly on the roof of the mansion. He shut down the engines and then asked, "So, how are my flying skills?"

"I'm impressed, but not surprised, Sir," I replied. I could feel a breeze on the rooftop when we exited the helicopter. I followed Mr. Frank and Mr. A.B. to what looked like an elevator. Mr. Bod`e reached into his bag and pulled out a walkie-talkie and radioed to his security staff to open the doors from the inside.

The inside of the elevator was soundproofed with red padding. We traveled down three floors before the doors opened. To my delight, Ms. Victoria greeted each of us with a hug and a kiss.

"Let me take that from you, A.B.," she said to Mr. Bod`e. He passed her the black gym bag he was carrying. She then looked at me with a bright smile as if we hadn't seen each other in months.

"Mr. Campbell, I will be fitting you shortly."

"Excuse me?"

"Your measurements for your outfits and I also need to know your shoe size." She stood with a clipboard under her armpit.

"Oh…ah… size twelves, ma'am." She had a curious expression on her face.

"Is everything as big as your feet?" she asked flirtatiously?

"Yes, very much so," I replied with confidence.

I believe she was trying Mr. Averie's patience with her comments. He didn't say anything; just gave her a look of disdain before she left.

Mr. A.B. motioned for me to follow him to the dining room. On the way, I couldn't help but notice the collection of vintage paintings decorating his walls. There were also more plasma screen televisions than I could have imagined in one house.

We passed the living room area, which had a huge

fireplace and a vaulted ceiling. All the lights were off when we entered the dining room. He clapped his hands and instantly the room illuminated, blinding me with the bright light of a thousand ceiling lights. At night, it would seem like the sun was out with all the lights shining.

"Are they too bright, Mr. Campbell?" he asked, smiling.

"I'll feel better with a pair of sunglasses." My eyes tried to adjust to the brightness so that I could view the large room adorned with more artwork and a thirty-foot-long table that could seat 18 people easily.

"This is where we'll eat breakfast and dinner every day." He turned to look at me for assurance. Breakfast is served at 8 a.m., lunch will be in the room where you write the story and dinner is at 6 p.m. sharp. I have a gourmet chef and a butler on site. Boshá is my chef and the butlers' name is Mr. Richards. They will both tend to your needs. The maids are Lucy, Naomi, Alicia and Holly. If you need anything cleaned, washed, or rooms tidied up, you can page Lucy; she's my head of maid staff. As was mentioned earlier, no alcohol will be served at any meal or in-between during this project."

I had a dejected look on my face. Hell, I needed a drink after all of this.

"After the completion of your assignments, there will be a great celebration in honor of you, Mr. Campbell. Oh, I almost forgot, you will have no contact with anyone over the phone, through e-mail, faxes or any other means of communication. And by the way, you had 22 calls from this morning wishing you an incredible birthday and to get out and do something you've never experienced. I should say, Mr. Campbell, it looks like you are doing just that"

I wondered who called and if any of the calls were from my daughters or, maybe even Olivia.

"Ms. Victoria will be with you shortly to get your measurements and there will be a clothing list on your bed. In the bathroom, there are over forty different fragrances for you to choose from. In the morning, the butler, Mr. Richards, will wake you at 7:00 a.m."

I tried to take all of this in as he spoke.

"I have a barber on deck to keep you groomed. As I said before, everything will be provided for you; shower slippers, house shoes, pajamas, robe, and earplugs – anything we can think of, we got them here for your convenience while you're here."

They seemed to have everything covered. He finally stated what I wanted to hear.

"For the next 30 days, our project will begin promptly at 9 a.m. and end at 12 p.m. for a break. You will resume at 2:30 p.m. and stop again at 4:30 p.m. These will be your working hours. If you decide to use music to inspire you, there will be an MP3 player at your disposal; you can select any sort of music you desire. Lastly, after tonight, your bedroom door will be locked every night at 9 p.m. with an alarm activation. One of my men will be posted outside your door each night."

I had to laugh at all the accommodations. What? I had to say something, "Am I in prison or something? Well, I have a request. I have to have fresh air for about 30 minutes every morning, so I will be sitting by the large pool I saw out back at 11am each day. Can you put that on my outlined agenda? Let me thank you in advance for it. I think it is time for someone to escort me to my room now?" As I looked around, I thought to myself, was all of this set up for me? This is better than the Waldorf Astoria, minus the security men outside the door and of course my lock downs."

"Mr. Campbell, your first half of the money has been deposited into your bank account in New York. Do you have any questions?"

"If I did, would you actually answer them?"

"I'd answer them accordingly."

"You had mentioned rooms, as in more than one."

"Yes, Mr. Campbell. You have the whole third floor as a comfort zone."

"Well, show me to my quarters please."

25

Mr. Bod`e had Mr. Richards escort me to the floor that would serve as my apartment for the next two months. It was everything I could ever want in a hideaway. If it wasn't for the occasional meals, I wouldn't have a need to leave that floor. There was actually an enclosed deck off my bedroom with retractable glass around it. I was told I could go out anytime and get that fresh air I needed. Who was the architect that designed this place?

He took me on a tour and showed me where my office was, the place where I'd be spending most of my time. There was a fitness room, Movie Theater, and a spa complete with a Jacuzzi and sauna. Alongside the spa was a handball court. It even had two wall-sized coolers stocked with bottled water. I wondered when I'd have time to play handball with a deadline on my hands.

The bedrooms were equally impressive. There were two of them, both soundproof. Both were furnished with king-sized canopy beds. The mattresses were some kind of Sleep Number beds. He explained how there were water tubes between the mattresses making for a more comfortable sleep. He also told me that the sheets were made of 100% pure Italian silk, two thousand dollars apiece; and the comforter was imported from Italy.

The room itself was like a huge suite, complete with high ceilings, painted to match a sky setting. It gave you the illusion that birds were flying through the sky during the day and at night it switched to dark skies with stars.

"Is everything to your liking, Mr. Campbell?" His baritone voice came out of nowhere. In fact, he came out of nowhere and startled me. I didn't even see Mr. Averie enter the room. Then again, the place was as spacious as a palace that he could've come in from any number of entrances. He's so secretive, there's no telling how many hidden passageways there were in this place.

"More than I expected, thank you. And please call me William, Sir."

"Okay, William. Do you have any questions about your living accommodations?"

"Exactly how long did it take to build this place?"

"Hmmm...approximately 16 months to create this one last masterpiece. From the recruiting of my security and staff to building this house, including getting to know everyone involved and their personalities. It all had to be precise, no matter how much time it took. The project has the same importance, in that it has to be told to the public."

My mind had already begun to form some ideas on how I was going to write this story. It had to be right and it had to be good. Like he said, he took the time to make every move precise, so I had to do the same. Otherwise, I might not get another opportunity.

There were certain things that I needed to evaluate about this whole situation. Maybe he feels like the story needs to be told because his time might be running out. I didn't know, I was just speculating. He was coughing might heavy.

"So, what's the price of this beautiful retreat?"

"Didn't cost me a dime. You should know that! He stared at me as if I should already know."

The place itself was $6.3 million, but with the security, which was an additional $1.7 million, that puts it at eight. Everything here is state of the art. Homeland doesn't have anything on this setup.

"You said there were rooms up here? There are others like this one?"

"You'll find out soon enough but for now, let's go see about dinner."

Mr. Richards, Mr. A.B., and I went back to the elevator that brought us up. Mr. Richards slid the plastic magnetic card into the slot to activate the elevator and open the doors. With an outstretched hand Mr. Bod`e politely allowed me to lead the way. In the elevator, I studied Mr. Richards and wondered how a man of his age could be working for such a man. He was in his late fifties, barely over five feet five inches tall. He had a bald head, not by choice, with a light brown shadow beard speckled with gray. Black seemed to be the attire for the day, because, he too, had on a suit and necktie of the same color; with a starched white shirt.

Moments later, we stepped off the elevator, following Mr. Richards toward the kitchen. I noticed that everything was voice-activated in the house. We did not have to touch any buttons on the elevator or down the hallway to the kitchen, lights came on automatically as walked down the hallway.

I observed the chef busy at his craft when we entered the kitchen. "Mr. Camp…William, this is my beloved chef, Boshá, preparing tonight's meal."

Mr. Boshá lifted his head at the sound of Mr. A.B.'s voice and I nodded to him.

"Hello, Mr. Campbell," he greeted me in a French accent.

"Are you ready for a mini feast this evening?"

"Why yes, Mr. Boshá. I'm looking forward to it."

"Good, I'll see you at six, Sir."

"Mr. Richards, will you show William back upstairs so he can freshen up and relax a bit before we eat?"

"Sure, Sir,"

We were back on the third floor and I was feeling more comfortable in my new home. There were more doors down the hallway that I hadn't noticed earlier. Each one was closed with a green light flashing; signaling that an alarm was set.

As we walked to the second room, the room they said was mine; we passed a total of eight closed doors.

"Here we are, Mr. Campbell, Sir."

We stopped at a set of mahogany-furnished twin doors.

"I'll leave you to get cleaned up for dinner."

"Thank you, Mr. Richards."

I reached for the handle and was surprised that it didn't require a key card entry, in fact, it was already opened; usually, everything was secured. When I walked in, the lovely Victoria was standing there in front of me looking as cute as she could be. She had a tape measure strung around her slender neck, ready to take my measurements.

Victoria was wearing an adorable pink and gray sweatsuit with matching pink Nike Air Max's that fit her tiny little feet. Her hair was pulled back in a ponytail, exposing the reddish-brown highlights. The earth tone lipstick set everything off.

"Well, are you going to come in or are you going to stand there staring at me?" She asked, smiling with perfect teeth.

"Damn, what a choice. Since it is my room, I guess I'll come in, but the view is wonderful from over here."

"Oh, just get over here, Mr. Campbell, I don't have all evening." Her smile was captivating. I would do anything she asked.

"What'd I tell you about that "Mr." Stuff?

"Okay, William, but I'll only call you that when we're alone. Now, what I need you to do is come and stand on this pedestal, so I can get your measurements."

I stepped up and allowed her to do her job. With my arms stretched wide, she ran the tape from my shoulder to wrist. It wasn't easy; she had to get on a stool to do it because she was a short woman. She did each arm then down my back for the length. She stepped down and faced me with curious eyes.

"Remember when I asked you if everything was as big as your feet?" She looked down at my crotch and then at my feet, and finally back to my face. That made me extremely nervous, but what she did next made it worse. She squatted a bit and then wrapped her arms around my waist and held it there for a second next to eternity. I just froze as she took her time reading the measure. She then ran the tape down the inside of my legs, starting at the crotch and moving slowly to the ankle. Her touch was enough to send off signals inside of me. I had to be careful not to let her movements arouse me or else she'd get an unexpected surprise.

"I guess you were right," she said getting up.

"Huh…excuse me," I was obviously lost in the moment.

"Your legs, they're long too, thirteen inches to be exact."

"Oh… ah… yeah, they are."

"Are you alright, William?" I liked the way she said my name.

"I was just wondering about something."

"Anything I can help you with?"

She put her tape measure back around her neck letting me know she was through for now. I stepped down from my stool to ground level. "Can I ask you a hypothetical question, Victoria?"

"Sure."

"What if two mature individuals, were to come in contact with one another in a neutral situation?"

"Well, hypothetically speaking, right?"

"Right…"

"I would say that if something were to occur, the two should remain mature adults about whatever took place, but they shouldn't be afraid to explore the unknown." She looked up at me with those eyes that held many secrets. Secrets I wished to learn.

"I'd say that was a good answer." I didn't realize she was that much smaller than me.

"What?" She asked, noticing me noticing her.

"You're just so short."

"Well, I'll be sure to send Mr. Richards in to finish the fitting," she replied like I'd hurt her feelings.

"No. I didn't mean it like that. Please accept my apologies. It's actually cute, you having to stand on the stool."

"Keep it up, William and I'll make everything an inch or

two short, especially in the crotch area. You know you wouldn't like that." She winked her eye like she knew something I didn't.

"All I was saying was I prefer my women closer to 5'3 to 5'7 inches tall that's all. But there have been exceptions."

"I guess I'll have to keep that in mind, hypothetically speaking, of course."

"Speaking of exceptions, how can I contact you, you know; if I want something?"

"My room is right below yours. You can stomp real hard if you want. I wouldn't suggest it because you might set off the sensitive alarm system and Mr. Bod`e wouldn't like that. So, just flush three times and I'll know it's you."

"I'll have to keep that in mind, hypothetically speaking of course." We both smiled at our private little joke. I could tell she was willingly letting down her guard; that showed me another side of her, a side I could really get used to.

26

When will my clothes be ready?

"Faster than you think," Victoria replied with a smirk as she left.

"What will …," The door closed before I could get the question out. What I wanted more than anything was a nice hot shower. I strolled into the bathroom and saw that it was set up identically like the one in the other bedroom I was in earlier.

While I was in the shower, I reflected on the events that had transpired since my last shower at my penthouse. I'd met several interesting people, learned some interesting facts, and traveled in two different states less than 24 hours.

After I got out, I went into the bedroom and noticed that someone had placed an entire outfit on the bed for me to wear to dinner. Everything was laid out; even the socks and shoes, a pair of Kenneth Coles in my size. There was also a designer black button down shirt and black jeans by Sean John. Just like everyone else, I too would be dressed in black.

I put the sleek ensemble on, splashed on a hint of Bond No. 9 (The Scent of Peace) cologne and admired my reflection in the floor-length mirror. Out of curiosity I walked into the bedroom-sized closet and couldn't make sense of what I saw. There were clothes lined up on hangers. Everything I could imagine was present and in my size, like the outfit, I had on.

"How in the…?" My thoughts were interrupted by Mr. Richards' voice on the intercom in the bedroom.

"It's 8:25 p.m., Mr. Campbell, you should be leaving now. Dinner is about to be served." Like a fool, I answered to no one.

I left the room still amazed at all the different amenities of this house. There wasn't a butler or a maid or a security guard to escort me to the dining area, but the intercom system in the hallway was there to guide me.

"Please walk to the elevator on the left side." Inside the elevator, Mr. Richards was sitting on a stool.

"We have five minutes, Sir."

We made it to the ground floor and to the dining room with seconds to spare. Everyone was there waiting for me. Mr. Frank, Mr. B., Tom, and Claude, Matt, Alex, and Rick were all sitting, wearing starched whitecollared dress shirts with black slacks. Victoria was the only woman present at the table and she was looking elegant in a black Dolce and Gabbana evening gown with house slippers. What a contrast, she was classy and comfortable at the same time.

Mr. Averie Bod`e was seated at the head, as he should be, dressed in a brown plaid blazer with a tan mock neck and brown slacks. He also had on house slippers and was reading a New York Times paper.

Everyone stood to greet me, "Good evening, Mr. Campbell."

"I'm glad to have your company this evening," Mr. A.B. said.

"Good evening to you lady," I winked at Victoria, "and gentlemen. Thank you for having me, sir."

Mr. Richards directed me to a seat opposite Mr. B.

"Please sit here, Sir." He pulled out a chair for me and explained to never put my hands on the table while eating. I agreed, it wasn't good etiquette.

I looked up at all the people present and Victoria was the only one who stood out with her smiling face glowing like the moon at midnight.

She was on Mr. Averie Bod'e left side. He was still reading the paper, oblivious to his company. The aroma of fine cuisine emanated from the kitchen. I could tell that we were close to serving time.

Moments later, the maids entered pushing carts with trays of our first course. They placed bowls with *buttered dinner rolls, peas, sweet carrots, garlic mashed potatoes, corn, and gravy,* all on the table in rows. Then they left, returning with house salads for everyone, along with a collection of dressings: *Honey Mustard, Thousand Island, Ranch and Italian.* On the salads were all the fixings. *Tomatoes, cucumbers, shredded cheese, olives, bacon bits, onions, and egg slices sitting on crispy fresh iceberg lettuce.* They left again, this time, coming back with a platter covered with the main course, carved lamb.

Before anyone touched a utensil, Mr. Bod`e put his newspaper to the side and said, "Could we all please bow our heads as we bless the food so carefully prepared by the chef." He kept the prayer brief but meaningful.

After he graced the food, all I saw were bowls being passed back and forth and utensils clanking against the china. Silence filled the room and chewing commenced. Then AverieBod`e spoke.

"How's your lamb, Mr. Campbell?"

"Everything tastes delightful. Very well prepared if I don't say so myself."

"We're here to please."

Then another round of silence. Mr. Bod`e noticed the befuddled look on my face.

"What's on your mind, Mr. Campbell?"

"Nothing...."

"Oh, you know I know you better than that."

He broke me down. "I was just wondering how you assembled such an organized and well-disciplined team."

"Well, I can honestly say, it wasn't easy." He looked around at his comrades, especially Mr. Frank and they laughed at an inside joke. "We've amassed a lot of time together mostly through unique experiences."

"Where do they stay? Right here at the house or in the other house I saw coming in?"

"Oh no, I wouldn't dare have them that far from me. They have rooms on the second floor. The other house was designed for the maids, housekeeping, outside maintenance and the chauffeurs."

"That was very generous of you."

"Believe me, Mr. Campbell, they are well taken care of, the same way that you are. You are now one of us."

As everyone was still eating, the chef, Mr. Boshá, entered and addressed the table. "How is everything?"

We nodded in agreement that the meal was excellent. He came over to me with a bizarre look on his face. I was curious so I had to ask, "How did you know lamb was my favorite dish?"

"Mr. Bod`e suggested it to me earlier, Sir."

This guy knows too much, I thought to myself.

We were finishing up dinner when the maids came in carrying an assortment of deserts. Cheesecake with graham crackers sprinkled on it, three types of pie; apple, sweet potato, and pecan, and there was even iced cake with numerous candles on it which they placed on an empty space on the table.

One of the maids lit the candles and everyone sang"happy birthday" to me in unison. For the first time, today, I actually saw the human side of these people. It warmed my heart to see they cared.

27

After eating a sampling of each pie and stuffing a slice of my birthday cake in my mouth, I couldn't fathom taking in another bite. I could tell I wasn't the only one who was full. This had to be one of the best meals I'd had in years, and if they kept it up, I believe I could enjoy living like a king.

Suddenly, Mr. Bod`e's voice interrupted my thoughts. Everyone was to meet at the theater in fifteen minutes. It was about a quarter to ten and I was fatigued from all the day's activities.

"Excuse me, but if you don't mind I'd like to get some rest," I said in the humblest tone.

"I do mind," Mr. Bod`e replied bluntly. "We always watch a good movie after our meal."

"I understand, but I'm tired," I argued mildly.

"Fifteen minutes in the theater, Campbell," he commanded like there wasn't a choice in the matter. And there wasn't.

"You can relax in the recliner," he stated while leaving the room.

Nothing more was said. I got up with everyone else and headed towards the hallway. Mr. Richards was there waiting to escort me to my room. We were about to step on the elevator when a quiet voice from behind halted my progress.

"I'll show him up, Mr. Richards." It was Victoria looking just as full as me.

The electric doors shut without either one of us saying a word. She swiped her key card and we moved upward. Our thoughts were loud against the small compartment while silence played the mediator. We stood side by side, both wanting to say something but not wanting to cross the line. Victoria made the first move by touching my fingers with hers. I could tell she wanted me to hold her hand so I turned to face her and moved within inches of her face. She closed her eyes anticipating the next motion. "Bing!" The doors opened interrupting what could've happened.

Victoria just stared at me as we strolled slowly down the hall. We stopped at my door and there was something on the tip of her tongue she wanted to get off but she was afraid.

"William," she whispered.

"Yes Victoria," my smile was used to calm her, warm her, allowing her to let down her defenses.

"I'll see you in 10 minutes. Don't be late."

Then she turned on her heels and left. She looked just as good leaving as she did coming. If she came to fish, I was dangerously close to being hooked. I opened the door and saw that someone had been in my room. My laptop, writing materials, and favorite pillow were all laid out at the desk next to my bed ready for a full day's work tomorrow. I went to the bathroom to relieve the pressure building up in my stomach. Before I knew it, eight minutes had gone by.

Then all of a sudden, I heard a banging on the bedroom door. When I opened it, I looked to the left and saw no one. Mr. Richards stood to the right, with his white serving gloves on. "Everyone's in the theater, Sir."

It seemed like I was spending a lot of time in the elevator because I was back in it again going down to the ground floor. At least I thought it was the ground floor; we continued to a lower level floor, one I didn't know was there. When the doors opened, the first thing I saw was a huge movie curtain. The room was already dimmed out, ready for the feature. The theater had black round tables with red and black leather recliners on each side. There were about forty seats arranged throughout the theater so people could see from anywhere. I wondered if they entertained large crowds in here, they could charge admission and make a killing. The theater was even equipped with a popcorn machine, soft drinks, and candy machines, as well as a cart for hot fudge. Victoria stood up and waved me over to her.

Mr. Bod`e was seated in the center with Mr. B. and Mr. Frank on his left and right side. The rest of the staff filled in the spacious room. I took the seat to Victoria's right and leaned back in the comfortable chair.

Mr. Bod`e controlled the lighting and movie projection from a panel in his lap. The curtain opened and the show began. The credits for "*Catch Me If You Can*" came across the screen. I thought, *how appropriate for us to watch a good guy/bad guy movie where the good and bad guys both wins in the end.*

I didn't care who won at that point because before the first action scene, I dozed off. I tried unsuccessfully to fight off the heaviness in my eyes but it was unavoidable as my body shut down. The next thing I felt was Victoria's soft touch shaking my shoulder. She offered to walk me to my room.

While in the elevator, Victoria's eyes became glassy when she looked at me. "What's up?"

"Can I ask you a personal question, William?"

"Of course, what's on your mind?"

"What happened with your marriage?"

I yawned and stretched and then said, "That's a little much to go into right now."

"I'm sorry I went there."

"No, that's alright. For some reason, I feel as if I can talk to you."

"I know that's a personal subject."

And it was, more sentimental than anything. It drudged up thoughts of our honeymoon back in 1994. My ex-wife and I decided to take in Toronto, Canada. It was the most beautiful experience of my life. We were so happy then. That was way before the problems, before the fights, before the misunderstandings, before my career became more important. That was a time when loving her was easy, and I could do no wrong. Then the children came and loving the girls was even easier. We thought those times would never end, but then reality hit and I had to deal with it.

Soon, we were back at my door.

"Will you be okay, William?" Victoria asked in a caring tone. "Do you want any company?" What an awkward position she had me in. I knew that the consequences for doing what I thought she wanted me to do, would be too great. I always remembered what a wise man said to me, "What looks good isn't always good for you."

"I'm fine," I said. "If I need you, I'll just flush three times, right? You're right below me so it won't take you long to get here."

She smiled and then turned away looking disappointed as she walked to the elevator. Coming off, as she got there was Mr. Tom. I guess he was my security for the night.

"It's about that time isn't it, Sir?" he said, walking up.

"Yes, it is. I'm exhausted."

"Mr. Richards will be here at 7:00 a.m. for your wake-up call. If you need anything, just hit the button on the wall and speak. Other than that, have a good night."

"Thanks, Mr. Tom, same to you."

28

As Victoria slowly walked to her room, a voice startled her from behind.

"Are you too sleepy to talk?"

"Look who's here and needs a friend," Victoria responded. "Yes Claude, I have a few minutes."

Before she stepped over the threshold, she removed her bedroom slippers and placed them in her hands. Claude began to follow her in.

"Wait a minute."

He stopped abruptly. "What?"

"You know my rules before entering."

"Lady, you are crazy!"

"Oh well, my rules. Either you take your shoes off or stay out here and talk through the door, your choice…

"Alright, cool." Claude started unlacing his boots.

"You seem bothered by my rules."

"Don't you see me taking my damn shoes off?"

She loved pressing his buttons. Once he was inside, she closed the door behind them.

"You must be worried about me seeing that big nasty toe sticking out of the hole in your sock." She was joking, but he really did have a hole and quickly tried to maneuver his bare toe out of her sight.

"This is some crazy stuff to be going through, but then I wouldn't expect anything less with your crazy ass."

"Anyway, what's up?" she asked ignoring his last comment.

"Look, Victoria, I know we've been on some bad terms lately."

"And why is that, Claude, can you explain that?"

"It isn't my fault entirely if that's what you're implying. You've got your own personal issues; when the pressure hits, then you blow your steam off on my ass."

"Then it is your fault, dammit. Look, you're the one who put me in this situation."

"No, your heart placed you and me in bad standings with Averie. You knew how he felt about you, and you call yourself getting back at him, so with Steve being the new kid on the team, you threw yourself at him just to see how Averie would react. It made me look bad because I was the one who brought Steve in."

"Okay, okay, you're right, Claude, damn. Are you going to keep beating a dead horse?"

"I'm just trying to get you to see that men like Averie aren't that easy to figure out. You see, he didn't react at all. He just let the whole thing play out and you ended up playing yourself. A man like Averie has a defense mechanism already installed in his mind, so trying to get inside is a 50/50 chance; you could get what you want or it could all blow up in your face. You kind of understand what I'm saying?"

"Yes, little brother."

"Hold up. Tom's the only one who can call me that." It was intended to make her laugh, but instead, her eyes began to water. Claude pulled her into a hug as she wept.

"Hey, hey, I didn't mean it like that. I know he hurt you, but he'll come around. It takes a little time.

"He's been focused on one thing and one thing only, and that's been this project." I know that's the problem.

"Damn! You women can be so selfish. You know he's been working on this for a while, yet he still managed to make sure you're straight. He could've easily cut you off.

Accounts, houses, assets, everything, but he didn't. And you still want it all with your spoiled fucking ass. That's what you are, a spoiled damn brat!"

"I'm not a brat!" Spoiled maybe, but a brat…no, at least not at this moment.

Finally, she cracked a smile. The light makeup she had on was smeared on her cheeks.

"Look, Sis, why don't' you go check on him and see if he needs anything. What's his favorite dessert?"

"Why?"

"Because, every man has a soft spot, and for some men, a late-night desert might be just the thing he needs, you know what I mean?"

"I think I get the picture. Wrap me up and serve it to him hot. He likes Vanilla cheesecake; I can spread it all over me while he watches."

"Damn, with a body like yours, that would get any man's attention. Even a man like our boss will melt like ice."

"Mmm-Wah!" She kissed Claude.

"What was that for?"

"Silly, for being there for me."

"That means I can start wearing my shoes in here?"

"Um… no! We're not that cool," she retorted, smiling.

"You just get your sentimental butt to that man."

"I'm on my way."

Victoria took a quick shower after Claude left. She went over her approach in her head as she freshened up. Little did he know, Averie was about to have a very good night.

29

Victoria dialed the chef and had him prepare the special desert for her evening escapade. She then ventured down to the main level to pick up the entrée. Then she strolled to the elevator on the main floor and swiped her personal key card. She pressed the 1 button three times. This was where Averie Bod`e had his chambers built. The elevator she was in was different from the one everyone else took to the movie theater earlier. This one only allowed exclusive access. It had a secret panel on the back wall that was controlled by Averie. It was designed as an escape route in case of emergency.

As the car came to a stop, the intercom sounded with his voice, "To what do I owe this visit?"

"I came down to check on you, is that ok?"

"I'm okay, thanks for asking," he replied bluntly.

"Well, I'd still like to see for myself if everything is okay."

"Why?"

"Will you stop with all the dumb questions and let me in."

"What's the magic word?"

"Please."

"Nope, that's not it."

"Please, Big Daddy?" A moment passed and the wall slid back. There were security cameras posted in each corner of the room. He could view everything, everywhere.

When Victoria entered, the wall immediately closed behind her. Right in front of her was another entrance; she stood in a sally port. The door was made of glass about 5 inches thick. But this was no ordinary glass; it manipulated the image on the other side so you couldn't make out the figure.

She couldn't go any further unless Averie permitted and he stood on the other side. He could see her just fine from his side; which gave him an advantage over anyone who intruded. He marveled at how beautiful she was.

"So, again, to what do I owe this honor?"

"I'm not going to beat around the bush Averie, I feel really bad about what has escalated between us. I was assuming you wanted to hear my side of the story."

"Not really," he stated flatly. "You're a grown woman, Victoria. You made your own bed, now lie in it."

"What?" She couldn't believe what she was hearing.

"You knew exactly what you were doing; you just didn't know the consequences, did you?"

"No. But you were…"

"I was what?" he interrupted. "There's nothing worse than a slick ass, two-faced vindictive she-dog, trying to play both sides of the fence." His words shot like darts through the thick glass.

"Averie, I was hurt and you weren't paying me any attention and it just happened."

"Well, I hope you were satisfied on the other sidebecause now my gate is closed."

"Averie, don't be like that. Aren't you going to listen to me?" He just smiled on his side of the glass but she couldn't see. "Look, I made a bad choice, I'm sorry; I'm human like everyone else. By the way, you are not spotless either. Don't think I don't have dirt on your cheating ass either? You think because you're the boss you can do and say what you please? I don't think so." Anger filled her insides. She was tired of talking through the barrier. "Open this stupid ass glass, you cheating bitch!"

"Excuse me?" he said in a calm tone over the intercom.

"You heard what I said,"

"You sound tough behind that door."

Suddenly, the door slid and she was facing the humbly amused Averie. "You have something to say now."

"You don't put any fear in my heart like you do everyone else."

He didn't respond. His stare was usually enough to manipulate any situation, but Victoria was a challenge to him, one that he liked. She wasn't afraid.

"You still haven't said anything."

"These are nothing but mind games, Averie. I can play them just as well as you can." Really, she couldn't, but she didn't want to give him the edge.

They stood, staring at each other for what seemed like an eternity until finally, she gave in.

"Damnit" Averie, stop this. I came down here on friendly terms. If you don't' want to talk, fine. I'll just eat this vanilla cheesecake myself." She teased him with the platter of dessert she had behind her back.

He hit a switch on a remote he had in his pocket and the glass door shut behind her and the room went completely dark. His voice was back on the speaker system.

"Look out for the wall, Victoria. Ooh, there's a sharp object about 2 feet from you," the voice echoed like he was at a fun park. "Don't move! Whoa, look out!"

She just looked around in disgust trying to hide her horror.

"Stop it, Averie. This isn't funny." A red light zoomed in on Victoria and bounced off the glass causing an eerie effect.

"Ahh, is little Vicki scared?"

"No!" she shouted.

"Oh, so you're mad?"

"You'll know when I'm mad."

"Well here's something sweet, how about some dessert?"

"I already have…," She noticed she no longer had the platter. Where did …,"

"Shh!" He could see her struggling to try and locate him in the dark. She listened for his voice. He continued to tease. "I had a taste for some cheesecake, and from the looks of this one; it looks like Boshá put his foot in it."

"Where are you?"

"Wouldn't you like to know? I told you I'm over here, eating this delicious dessert. Yum," he teased.

She decided to play along. "I want some."

"Well come and get it." He lifted the darkness a bit to a dim. "Walk over to the fireplace so I can see your beauty in the light."

She did as she was commanded, slowly sauntering into the illumination. Victoria seductively slid her robe off and let it hit the floor. Her shadow moved just as gracefully as the real thing. She knew he was somewhere in the darkness watching as she continued to perform her sensual striptease. The next to go were the straps to her silk negligee; it met the robe on the carpet. All she had left to remove were her Gucci slingbacks; those stayed on.

Averie was now ready for the show and Victoria didn't disappoint him. She began playing with her full breasts, twisting her erect center buns between her thumb and forefinger, causing her to emit soft moans. Averie was entertained. Tonight, she was on a mission and she wasn't going to stop until she completed it.

With both hands, full of her 36C's, she pulled each one up to her mouth, one at a time, and teased her own nipples, then she dropped them making them bounce uncontrollably. She then turned around and bent over exposing a most perfect round ass anyone had ever seen. She started smacking herself on the ass, demanding his attention. Little did she know he was getting extremely turned on by her act.

Her right hand went from smacking to rubbing to moving dangerously close to a land close to her heart.

Before she realized it, two fingers slid inside the opening to her pleasure palace and started rotating in a slow motion. Her moans became more audible the more she played with herself. The passion was almost too unbearable for her.

She hollered through her own gasps for Averie to join her. Finally, he emerged out of the darkness and made his way over to where she was. His body heat gave him away, as she used her free hand to feel around for him. What she found wasn't what she expected, but was surely welcomed.

His hard member met the palm of her left hand with warm greetings. She stroked his ego, signaling that she'd won the battle.

He turned her around, and put his hand on her head, pushing her toward the intended target. She looked up with willing eyes as she took him into her mouth. After a few minutes kissing him, she was fully into it. Even with her best work on him, she still couldn't get anything more than some juices, he was hardly near exploding.

Averie pulled Victoria's head back in an aggressive manner, which meant he was all about business from that point on. She rose quickly and bent over a chair without being asked. Her melon pulsated, anticipating his arrival.

He entered her slowly and then began. At first, Averie controlled the pace but soon lost out to her rhythm as she threw her buttocks back against him. She clenched her cheeks together, pinching his tool to where he couldn't move the way he wanted to.

"Ooh…. Baby, he moaned out. "This melon is good, baby girl."

"You like it?"

He responded by grabbing her hips and banging them angrily, making them slap against his pelvis. Deeper and deeper he went until she screamed unmercifully. She wanted to explode right then but he wanted it done together. He pulled out of her just long enough to sit down and have her mount him again. This time he took the lead and controlled the flow. Victoria began riding him like a cowgirl on a wild horse. The more he thrust, the louder she screamed. "Averie, baby, I love you… oh yes, baby…right there."

Her back was turned to him, so she couldn't see how suddenly, he became disinterested. His mind drifted to his case the feds felt they had on him and Mr. Campbell.

"You love this pussy, don't you?" she asked, still riding reverse style. He didn't respond, he just let her think she was working him but the truth was, boredom had set in.

"Ooh, baby… I'm cumming… I'm cumming… I'm…" she slowed to a rocking motion until she stopped, resting on Averie's chest.

She started mumbling to herself and then she whispered to him that he was forgiven of all his wrong doings. Averie tapped her. "Get up, Victoria."

"Ooh baby, wait. This feels good right here with you in me."

"I want you to go over to the Jacuzzi and relax in the hot water, maybe eat some cheesecake. Would you like that?"

"Of course, you're joining me, aren't you?"

"Yes, sweetie, you go ahead. Let me get the cheesecake and make a call and then I'll join you in a hot minute."

"You promise?"

"Now, when have you known me to make a promise? I said I'll be there," his tone changed, alarming her. She backed off.

"Alright, damn Averie. Just like a man, as soon as he gets an erection, he's through with our ass," she mumbled under her breath. But he heard her.

"What? You're the one who came running your hot ass down here to me, not the other way around. I had other stuff on my mind, and I didn't even have an erection!"

"Oh, no, you didn't go there, you----!"

"I think you need to watch your mouth. Your ass could come up missing down here, no witnesses. There is nothing you could do about it. Now watch it, you hear me." He had to put her in check.

She didn't know which way her emotions flowed. Tears

started to form in her eyes wondering where all this was coming from.

They both stood from the bath seat and she tried to walk away. Averie took one look at her, realized he was wrong, snatched her to him by the arm, and kissed her vigorously as a form of apology. Her eyes were still full of tears as she fell into him and his warm embrace. She was completely lost in his love. This was the same love that caused her to quit her last employment, the love that drew her to his side.

"Jump on," he told her as he knelt down. He gave her a piggy-back ride to the Jacuzzi room. He turned the jets on making the water bubble to a boil. Steam rose, warming the area. "Alright, slide down."

"That's almost five feet, Averie"

"You don't trust me?"

"Of course, I do." And she did as she was instructed, landing safely into the bubbling pool. She could only smile at Averie realizing the love of her life was capable of doing the impossible. With anyone else, she felt vulnerable, but with him she was safe.

She could still smell the faint scent of his Bond number nine cologne, now magnified by the humidity in the room; it made her want to touch him again.

"Thank you, Sweetie," she said for nothing and everything.

"I'll be back as soon as I get off the computer. Is that alright?"

"Yes, baby." As long as he wasn't' leaving her life, everything was alright.

Leaving her sight, he walked over to the other side of the room, entering his sound-proof 10 x 10-foot dark secret room. He thought if Steve doesn't have his camera device linked on his cell phone, it would be difficult reaching him. The monitor was activated and there he was…

30

Steve's visual showed up on Averie's screen pixilated, but clear enough to make out his expression. He looked confident in his posture and his voice. He was out on the streets to handle a special assignment for Averie.

"Steve, how's everything?" Averie asked in a chipper tone.

"It's a go, Sir."

"Was she as expected?"

"Very much so, Sir."

Averie studied Steve's body for any changes in body language. That was a telltale sign of any disloyalty. Right now, Steve didn't show any.

"I have to admit, I didn't have to persuade her like I thought I would."

"Excellent work, young man," he praised him as he looked at his watch nearing close to 1:00a.m. If you keep this up, you'll move into a more responsible position on the team."

"Thank you, Sir,"

"No problem."

"Sir?"

"Yes, Steve." Now, this is where Averie saw some

fidgeting with Steve.

"I wanted to let you know, you shouldn't have doubts about me or my work."

"What are you talking about?" He kept his tone even until he heard Steve out.

"The dynamic duo you sent to follow me." Averie smiled knowing Steve couldn't see him. "Well, they're both resting in their trunk on the side of the road."

"What!"

"I knew you'd have someone on me, so I took precautions. I was planning on delivering them to a secluded location."

"What did you do to them?" Averie was concerned now. He was responsible for the wellbeing of the two trailers.

"Let's just say for the next few hours they won't be available."

Steve went onto explain how he pulled off the move. He had acted like he was having car trouble. When he flipped on the hazard lights, the persons pulled up behind him and attempted to assist him with the problem. Steve told them the problem was under the hood and like two dummies, they went and looked when he popped the hood open. It had surprised him to find them so gullible, and that was their mistake.

He had eased out the car with his twin automatic 380's and a set of handcuffs he had in the glove box. He crept up behind them and told them, "Spread em." He cuffed them to each other and did a pat down search. They were carrying just as he expected, both had glocks and didn't mind relinquishing them.

Even though they each had a free hand, they didn't put up any resistance when he escorted them to their 2017 black Cadillac SRX. He made them face each other and retrieved the car keys from the taller of the two. He pressed the button to open the trunk space. Luckily for Steve, it opened; unlucky for them.

From the pocket of his carpenter's pants, Steve pulled out

a high voltage stun gun. The taller one was the first to get hit with the 50,000 volts. His body shook violently until the smell of feces filled the air; he had shit on himself involuntarily. The other one tried to cop a plea; explaining to Steve that they were on the same side. That only angered Steve the more, especially when he said that they were ordered to follow him. He hit him with the stun gun too, producing a pissy smell.

"I remembered what you told me earlier about mistakes, we can't afford mistakes. You remember saying that, Sir?"

"Yes, Steve. What's your point?"

"If you must know; I didn't kill those guys. I just kicked them into the trunk. They were fumbling so hard, it took me nearly four minutes to get them in."

"So, what you're telling me, Steve, is that you are making decisions on your own now?"

"No! But, I felt it was necessary to send you a message that I'm your guy."

"No, Mother Fucker, what you did, was what you wanted to do!" If anyone of my men gets into a situation they should first contact me. I take care of problems, not you! And to top it all off, you said you knew I had you followed; so why did you continue with the bullshit?" His commanding tone was just as frightening as if he were right there in front of him physically.

"I… I…"

"I what, Motherfucker? Say something worth understanding."

"I was just trying to impress you."

"Steven A. Jackson, you want to impress me? Have your impressing ass here with the package in the morning at the specified time that you were given. I guarantee no one will be trailing you. I won't contact you anymore. If you fail me, Steve, I'll be the one doing the impressing real swift like. Now, where are my men so I can clean up your mess?"

"They're…"

"Wait, that's them chirping me now. Steve, how in the

heck are they chirping me? I thought you said they were out of commission? Oh, never mind, just do what I asked. Goodbye." Averie blackened his screen out on Steve and dealt with the two dumb-asses.

"Kevin and Mike, where are you?" Kevin grabbed the phone from the console and spoke.

"Sir, we're on route to the package."

"Is everything alright?"

"Yes, Sir."

"Where's Steve?"

"Ah... He took a quick turn and we lost him."

"Oh, really. Put Mike on the phone."

"Here man he wants to speak to you," Kevin gave Mike the phone.

"Hello, Sir,"

"Why do you sound like that, Mike?"

"Well, Sir, the truth is, Steve tricked us into stopping, and then locked us in the trunk of our own car."

"Oh, really?"

"Put Kevin little ass back on the line."

"Can you hear me?"

"Yes, Sir." He held the receiver while whispering to Mike. "What did you tell him that for? That was some dumb shit!"

"Kevin!" Averie shouted so loud Mike heard him. I want you two dumb fucks here in the morning and to continue trailing Steve, this time un-noticed. Goodbye." Averie hung up with the press of a button.

"What 'did he say?" Mike asked.

"He said you're a dumb, stupid, no thinking ass, and we're a couple of fuck-ups who belong together. We have our assignment, so lets' just do it. Afterward, it's you and me one on one."

"Shit we don't have to wait, I'll kick your little-tight ass right now, short funny looking ass."

You're just saying that because I'm driving!"

"Well then, pull over. We're already behind on time so hell another 5 minutes won't make any difference."

"No, but me whipping your light skinned-curly hair ass will. As a matter of fact," Kevin hauled off and hit Mike with a right hook to the jaw.

"Oh…Hell to the Naw! Pull this motherfucker over."

Moments later, they were on the side of the road brawling. A kick in the butt, then a swift kick to the knees. They wrestled a round or two and then stopped when cars passed beeping their horns at the two of them. Mike hopped in the Chevy, fully intending to leave Kevin, as he laid on the ground with a bloody nose.

"Asshole, get up. We have a job to do. Don't' make me leave your little dumb ass out here alone on the road with these deer's."

"Help me, man, I'm hurting, Kevin cried out like a wimp."

"Ooh… you better get up before that big ole' snake bites you in your tight little black ass."

"Where? He hollered, jumping up and high-tailing it to the Chevy Camaro."

"I knew that would get you moving. Now, close the door so we can get on the road."

"Just wait 'til we get back to Georgia so I can get your ass in the boxing ring. You with all that wrestling, I want to see how good your hands are." In mid-sentence Mike slammed on the brake, causing Kevin to bang his nose on the dashboard. It instantly bleed.

"You need something for a bloody nose," Mike joked?

"Just drive the damn car man."

"God, you're lucky I had the spare key or our asses would be stuck and that damn Steve motherfucker going to get his."

"No, you're lucky we have important business to attend do."

Their friendship had been like the odd couple for 15 years; yet they had always remained close. One thing was for sure, if they failed Averie again, he'd find a way to separate them permanently.

31

Olivia was right. I have a tendency to put my work before my family and other things that should be more important to me. If she only knew how this new writing project has consumed me. Over the past two months, I've really lost touch with who I am. Detailing all the sordid events Mr. Bod`e encountered gave me a grave understanding of the underworld that he controlled. So many different characters have entered my life; I don't know who is friend or foe. Trust is something that is thrown around loosely, only valued by particular members of the team. And yet I trusted Averie to keep his end of the bargain; to keep me safe during the writing period and to deliver the other half of my money as promised.

And he did. A two-million-dollar contract was awarded to me, a million upfront when I got to Atlanta to start, and the rest when I finished the book. I even received a bonus for finishing early. So, overall, it accounted for 2.3 million dollars that I decided to have transferred to a bank in New York. He proved to be a man of his word.

What was I going to do with the money? For starters, I'm

going to start my own publishing company, to enable upstart authors an opportunity to have their works in print. By publishing books, I'll be giving back to the same institution that engaged me to be a Pulitzer Prize winner.

I also planned on living life to the fullest, something I didn't do with Olivia and the girls. I was a decent father, but I could've been a better husband. So, I'm starting fresh with Victoria. We found love through the strangest of circumstances. We weathered the storms of our pasts and came out victorious.

The first thing I did was charter a private jet to San Pedro. This trip was to be an escape from the rat race of the New York life and a treat for Victoria for being so committed to starting over with me. The island's seclusion allowed for me to download all the intense drama that took place over the past 180 or so days of my life.

If you had asked me at the beginning of all this, "Do you see yourself relaxing on a beach with a beautiful lady and two million dollars richer?" I would've responded adamantly, "Hell No!" But, here I am, sipping on a daiquiri with one of those little wooden umbrellas poking out.

Victoria was cooling her freshly manicured toes in the bluish-green water while twirling her bikini top around her fingers. She enjoyed walking around the private beaches topless. It made her feel uninhibited, free from all the restraints she'd been held down with for far too long.

And I enjoyed watching her prance around to the beat of her own drummer. She is a beautiful woman and I think I love her.

My time was spent typing away at my memoirs, something I vowed to do once I had some spare time. It's amazing how a couple of million can free up your life.

The waiter was so attentive and courteous. He kept our drinks replenished before they were close to being empty. It was like he had a beam on how quickly our glasses got low. It had been two months of me not consuming alcohol and my taste buds welcomed the tanginess of the liquor. Victoria was back at my side reclined in a lawn chair soaking up the suns' rays. Her body glistened. Her perfect breasts were begging for attention. She sunbathed with her Prada sunglasses on while the tropical breeze blew through her hair.

"Excuse me, Señor." The polite young waiter said, returning, this time with a gold platter with a burgundy handkerchief draped across. I was busy typing, but his presence alerted Victoria. She sat up and acknowledged him with a nod. "I have a message for you," he said in a thick Spanish accent.

When I looked up, he was brandishing a chrome handled 9mm with a silencer attachment. I was speechless for a moment. Where did all of this come from? Everything was going so beautifully. Instantly, sweat started drenching my face and it wasn't the humidity, I was literally staring death in the face.

Everything moved in slow motion, everything except my thoughts, they sped a mile a minute. Maybe I'd harmed someone earlier in my life, or maybe the wrongs I'd done had finally caught up with me. I glanced over at Victoria and she looked at me. She took off her sunglasses and I saw the gleam in her eyes. One I'd never seen before; it was a look of betrayal. She nodded once more, and the waiter moved closer to me. Sweat was pouring uncontrollably now and my heart pounded in my chest. Could it be that Averie sent this man to kill me, and Victoria was in on it? I heard the click from the trigger, then nothing but blackness.

There was no noise. No blood. I looked to my right and there was no Victoria. The room was still dark, the way it was when I laid down. The only thing that was real was the sweat-soaked pillow that my head laid on. My body was cold from the perspiration and cool air in the room. The "Kill Bill" experience" had only been a dream.

******

A dark figure was standing in the shadows, maintaining a

stillness that was eerie to me. Whoever it was moved closer into my space, yet, I still couldn't make out who it was. I really didn't know what was real anymore. Was this also a dream? Was everything that happened just a dream? I was still breathing, so I knew I was not dead. Who is this person standing before me? I called out, but I couldn't hear my own voice. What was going on? Then a voice broke the silence in my mind.

"Mr. W.D. Campbell," he said in the softest tone. "We need to have a serious talk."

What in the world was this person talking about? He sounded like Mr. Richards, but his voice was much more reserved, more sensitive. I got a closer look when he stepped to my bedside. It was him, the butler. He smiled curiously as he touched my arm. I knew then that this wasn't a dream because I was awake and he was still there.

32

The project was about to enter its' most imperative stage. Everyone on the team was responsible for playing their part to make everything successful. That meant doing things one might not be too comfortable with. To Averie, this was a time for sacrifices.

"Victoria, I need for you to get as close to William as possible. Use any means you can to make him comfortable, understand?"

"My pleasure, boss. But I want you to know that I'm yours forever."

"I know, sweetie. Now, go check on your guest."

A few minutes later. 'Knock! Knock! Knock!'

The rapping on the door startled me. I'd been on edge since the dream last night. I couldn't quite understand the meaning behind it. Was it a foreshadowing of what was to come? But, I knew one thing was for sure, I would be watching everybody very closely from now on, especially Averie Bod`e.

"Mr. Campbell, are you awake, Sir?"

Just hearing Mr. Richards' voice made my stomach knot up. I hadn't had a chance to ask him about last night, but something inside of me was telling me to let it be and allow it to play out. Sometimes it's better to let people hang themselves. I kept my response cordial.

"Good morning." There was an eerie silence in the room before the door opened.

"Good morning, Will...Mr. Campbell, time to get up, Sir."

My eyes diverted from Mr. Richards' and focused on Victoria's as she entered the room.

"I was just about to get up."

She was standing over me and I wondered why it took two people to wake me up. One of them wasn't supposed to be here.

Mr. Richards excused himself, feeling the vibe that he was the third wheel. He was always going to be the third wheel to me, not having a thing for men. That had me look at him in a whole different light. Victoria was already dressed, hair wrapped in a bun, and wearing a navy-blue business suit. Her legs seemed to flow from the material.

"I'm sorry I disturbed your beauty rest, but I didn't want you to oversleep, breakfast is at 8 a.m. Mr. Bod`e sent me to make sure you were up and ready."

"You sure it was him that sent you or did you come on your own?"

"Well, it could've been me," she said smiling.

"I kind of figured that."

As I rolled out of bed, Victoria approached and gave me a warm hug. I immediately got excited; beautiful women early in the morning did that to me.

"I can feel you down there, William," she leaned up and whispered in my ear.

Remembering that I had chronic morning breath, I covered my mouth.

"You can say I'm happy to see you."

"I'll find out how happy you are soon enough."

"I'm sure you will."

We parted bodies and I headed towards the bathroom and she went to the door. "I'll see you downstairs in a half hour, she said before making her final exit."

"Alright, Vicki, I'll see you soon," I said in response. Look at me I was already giving her a nickname. She just laughed, noticing the same thing.

*****

I looked up to the painting on the ceiling that had changed to a heavenly scene and it brightened my spirits. I finished gargling, brushing and flossing my teeth, prepping myself for the day's activities.

Then I sat on the edge of the bed, collecting my thoughts before I dressed. Diamond popped into my head unexpectedly. Being in the same state she was in and not to think about her would be awfully insensitive.

What would she think if she knew I was here? We hadn't spoken since 2002; fifteen years can put a lot of distance between two people who loved the way we once did.

The miscarriage had been rough on both of us. Diamond and I had an argument the night before. We were at each other about trivial things, like, who's more of a financial benefactor in our relationship? Diamond worked as an in-house child developer, working with children of all ages. It didn't pay much, but it was sufficient at least until she renewed her physician registration. We even talked on several occasions about launching our own business, but she disagreed with the restaurant idea. That sparked more arguments and they didn't stop for at least a week. It was stressful for both of us.

The night before, I had to take a flight to Greenville, South Carolina, to do a book signing, we argued until she cried. I knew then that I had to take control of the situation. Being a spiritual person, I could feel something tugging at me from the inside. Something kept telling me we were destined for trouble. So, I told her we should pray to God to forgive us and expel the unclean spirits from us. On most occasions, she agreed, but that night was different, the devil had his way with her and she refused to pray with me.

Needless to say, she lost the baby while I was away on my trip. In fact, it was the day after I left. I cut my stay short and hopped on a plane to go back to Minnesota to be with her. It was a terrible time. She cried and blamed herself for a long time. She kept asking me not to hate her. How could I?

What happened was not her doing. It was God's will.

I waited for a couple of days to ask her why she didn't pray with me, I always thought it might have helped. She just looked at me with disdain and spewed some words at me that I couldn't understand. Days went by and the distance between us grew. Again, her attitude changed suddenly and I believe, with the help of her family and friends, she decided to leave me. That's two women I adored who left me. Why don't people just mind their own damn business? A month and a day later there was a note attached to the inside of my door at my penthouse.

It read: "*I love you William, but I need time to evaluate my thoughts. I'll be in contact with you when I get myself together." Love, 'Diamond'.*

The last thing I heard about her was that she had moved to Atlanta. I knew she was capable of holding a grudge, but this was different. Just thinking of those dreadful memories erased the thoughts of contacting her. I told myself, it would only make things worse.

I stood up from the bed, clasped my hands together and got ready to tackle whatever was in store for the day. The next fifty-nine days should be very interesting if they are to be anything like yesterday.

My closet doors were partially opened; I slid them back fully to expose the array of clothing that had been tailored just for me. There was a lot to choose from, but I wasn't quite sure which outfit would be appropriate for the day. I saw something casual that caught my eye and chose it since I'd be doing a lot of writing. It was cool inside the house, so I selected a cream, brown and blue long sleeve pullover. I matched the slacks, socks, and shoes to coordinate with the Hershey brown in the shirt. All that was missing was a smooth fragrance to accent my look.

The bottom drawer in the bathroom held a collection of high-end colognes. I splashed on some *Happy by Clinique* and declared myself ready for breakfast.

Once again, I was met by Mr. Richards when the elevator opened. I understand it's his job to be everywhere to serve, but I was somewhat leery of him after he mysteriously showed up in my room late last night, and how in the hell did he get past Tom?

"Are you ready to join everyone for breakfast, Sir?"

"Yes, I am," I responded without any emotion.

"Oh, by the way, there will be a special visitor joining us at the table."

I wondered what that had to do with me. "Mr. A.B. would want you to know that."

"Okay."

We stepped into the dining area, one after the other. Everybody was already seated. Mr. Bod`e stood and greeted me.

"Mr. Campbell, it's an honor for you to join us this morning. How did you sleep?"

I flashed back to the dream and thought, *you're the same one trying to kill me,* but I kept my comments cordial and didn't say anything about Mr. Richards.

"Just fine. The bed is very comfortable."

"Good, good. Please, sit here, by me."

Everyone's eyes were glued to me as I sat down between Averie and Victoria who was on my left.

She leaned in and whispered, "Damn William, you smell wonderful, and that outfit looks good on you."

"I know," I said with a certain arrogance. "But thank you anyway."

"Aren't we cocky? I think we've created a monster."

"No, when you got it, you got it." Victoria smiled and then pinched me on my leg.

Mr. Richards returned and announced to Mr. Bod`e that the package had arrived. Mr. Steve appeared from behind Mr.

Richards. I hadn't seen him since the previous morning in New York, which seemed like months ago.

"Thank you, Mr. Richards. Please take care of her and show her to the restroom to clean up so we can eat."

"Very good, Sir," he left as ordered.

"Steve, glad to see you've made it."

Out of the blue, Victoria whispered, "no matter what, William, you're mine, you hear me?"

I gave her a puzzled look, "What are you talking about?"

"Victoria, what is all the whispering about? It's rude not to share whatever it is you feel obligated to only share with Mr. Campbell."

"You're right, Sir, I'm sorry."

Mr. Boshá and his staff came out with the table settings. The fine china was labeled "Christofa" and I wondered how much it had cost. Victoria noticed my curiosity and despite Averie's warning, she again whispered in my ear, "The cost was $650 a set."

"$650 my ass!" I blurted out. Her face reddened as she smiled. I counted each piece and then did the math. "That's $7,800.00."

"The whole set is somewhere in the area of let's say…umm…$60,000.00. As I was about to say "What!" Mr. Bod`e interrupted us and called out my name, "Mr. Campbell?"

Mr. Bod`e chuckled to himself, "No sir. I did not use anything that wasn't in the documents I showed you." The china was not charged to your card.

"However, it was purchased in another person's name?" I regretted asking the question, but it was too late. I already knew the answer.

"Yes. Yes, it was."

Nothing really surprised me about these people. They had access to everything and I'd be a fool to think I could figure them out. By now, I figured I'd seen just about the most shocking events I could have expected to see. Then, in the next instance, I was blown away once again.

33

"The Twist"

There she was, looking directly into my eyes in a disheveled manner. She entered the dining area timidly, but once she saw me, her demeanor changed to anger. I wondered what the hell she was doing here. With a disturbed look on her face, she approached me.

"William, what is going on here? And why was I pulled into this crazy situation?"

She had plenty of questions and, if I knew her correctly, she was going to have plenty more.

"And, who is this woman sitting so close to you?"

I knew it wouldn't be long before her jealousy emerged. I didn't have a second to respond to any of her inquiries.

She pointed to Mr. Bod`e on my right. "Who are you?"

"Mr. Averie Bod`e, ma'am, at your service."

"Oh, so you're the one who woke me up late last night, blackmailing me into this circus."

"Actually, ma'am...,"

"You and I will talk later."

She took a seat on her own, one directly opposite of Victoria. They stared at each other with the anxiousness of two feuding cats in heat. She kept looking from me to Victoria, shaking her head like she knew something we didn't.

"Honey, don't even think you're going to get any from that man. He's already taken." I wondered where all that came from, my eyes bared down as if to ask the same. Victoria just gritted her teeth, trying her best not to explode on this rude, unexpected guest. Averie would have no combative scene at his table or in his house for that matter.

Mr. Boshá and his staff carted in the food, breaking the tension.

"Breakfast is served," he announced.

Trays of pancakes, waffles, eggs, sunny-side-up and scrambled, turkey sausage and bacon, crepes, sliced oranges, pink grapefruit, bananas, and apples all adorned the decorated table. Milk, orange juice, and coffee were served to wash it all down; even my decaf with two sugars and cream. This was virtually the same breakfast as yesterday.

As we ate, Mr. Bod`e glanced over at the mystery woman, obviously quieted by the food she was eating.

She, too, watched him.

"So, how was your flight? Was Steve helpful?" Frank asked, trying to lighten the mood in the room.

"It was just fine. And who might you be, if I may ask?"

"I'm Frank," he responded and then went around the table introducing the others. "This here is Tom and Claude, Rick, Alex, Kevin and Mike, Matt, Frank and Mr. B. You've already met Steve."

"Indeed!" She then turned to Mr. B. "Why is it just 'B.', you don't have a regular name like everyone else?"

I interrupted, attempting to keep the confusion down, "He's a very private person, that's pretty much all you need to know."

"What!"

"Excuse me, ma'am, but why are you raising so much fuss over things that really are none of your concern?"

"Excuse you!"

"Wait I'm talking."

"You can talk, go ahead!"

"First, you come in here full of attitude, rudely disturbing everyone's mood and displaying jealousy. Then you insist on asking questions when we haven't even explained our purpose. Now, my personal life is just that personal. There are repercussions behind knowing such information and I don't think you can handle it. If I were you, I'd be the quietest woman on earth right now."

She didn't take well to her public lambasting and in a show of total disrespect, she dropped the heavy sterling silverware on the expensive china to the surprise of everyone, including Averie.

"Excuse me, Mr. …"

He didn't even give her a chance to finish her sentence. Mr. B. moved swiftly towards her and squeezed her right shoulder near the collarbone. Instantly, she passed out, body slouching in the chair. The room went quiet watching Mr. B. operate as if he was trained by the secret service; knowing A.B., he probably was.

Tom smiled, amused at Mr. B.'s maneuver. "I haven't seen that in a while, but I'm sure we all thank you."

"Believe me, it was my pleasure."

I was concerned and these two were talking as if this woman wasn't unconscious. Mr. B. placed her head back upright and rested it on the back of the chair.

"Relax, Mr. Campbell. She'll be alright in a few; she's just out temporarily. Besides a stiff neck, she'll be back to normal, and hopefully a bit humble."

"Where did you learn all that Mr. B.?" I asked.

"Mr. Bod`e will explain our strengths and our relationships in due time. Now let's finish eating, shall we?"

I turned to Victoria and noticed the frustration on her face. "Are you okay?"

"She has one more time to disrespect me, you, or any of us, and what I will do, won't be temporary."

After what I just saw, I had to believe that she knew what

Mr. B. knew.

We continued eating, periodically looking at the limp woman; waiting for her to come to. Mr. Bod`e decided it was time to wake her. He grabbed a pitcher of ice water and handed it to Mr. B. I immediately knew what it was for.

"If you do that, you lose me, Sir."

"Well, what do you suggest we do then, Mr. Campbell, kiss her on the lips like Prince Charming?"

"Actually, that would wake her."

"I'll do it then," Claude jumped into action.

No, Mr. Bod`e stated. "That wouldn't be appropriate.

I'll kiss her."

To my surprise, Victoria stepped in and said: "and that would…?"

"Now, now, Victoria, I was just testing his passion for her. You love her, don't you, Mr. Campbell?"

I thought for a second but my answer was sure, "Yes, Mr. Bod`e."

"Then kiss her," Victoria said reluctantly.

I rose from my seat, walked over to where the slumping woman was, gazed at a face that was all too familiar, and then planted a soft kiss on her. It was something out of a fairytale, watching her inch around a little and blink her eyes, struggling to consciousness. She recognized me as the one who had broken the spell and reached up to give me a warm, loving hug. Her eyes teared up at the reality of what was going on.

"What are we doing here, William?" she whispered. "And why did they pick us?"

"I don't know."

"Did they destroy your credit and put you in financial debt, too?"

"Yes, they did. Be very careful what you ask or say around here, we're under a microscope."

"You don't have to tell me twice. I'm sorry I reacted the way I did. It's just…. that woman was all over you at least that was the first thing I saw when I walked in."

"She was just telling me something she didn't want the others to hear. She's actually very nice."

"Do you like her, William? I know you, you're attractive, she's attractive; there must be something you both have in common. Were you planning on not seeing me anymore?"

"No. And to answer your next question, I still love you."

I must admit that seeing Angela again stirred up an assortment of feelings that I thought were long buried. Unconsciously, I was comparing women I had dated after our break-up to her. It had to be her independence and conservative nature that had me intrigued. Angie's overall zeal for life lifted my spirits by just being around her.

Angela Jones, I called her Angie, had captured my heart a few years ago. She was a fellow writer, one with whom I instantly found common ground. Soon, other things caught our interests as well. She was divorced, so we spent many late nights on the phone comparing notes; consoling each other. She had two children who didn't mind their mother having an intimate friend. Although I didn't see them often, when they did come around, we got along great. Her daughter, Seven who had just turned 27 resides in Albany, New York. Her son Jamie stays with his dad and is preparing to go to Syracuse on a basketball scholarship. Angela and I remained friends and kept in touch after our break up. Us on again, off again relationship never resulted in ill feelings towards each other. The only distance between us came when her job transferred her to Stone Mountain, Georgia. Since then, we had lost contact; of course, until now.

"Ahh…Isn't this special," Mr. Bod`e interrupted. "We'll have to continue this little reunion later. Right now, we need to eat up. We're on a schedule today."

Angela gave a menacing glare at Mr. B. realizing he'd been the one to put her out.

"Should I be worried about my food?"

"We're not killers, ma'am." Mr. B. reassured her. "I had to put you to sleep because you were getting out of line. Everyone here is family and we don't tolerate disrespect of any kind. You brought that on yourself, by your conduct. My job is to make sure you and Mr. Campbell are completely safe."

"I apologize to all of you for my behavior. You must understand this has been a very tough situation to deal with. I was literally dragged into something I had no clue about. My whole livelihood is at stake. I'm $50,000.00 in debt because of this and someone comes out of the blue and says he'll pay it all off, plus give me one hundred thousand dollars for 60 days of service. That would have been hard for anyone to believe. I couldn't take it anymore; I just blew up out of frustration. How would you feel?" she directed her question at Averie.

Claude took the question. "We all understand how you feel, ma'am."

"How could you, unless it actually happened to you?"

Claude mumbled under his breath. Frank kept him from saying something he wasn't supposed to say.

"You will be filled in on all the details about us during the project."

Everyone finished what was on their plates without any more questions. Victoria still had a scowl on her face when she eyed Angie.

"At 9 a.m., you'll have to prepare, Will… I mean, Mr. Campbell, for the interview." That leaves only eight minutes to gather your items."

"What about me?" Angie looked confused.

"I'll show you to your quarters, ma'am. Follow me."

Angie came over, hugged and kissed me and then left with Victoria. I eyed Mr. Averie Bod`e.

"Is it wise to leave those two alone?"

"I think our guest has learned her lesson about respect."

"She's not the one I'm worried about."

34

Mr. Frank and I went back up to the third floor where my elegant room had been put back to its original condition by the housekeeping staff. I saw a different side to Mr. Frank this time around, he seemed more relaxed when he spoke to me.

"It must be nice to have two beautiful women competing for your attention."

"Yeah, I could really get used to this. Being paid two million dollars to do something I love, plus living bill-free and having everything at my beck and call, I'd say I'm pretty happy."

"Quite a change from 24 hours ago when I first met you."

"I would have to agree."

Frank deactivated the alarm system to my suite. We walked in and all the things I needed were placed on the bed. It wasn't even a mystery anymore how things were done around here.

"Don't forget your reading glasses, Sir."

"I wouldn't feel right without them, thank you."

I grabbed my laptop, favorite sitting pillow, my novel, pen collection and prepared for the biggest story of my life.

Mr. Frank turned the alarm back on once we left. We walked down the long hallway towards a room at the far end, beyond the elevators. I'd seen the room numerous times but never knew what it was for. Butterflies fluttered around in my stomach as we approached it. Mr. Tom, Claude, and Rick were all outside securing the entrance. They each nodded as Frank showed me in; it was secured after we entered. A loud beeping sound told us an alarm was set. With this much security, I thought I was entering a bank vault.

Through another doorway, there was a meeting room.

I didn't realize the room was so big. Mr. Bod`e and Victoria stood there, looking out at a huge bay window with their backs to us. Frank excused himself, shutting the door behind him. Averie and Victoria then turned around and faced me.

"It's time we begin," Averie said. "Have a seat."

He pointed to a tall black chair while he and Victoria sat on a couch next to the oak boardroom table.

"Victoria set his computer up. There is an in-house sound system that will play whatever you want at your command. It is already set up with your voice recognition. The room is also soundproofed so nothing will disturb us, except the hourly checks by Victoria and Mr. Frank. Would you like to have something before we start?

"A hot cup of decaf."

"One sugar and cream, right?" she smiled.

"Correct."

"Mr. Richards will bring it right up," she said grabbing a nearby walkie-talkie.

Mr. Richards arrived shortly after the call was made, with a coffee mug covered with memorabilia from the 01 and 09 World Series Champion New York Yankees and 1907-2016, Chicago Cubs, with cream and sugar saucers.

"Good luck today, Sir," he said, smiling as he placed the tray down. Mr. Bod`e looked at him strangely as he sashayed out of the room. I wondered if he knew what I knew about this overly happy butler. With everybody in place and all parties now seated and comfortable, Mr. Bod`e placed a tape recorder on the table and then pressed record.

"The time is 9:15 a.m., August 4, 2017."

35

"The Untold Story"

Let's introduce ourselves for the record. "My name today will be Averie Bod`e, I'll be navigating this journey. And what's your name?"

"My name is Mr. William David Campbell. It will be today, tomorrow and for the course of my life."

"If I've asked anything too personal up until this point, I'm sorry," Mr. A.B. said.

"It's a bit too late for that."

"Alright, Mr. Uptight, let's move on."

"Yes, please."

He leaned back against the sofa's comfortable cushions and spoke calmly.

"It took several journeys and plenty of hard work to provide the information I've gathered for you and the public. I'm sorry it's taken as long as it has, but I promise you and the American public that you won't be disappointed."

"I'm excited and honored to be able to bring this story to the world. I have to admit it has been challenging but I believe it will be well worth it, and not just financially."

"That's good. We have very little time and so much information to discuss."

"Well, are we ready to begin?" Mr. Bod`e held his balled up fist to his mouth and started coughing incessantly. My concern went out to him.

"Sir, are you alright?"

"Yes, nothing to worry yourself about. It's just something from my past that's caught up with me, I'll discuss it later."

I didn't pry into it. He looked as if he appreciated that and continued when he gathered his breath.

"People of the world, I want you to be very cautious and aware of your everyday surroundings. The people you generally encounter, those you might consider as your friends, business associates, or even a classroom school teacher, may not be who they appear to be. In fact, they could very well be complete strangers while perpetuating someone else's identity. There are over one million men and women today who are living a double life as "imposters." I feel there is a grave importance and urgency to inform people, that this does exist. We must learn everything about the people in our lives as well as those we associate with daily. Who's to say the neighbor next door is who they say they are? Do we really know?"

I interjected out if instinct, more so because I was engulfed in what he was saying. "I suppose not."

"You suppose right. We don't really know. There's only one solution if you're not 100% sure about that person, and that's to acquire a solid background check. That means get some type of positive description, personal information, and maybe even fingerprints. It's that serious when you're talking about protecting your family, business, or things that are valuable to you."

Averie seemed very passionate about what he was discussing. It was as if he was warning every single person in America personally. Little did they know, He was the one they really needed to be aware of.

"Close to 110 million Americans have their personal

identifying information placed at risk of identity theft each year. When records maintained, not just in government and corporate databases, are lost or stolen at hotels, restaurants, bars, libraries, and at night clubs they usually go into the wrong hands. These alarming statistics demonstrate identity theft may be the most frequent, most costly and pervasive crime in the United States."

"You never know who is who. He or she may be on the run from the law as I was; or maybe they could be a mugger murderer, molester, rapist, or worst-case scenario, even a terrorist. It may be scary, but these are the hard facts."

"Here's another hard fact, your marriage might even be falsified. There have been cases where spouses were imposters."

This was obviously Averie's story, to let the public know what's been on his mind for years. He wanted me to write his story; he wanted everything laid out in written form. He inched up to the edge of the couch and placed his elbows on his knees.

"America, hear me out. If I had access to unlimited amounts of money, wouldn't you believe too that there are others, even millions of men and women who have stolen someone's identity and have used it for financial gain? Hell, right now you probably know who I am talking about. One hundred million consumers have been victimized in this country already and the numbers are steadily increasing daily." Who are the people being sought out to be victimized? Everyday people; family members, law enforcement, churches, businesses, consumers, and even the deceased, have been used for profitable gain. Oh, I forgot one of the most selfish and insensitive methods; using a child's identity. Parents have been known to use their children's identity to re-establish credit, re-activate phone lines, or use them for residential purposes. It's not as serious as the other ways, but it's still wrong.

"The main issue here is that you can't recognize who might be the ones doing the crimes because they're everyday people around you. Just look around you, right now. Who do you really see? What do you know about the people who surround you? Do you have 100% knowledge of everyone's true identity?"

He paused for emphasis as I took down some notes. In fact, I shorthanded basically everything he recited.

"Not knowing certain facts could be dangerous to your health as well as your wealth. I'm merely stressing this point and providing this information because I have to, and no one else will."

"This, America, will be your wake-up call!"

Averie stopped the tape recorder, so he could say some things off the record. He knew, very well, the importance of this project and the anonymity of every detail.

"I want you to peruse these documents before we continue. They will give you some necessary background that you'll need to give this story credibility."

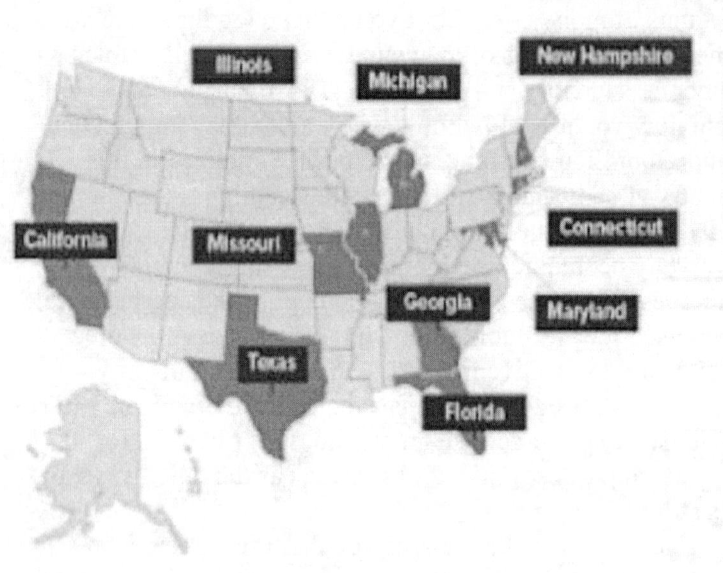

36

The Breakdown of F.I.F. "Financial Identity Fraud"

The Term Financial:

To conduct financial operations.
To manage the financial affairs; the management of money matters.
The science of public revenue and expenditure.
Public funds or resources of money

The Term Identity:

Sameness as,
Distinguished from
Similitude and every possible circumstance

The Term Fraud:

"Unlawful Gain"
The term in English: "Imposter," "Deceiver," "Cheater," "False Pose," "Perp," "Swindler," "Deception"

FTC Releases Annual Summary of Consumer Complaints
Imposter scams are now the second most common source of consumer complaints

This is a legal Identification Document:

Any document or card issued to an individual by a government agency or by any authority of a government agency, containing the name of a person or person's photograph or both, and includes without being limited to, a passport visa, driver's license, military Identification, or an Identification card.

The Term *Legal* Means:

According to, pertaining to, or permitted by law; Lawful; judicial.

This is an Illegal term:

Not legal; contrary to law; prohibited; illicit.

Altered and Forged Documents:

Any documents or card issued to the wrong individual by an inside source of a government official containing the name of the victim and description or such imposters Photograph, without the legal authorization of the sole victim.

Consumer Victim:

Any individuals whose personal identifying information has been obtained, compromised, used, or recorded in any manner without the permission of that individual.

Current or former names, social security numbers, checking accounts, driver's license numbers, credit and financial transactions, debit card numbers, medical identification, birth dates, personal identification numbers digital or electronic signatures, credit card numbers.

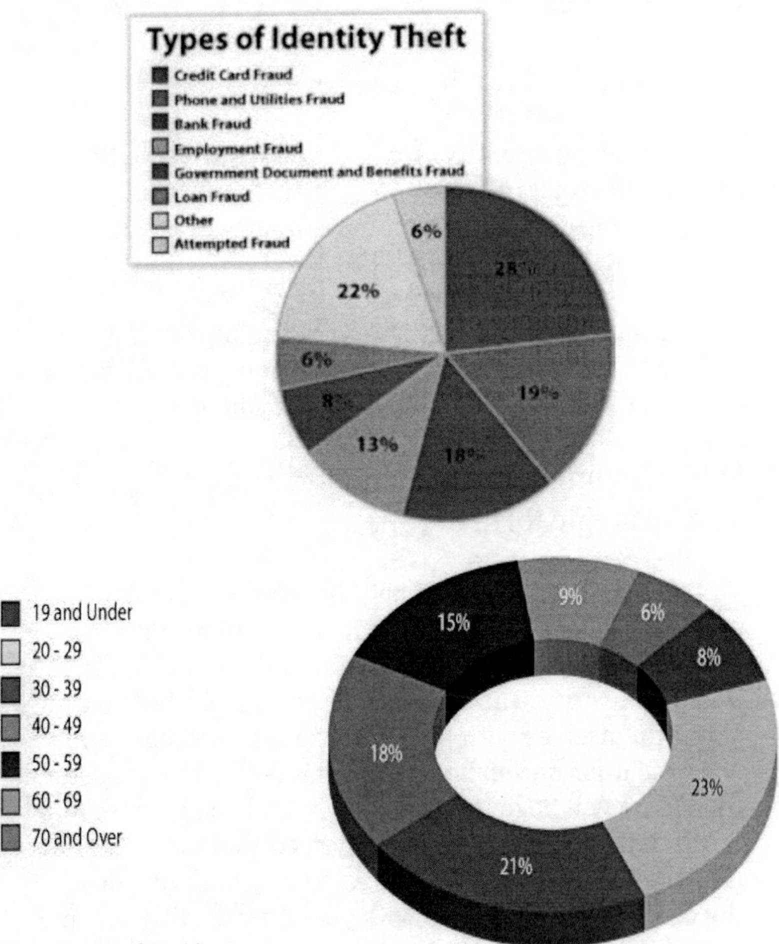

Business Victims:

Any individuals or entity that provided money, credit, goods, services, or anything of value to someone other than the intended recipient where they had not given permission for the actual recipient to receive it and the individual or entity that provided money, credit-goods, services of value has suffered financial loss as a direct result of the commission or attempted commission of a violation.

Resources:

Includes, but not limited to:

1. A persons or entity credit, Credit history, credit profile and credit rating.
2. Real property and Personal Property of any kind.
3. Credit, Charge, and Debit Accounts.
4. Loans and Lines of credit.
5. A person's personal history, including, but not limited to records of such person's driving records or insurance history, education or employment.

Social Engineering: (Telephone Fraud) The Strategic form of (SE)

To consumers of personal information over the telephone lines with only standard questions with the intent of receiving information about the individual's personal history. The victims will provide a whole outline about themselves with the trust of a total stranger and after the information has been obtained by the imposter, the victim will begin to think of what just happened. But it's toolate. He or she has already recorded the information and have initiated a credit check on you, during their conversation with you, now they've become you destroying everything you've worked your entire life to achieve, just for it to become a nightmare in the days to come.

In addition, here are the statistics by the Federal Trade of Commission and the Javelin Strategy & Research.

The 2017 **Identity Fraud** Study, released $16 billion

was **stolen** from 15.4 million U.S. consumers in **2016**, compared with $15.3 billion and 13.1 million **victims** a year earlier. In the past six years **identity thieves** have **stolen** over $107 billion dollars with no recovery.

Past decade and a half, identity theft is the #1 multi-billion-dollar financial crime in the country. In less than 3 seconds someone becomes a victim. Over 35 million American's is expected by the year 2020. Question is, when will you become their next victim?

These are your supportive facts
"America it's time for a change!"

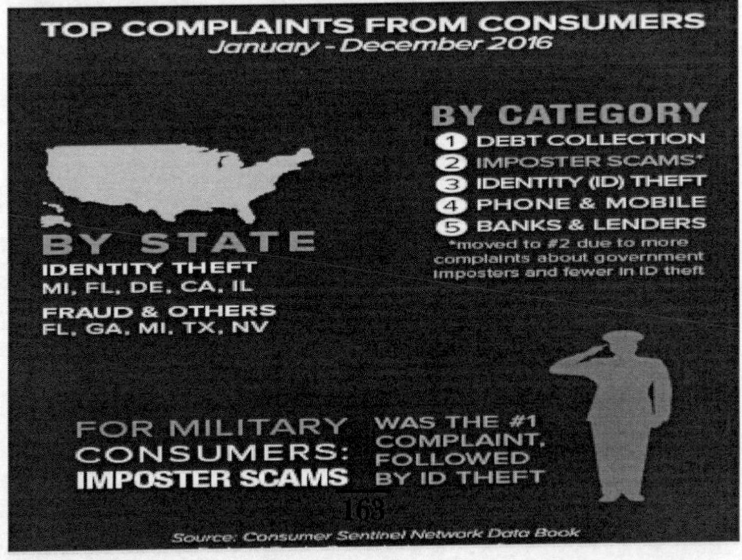

Total Fraud Victims Reaches Record High

Source: *2017 Identity Fraud Study*, Javelin Strategy & Research. **JAVELIN**

Then Mr. Averie Bod`e placed the recorder back on top of the table as he only stared at me without a sound. Thirty seconds went by and finally, he gave the okay to re-start the interview.

37

I had just finished reviewing the material breaking down F.I.F. that Averie had handed to me. As we started into the interview again, everything was beginning to flow smoothly. I inquired about some things and Mr. A.B. answered my questions in a clear, concise fashion. Then suddenly there was a pause.

"Stop the tape! "He abruptly rose to his feet and then began pacing back and forth in front of the sofa, like a caged lion. He reached down and unfastened a manila legal folder and poured its contents out onto the table. There was an 8 ½ x 11 photo that he held close enough to his face to breathe in its fumes. With an angry scowl, he then flipped it in my direction, having it land face up.

I was afraid to ask, but my lips reacted first.

"Who is this?"

"Think back over the year 2001," he shouted. "That son of a Bitch!" He took a deep breath as if to take in all the pain and frustration this man had evidently caused.

"His name was Abraham Abdulla. He's from New York and a real character. I spent months, even years, profiling potential victims, and this Abraham, who worked at Zaytoons, the Brooklyn restaurant making $350 a week as a busboy-dish washing motherfucker (not implying to anyone else) comes out of the blue and red flags everyone. I mean, he fucked up everything! I just don't understand these stupid fucks. They think they can pull off the billion-dollar plan, but it always backfires on their asses. Do you have any idea who was involved?"

"No Sir."

"Big names, that's who. Think of all the big names out there and you got your answer. Political, business, celebrity, you name it!"

I couldn't believe what I was hearing. As he read each name, my mind traveled to all the different areas of media and entertainment and the prestigious people touched. Mr. A.B.'s body trembled and anger shot through him at the mere mentioning of these people.

He slammed his hand on the glass top table, nearly shattering it. "That was my target list!" Tears began to form in his eyes as he turned in silence. He bowed his head to gather his thoughts. This person, whoever it was, affected him seriously.

"Sir, whatever happened to this fella Abraham?"

"The feds caught his ass, locked him up in Ohio, and he's been quiet ever since. And I hope he doesn't go backward from this."

"From that point, Averie turned again, this time with a menacing glare, "his ass or no other one better fuck up my plans with the selected list I've profiled to expose for the ending of this story. For starters, LifeLock, I.d. Watch Dog, Identity Force, and Credit Sesame. Then 3 of our major credit Bureaus. I have information here on over 1,000,000 consumers right in front of me, enough to target them all. Now wouldn't that be something? as a test saying each of their company's identity theft proof. So, let's challenge each. They guarantee up to a million dollars to each client. As of today, their client count is up about one million and a half. So, hypothetically, if their clients were victimized by chance, it would cost them somewhere say in the neighborhood of one and a half- trillion dollars to recover.

"Now that maybe a slight exaggeration, but I'm not far off. The point I'm making is it will not only dispel these corporation's theory but also cost their credibility and company. Now, if their services are as good as they guarantee it is, then I will personally endorse their product of service to the world. Wouldn't that be something?"

"What's that, sir?"

"The Mr. Averie Bod`e challenge."

"I'm following you with this. Your story will, in fact, place selected ones at the top of their competition. That's a very smart thing there."

"But first, we must see if there all up to it."

"Mr. Campbell, I must tell you there will be major collateral damage."

"How many consumers are you estimating, sir?"

"We're talking about in the millions easy, Mr. Campbell, beginning with the first target."

These companies seemed to challenge Averie. I could see the fire in his eyes just at the mentioning of his name. I wondered if any other household names like Sean Carter, Sean Combs, Russell Simmons, Stephen Curry, Stephen Harvey, Curtis Jackson, and Josh Goldstein to name a few that came to mind, would be on his list."

Through it all, Victoria didn't say a word.

I felt sorry for whoever got in his way. Murder seemed like the only thing that would clean his conscience. His voice returned to its normal tone.

"Mr. Campbell, please forgive me for my outburst. It's just that it pisses me off how these knuckleheads can sabotage someone's operation. Please forgive me, sir!"

"No problem, Sir" I responded, startled by his unbalanced emotions.

"Let's continue with the interview. By the way, Mr. Campbell, did you take your meds and shot today?"

"Yes, I did. Thank you for your concern."

"I only asked because we don't need you falling out on us, oh great writer of mines."

His sarcasm was disgusting at times, but I bit my tongue as often as possible to see things through.

"No sir, we don't want that."

"Good. Now let's continue."

Victoria then picked up the recorder from the carpet and placed it back on the table. I readied myself for what was to come next.

"Mr. Campbell…let's get right into it, shall we?"

I figured in order for the world to get a good grasp of what AverieBod`e was about; they would have to know the origin of his existence in the capital gains industry.

"Mr. Campbell, if you don't mind I'd like to go back to where it all started."

And with that, he began his story as I sat back and listened like I was at the theater watching my favorite movie.

38

"Into the Wrong Hands"

God must have had a plan for my life because he restored me and made it possible for me to see my first day. See, inside my mother's womb, I already faced a struggle to survive. My breathing was labored, my heart rate was weak, and the doctors tried their best to keep hope and me alive. Before I saw the light, my world was dark. Then I overcame the odds.

That was the story of my gift, overcoming the odds. Born on the south side of Chicago, the odds remained against me. Growing up I was gifted in school, very active in activities, athletically inclined, plus my parents kept me involved with community affairs. This made me well-rounded and a more responsible individual. My intelligence made me the envy of those around me, my popularity drew jealous stares and created a hatred that I viewed as undeserved. Eventually, my perception of the world became distorted. I wanted to win. I saw those around me winning and my goal was to obtain it all. And in the end, I became a time product of my own environment.

My adult years proved to be equally as challenging as my youth. Obstacles were continuously placed in my path, causing the frustration to mount like Lego blocks. At every turn, I felt opposition. It seemed like everything was against me, making it difficult for me to see the light at the end of the tunnel. Yet, I was determined to make it, some way, somehow.

Mr. Bod`e, can you tell me about some of your challenges you faced as a kid? You said the world became distorted. Can you explain that? He did not answer any of those questions, I was given a nasty look as he continued to talk.

The move to Atlanta was supposed to be the beginning of a new era for me. Averie Bode' introduced me to this new world. The music business was going to be my doorway into the future of wealth and fame. To me, it was the perfect match, a young Chicago dude fresh full of ideas and ambition, living in a city that was waiting to show the world that it had just as much fanfare and excitement as other major cities in the country. The way I saw it, I was the key to putting Atlanta on the map.

The fall of 1997 through the summer of 20?? was a great time for me. I chose concert promotions as a solid avenue to make my mark. Hustling was a part of who I was, so with a few connections with some people on the inside, getting in the door wasn't going to be too difficult of a task. My personality and ability to "talk the talk" would make me a force in this industry, or so I thought.

The music scene was electric. Everyone in the promotions arena was anticipating the upcoming tour season. For us, this was where the most lucrative moves were made. Touring was a chance for artists to perform their hit songs in front of crowds for further fame. The interactions at these concerts made things personal and very rewarding for the artist and profitable for the promoter who put it all together.

It was an exciting time for groups who needed to rejuvenate their careers, groups like the Spice Girls or New Edition. To them, touring meant bringing out fans, both young and old, who enjoyed their music.

New releases were opportunities for artists to keep fans connected to their favorite stars. Mary J. Blige had just released her self-titled album "Mary" and she hit the road accompanied by a newcomer in the hip hop game who was straight out of New York's Marcy Projects, Shawn "Jay-Z" Carter. For him to share a plaza with someone of Mary J's caliber would do wonders for his fan base, not to mention his career. They were all making various appearances around the country promoting the release of their new album, hoping to increase sales.

I took it upon myself to be anywhere the party was; I had to have my face in the place. I understood the game, learned it quickly; *get to know the ones you need to know and be in the right place at the right time.* Radio show hosts, disc jocks, recording industry executives, all these were people I needed to meet and build a working relationship with. This is what's known as networking or making "power moves." Learning this skill was necessary to having success in the promotions game. Being in the Atlanta area, which was considered the new haven for the recording industry, gave me great exposure to the budding scene. Night after night, I attended various events or frequented clubs to get my face and name known. I literally talked my way into where I needed to be. I was born with a gift and I used it to help me move through life.

The chance to make my mark finally came when I booked my first show at the Atlanta Civic Center in downtown Atlanta. It was "Master P's *I got the Hook-Up* comedy tour. And boy did I get hooked up alright, more like hung up. I sold out the show! Put all the pieces together. Made all the right moves.

Two people were responsible for my failure, Mr. Campbell. Ms. A, the event director, and Ms. J, special-events coordinator. Both names will never be erased, especially that of Ms. Ann. I hold her fully responsible for canceling my show.

Let her tell it. She said I breached the contract we signed. According to her, the contract agreement was that she wanted to be present at the event. You see, Mr. Campbell, during the scheduling phase she stated that she had family coming into town at the time of the event. It was a conflict for her schedule. I didn't see the conflict, considering that I had everything under control. She, however, saw things differently. She tried to find any negative thing to shut me down, and she did" he stated empathetically.

If you calculate the proceeds from all the ticket sales from Ticket Master and walk-ups, it totaled $166,378.23. My name was shamed after that as a promoter. I looked like a fool to the Atlanta radio industry and lost support from all the sponsors I had convinced to give me a chance and support my efforts. I lost credibility with a lot of the movers and shakers in the city at that point. Especially from radio personalities at the top stations. Local on-air radio personalities both Ryan Cameron and Wanda Smith from the radio show V-103fm got in on the jokes and blasted me all over the city. Yet, even with all the bad publicity, still, I never quit.

39

My persistence paid off when I got the opportunity to make a solid connection with a promoter who had major clout in the game. Terry Bradley was the manager-co-owner with his pops Big Terry of the Atrium night club in Stone Mountain. The Atrium was one of the industry's hot spots where many of the flashiest artists came to have a good time. I was introduced to Terry by V-103 radio personality, Rick Party. Rick put his stamp on me which gave me credibility, Terry and I gelled instantly after that. In this game, trust and loyalty are the pillars of long-lasting relationships, I earned that with him.

Terry allowed me the opportunity to learn from him by working alongside him while he put together a major event featuring the Bay Area Legend, Too Short. Because he was a resident of Atlanta's Southside, Too Short had a large following. This would prove to be a positive draw to bring in a nice crowd and turn a substantial profit. In order to partner up on the event I had to put in $15,000 to advertise; this was called a working budget. Shows must be planned carefully and radio promotions are a must, budgets are required to make everything work. We anticipate a good turn out and my launch would be a successful one. That could have been the farthest thing from the truth. The show was in my hometown of Chicago, featuring Queen Pen and Teddy Riley. Queen Pen was sort of a newcomer but with Teddy and his past success with the group, *Guy,* and his new project, *Blackstreet*, it wouldn't be too hard for her to be accepted. He was backing her record release party and after some hard negotiating for a period of two months, I finally got the deal done, contracts signed, convincing them that I was the top man for the job. This was my one time to shine and I had only 3 weeks to prepare, so I began by using my resources to get things in motion. You get one chance to make a first impression, that's why I decided to make it the biggest event possible.

2300 South Michigan was the happening spot where all the celebrities came to party, that's the venue I wanted and had to ensure there would be a draw. I could not afford another loss, so making the same mistake as last time was not an option. To help in my cause, I made a connection with all the major DJ's from WGCI, 107.5 FM, which was the top radio station in the Chicago area. Everybody from Ramonski Luv, Tornado, Sam Silk, Stone Pony (Davonte Stone) were targeted and put on the guest list. Having the radio and media outlets helped to get the proper exposure for the show. Gathering the celebrity guest list was next on the agenda.

On the night of the show, my nerves were going crazy. All the "what ifs" crept into my mind as I paced up and down Michigan Ave. The forecast was for rain, and Mother Nature didn't disappoint us when I felt the light drizzle. That added one more concern to my list, I didn't want the weather to deter the people from coming. I had invested over $1,300, so recouping what I spent was a must. With general admission starting at $20.00 and VIP at $100.00, I knew it would be a good night.

This guy named Kirk, one of Terry'smen was put in place to handle the door for the night. Because he came highly recommended, I felt the need to trust him. Kirk and I met up when the patrons began to show. To calculate the number of patrons that paid to get in we used a counter. Kirk was to keep track of the numbers.

As the rain fell steadily, surprisingly, more and more

people lined up.

"Kirk, make sure you do not leave this door," I instructed knowing the importance of his presence. He told me not to worry, he got it covered. The club positioned one of their own people, this woman named Katrina, to help Kirk out at the door. When I saw her, I immediately questioned why she was there but because this was my first shot at a gig, I didn't say anything to her. However, I did make mention of it to Kirk.

"Look, man, that woman at the door with you, they put her there for a reason. She can't be trusted, so, by all means, do not leave her here by herself." Once again, he assured me that everything was under control.

Limousines were pulling up left and right, with the celebrity guests started spilling out. They flowed through the front entrance escorted to the V.I.P section. When I came back to where Kirk was supposed to be manning the entrance, all I saw was the crowd of people lined up around the corner. The woman, Katrina, was there ushering the people in, but Kirk was nowhere to be found. I searched in all the usual spots, bathroom, coat check, baruntil finally, I spotted him in the back stairwell flirting with a tall caramel colored sister with a dress so tight it squeezed the sexiness right out of her.

"Kirk, what the hell are you doing man!" my outburst startled him. The tone of my voice shook the woman, causing her to walk off.

"Aw man, I just left for a couple of minutes." I knew he was lying because I'd been looking for him for at least 20 minutes and there was no telling how long he had been gone before that. I made him return to the door and finish collecting the entrance fees. Just as a safety measure, I stayed until the last of the people who could get in, got in. The spot reached full capacity with about 1,500 patrons. That was considered a success, at least that's what I thought until I walked into the office at the end of the night to count the proceeds. My cousin, Kalvin, who was also my money man, had to break the news to me that we only cleared $16,000. I nearly went ballistic when I heard the total. Even though I trusted Kalvin's count, I asked him to count it again just to make sure. He was right. The stack of bills didn't even measure up. I was anticipating pulling in at best $40,000 easily.

Kirk was called into face me and Calvin. He immediately went to explaining. I didn't want to hear it, the fire in my eyes was enough to silence him.

"No one steals from Averie Bod`e. No one!" I shouted, slamming my fist on the table, scattering the money all over.

"Ah... Averie... let me explain." He stuttered, with wide eyes. I tried to get close enough to him to put my hands around his neck, Calvin impeded my progress. Kirk saw my attempt and didn't offer up another word. There was nothing else to be said. He knew he was responsible for my loss, but there was nothing to be gained by roughing him up. The money was never collected so it couldn't be recovered, they just got a free night of partying courtesy of me. We sent him back to Atlanta the next morning, first thing smoking.

40

Over the course of two years, I didn't have the best of luck. I made several investments in the entertainment business as a concert promoter which didn't pan out the way that I had hoped. Even a hundred thousand dollars was squandered in that period. This not only drained my pockets but sent me into an extreme depression as well. I was in a tight spot and needed to find a new path. I was broke, homeless, discouraged, with no direction, my mental state was very unstable. Doing something unlawful had crossed my mind, I needed to shake it; I needed a change.

I reconnected with a partner of mine who lived in the Cobb county area of Georgia, Marietta to be exact. We would frequent the nightclub nearly every night. On Monday, we were at Club Chaos followed by early morning hanging out at P. Diddy's restaurant, Justin's. On Tuesday, you could catch us with our boys, Alex and Mike, at Club Visions, Wednesday, the spot was Glady's Knights chicken and waffles, Thursday, it was Vegas Nights. Fridays, we hit the Velvet Room with my man's, Alex and his brother Gabriel Gideon of AG Entertainment. 112 on Saturday when it was ladies' night, and on Sunday, I rested, getting ready to do it all over again on Monday.

These days the chill spot with my all the ladies "Club Bolts." While rolling with Mitch from Marietta, I witnessed him shell out a lot of cash in a short period. I wondered how in the world he could afford the things he was doing. Nice house, nice car, partying night in and out, entertaining, fine dining, all with no signs or a job. What was I doing wrong?

But I didn't ask any questions. I just watched, took heed of everything that we experienced and just enjoyed myself. Mitch took care of everything. Watching him whip out one credit card after the next. I figured he was into some sort of illegal activity. At only 31 at the time, he couldn't have had that type of credit to do the things he was doing. But it wasn't my business, so I didn't say a word.

In the course of our daily escapades and wild living, Mitch just up and disappeared.

One day while at Justin's in Buckhead, I was talking to the co-manager named Steve, and sipping on a Long Island Tokyo Tea. To my left side, over at the bar, I heard a loud raunchy voice that sounded vaguely familiar. I couldn't see his face but the voice barked out orders to the bartender sending drinks his way left and right. Anyone who was near him could get a drink on him.

I strolled over to him and asked where my drink was. He heard the recognizable voice and greeted me with a manly hug. "Aww man, what's up cousin?" It was obvious he was just as excited to see me as I was to see him. He announced to the bartenders and anyone in earshot that I was his ace, his number one partner, his cousin and to give me whatever I wanted for the rest of the night.

So, we drank and drank, then drank some more until I became woozy. I really wasn't a drinker and the excess went to my head. I realized that I had had enough and needed to make it out of there before I couldn't function anymore. We exchanged numbers, and I watched as he continued to toss around one hundred dollar bills like they were confetti. I wondered what the key to all this wealth was.

Days later I would get all the answers I needed, just not as I expected.

There were three men who introduced me to the world of credit card and identity fraud. Mr. Black, Mr. Chase, and Mr.

Colby, all three had an influence on me in different ways. Mr. Chase Allen was the first to bring me in by showing me the proceeds from the scams he was into, this was proof that what he said did indeed work. Mr. Black wasn't in too deep but still taught me a few tricks of the trade. Mr. Colby Smith, on the other hand, would end up becoming the inspiration for what I am today. He is the reason that now, after 15 years, I have resurfaced to tell my story.

Chase, being the creative one, had plenty of business sense, plus the money to back it up, but he had one flaw, "too damn much attention on him" he could be a loud, boisterous character when he got drunk. That didn't get in the way of him succeeding; he was always able to put the pieces together. One day, Chase mentioned that there was someone very important he wanted me to meet. That person would happen to be Mr. Colby. I would soon learn of his intellect and his cunning ways, both were necessary skills needed in this line of business. It would be his knowledge that opened the door to a world I knew existed. This doorway ended up causing total devastation and chaos to Americans and people worldwide; identity theft was born.

A few days later, I was at Club Visions in Atlanta for a grand event. It was a birthday party for my cousin, Chase, and there were lines of people that stretched down the sidewalk and around the block. Word was sent to me that I was on the VIP guest list, which meant there would be no standing in line and no ushering in through the general admission area with the wall to wall patrons. I would be escorted directly to the exclusive section located behind a set of velvet ropes, heavily secured.

Waitresses walked back and forth carrying several bottles of champagne. Two trays each of gold bottles went to the back section where I assumed the real party was. I grabbed an Apple Martini off another tray of drinks and headed in that direction, sipping my drink.

The booming sounds of hip-hop music led the way. I was let into the VIP area with no problem whatsoever. People were mingling everywhere. You wouldn't have even known all this was going on in there. Tables were adorned with golden Cristal bottles, one after another being popped and pour to the tops of glasses.

Conversations of various volumes crashed into one another. It wasn't hard to tell that this was the place to be.

"Hey cousin, over here," I heard the loud familiar voice summoning me to his table. I finally saw Chase in the midst of a sea of women, he had to climb over a few just to get to me.

"Everyone, this is my cousin, Big Averie," he announced to the partygoers.

"Hey Big Averie!" they sounded back in concert as if it was orchestrated.

"Well happy birthday Chase!" We embraced again.

"Excuse me, sir. There is someone insisting on coming up." I looked over his shoulder and saw my man, Mr. B. standing on the other side of the ropes. Evidently, he had tracked me down because I had left him at the hotel by the airport. He was never too far and always there when I needed him. Mr. B. and I go way back to my days on the block, in grade school, and then when I first started out in the promotions business. Mr. B. served as my personal security when I was in Chicago working on the Teddy Riley and Queen Pen show. I noticed his work at the club and he admired my ambitionand organizational skills. After 22 years, we were reacquainted by a neutral associate. We instantly clicked, and the rest, they say, is history. I was kind of skeptical at first when he wanted me to call him Mr. B

"It's better this way!" he explained.

"But I know your name, B????"

"Yes, and only you!" It'll be safer for us all to refer to me as Mr. B. Never trust anyone, bro."

"Okay, out of curiosity, what does the "B" stand for?"

"Business!" I never inquired about it again and he has been just that ever since Business.

However, I was a bit surprised to see him at the party. Mr.

B. didn't do much hanging out. True enough, he was security to me but it wasn't as if I was some sort of celebrity who required constant watching over. His presence was welcomed.

"That's my guy, cuz."

"Oh, he's with you? Let him up!" he motioned to the bouncer.

"So cuz, where have you been all these years?" I asked as he made room for us at the table. There were a group of women already seated but he quickly shooed them away.

"Busy," was his simple response.

"I see." I looked around." So how were you able to do all of this? The party, these bottles, this stuff isn't cheap, you know."

He chuckled at my innocence. "I'm quite aware of the cost. In fact, I requested the 1995 vintage selection personally which values at $800.00 a bottle. I believe $350.00 in stores, but hey, who's counting the pennies?" Chase let out a hearty laugh at his own humor.

"You must have hit the Georgia lottery Mega Millions or something." The whole table burst out in laughter.

"I'll have to sit down and explain how I got to where I am today. Some other time; some other place. Right now, let's enjoy this celebration."

At the close of the evening, Chase invited us to join him at the Four Seasons Hotel around the corner from Club Visions. When we got to the front desk, a woman named Brandy personally came to assist Chase. He slid her a V-Platinum credit card which she thanked him for with a wink. The whole exchange seemed to be harmless flirting, so I dismissed it.

41

After sitting with Chase nearly all night and soaking up every piece of information like a sponge, I realized that he had his plan and I had to come up with one of my own. I started putting some people in place to assist in making things happen. Our meeting extended to him linking me with his inner network of professionals. His man, Colby, would be a major piece to the whole operation, so making that connection would be vital.

Credit cards and driver's licenses went hand in hand, they had to match and they had to look authentic. Learning from Colby really put me in position, because he paid attention to every detail and didn't mind teaching me. It took a couple of weeks of relaying information to finally get it. I was confident in what I learned, now I was ready to work the plan.

I began by creating an underground company called Travel for Cheap. I booked trips for everyone, beating my competition with the fair rates and packages. Most of my business came from an online company called Sleepwell.com. They were good at what they did, and I endorsed them. With their references, I could build clientele, that's all I needed to work my network.

"We Got What You Need" became my motto for all those I encountered. From flights to hotels, I was the man you needed to see. If it was Miami, I got you there. Las Vegas, Los Angeles, Atlanta, Chicago, Houston, New Orleans, New

York, the Islands, pretty much every major city and even countries abroad, I serviced. Wherever planes took off and landed, my business was there.

There was a lot of easy money to be made if I had my paperwork in order, and as long as I had credit card numbers, I was making money. People don't realize that it's not about the plastic, it's the credit score, the credit history, that's what's important.

Through my connections, I could come across the right people to provide me with personal information. I needed spreadsheets of credit card information, then after a few days, we could compile a healthy list of potentials to work the next phase. Assisting me would be Cynthia Crawford, an attractive Caucasian woman in her late twenties. She was very smart, just caught some bad breaks early on her adult life. Right when she was finishing up her degree in accounting she got pregnant by a man she described as a deadbeat. Because he basically left her with the full responsibility, she was unable to handle the rigors of school and childcare. Now, with two children, she was ready to put her intellectual skills to work. To me, she had more hustle in her than any other black sister, minus the attitude.

Cynthia brought in one of her associates, a girl named Ramona, to help her in our efforts. Ramona was good with detailing and researching. I felt like they were the perfect pair; Lavern and Shirley, Cagney and Lacey, the way they complimented each other made the operation click. They were to provide spreadsheets containing hundreds of clients' personal information. Cynthia was genuinely interested in helping me even though we were doing something illegal. Over time, she proved that she was down for the cause.

Ramona, on the other hand, came from a different background. Before she and Cynthia had crossed paths, Ramona bounced around from job to job in various cities doing everything from small-time credit card scams to account fraud when she worked in the accounting department at a local bank. She tried to straighten up after losing her last job as funds manager, and that's when she met Cynthia. They worked together part-time for a bonding company. Ramona had an itch that she couldn't quite scratch and was waiting for the next opportunity to work her hustle.

The two dealt directly with accounts and had access to exactly what I needed. I would give instructions and they would follow through. Names, addresses, phone numbers (home, cell or work) and, of course, the ones I needed the most, credit card numbers and pin codes. Blue and Red cards beginning with the 4's and 5's were the ones I wanted, but at times the 3's would be processed for higher scale packages. While the girls worked, I had time to connect with potential clients.

By working brief stints in the music industry as a promoter, I could rub elbows with some of the biggest and wealthiest celebrities in hip-hop and the entertainment of sports. Those would end up being on my client list. Not to exclude the drug dealers and every day 9 to 5 taxpayers.

Travel for Cheap became our brand that we shopped to the business world and our selling point was to do it for cheap. In America, everyone was looking for a way to save money, so people were always looking for the cheaper route. What we were providing fit the needs of the public.

All I was concerned about were the spreadsheets because I knew how important they were to the operation. As Cynthia compiled them, she notified me. Together they could pull in about two hundred to three hundred; that was solid, which was a nice quota. However, before I could collect on the fourth batch, a problem surfaced.

"Hey Averie, I feel like Ramona is going to be a problem."

"What gives you that impression?" I asked, curious about her concern.

"For one, she's wondering what her take is going to be if she continues to work with us."

"I believe I made that clear to you two that you would be taking care of the increase of information." I thought for a second about what she had just said. "Wait a minute, what do you mean? She has the spreadsheets? They're not all with you?"

"Once she finished her portion, she collected them and said she preferred to deal directly with you on the business from now on."

I gave her an incredulous look, then I agreed to speak with her.

"Give me her information, I'll handle this!"

"Averie, are you sure?"

"I'll handle her ass. You just keep doing what you're doing. Good work, Cynthia."

I contacted Ramona and we had a heart to heart. From her tone and the way, the conversation was going, I could tell that she was trouble. I usually did the screening when pulling in members of my team, but in this case, I took Cynthia's word on this.

I assured Ramona that I had a package ready for her and instructed her on how and where to go to pick it up.

"Mr. Averie, okay, but what about my money?"

"Ms. Gillard, your money will be delivered to your mothers' house this evening, Ms. Garcia in Norcross I do believe."

"What, but how?" How do you know where my mother lives and how do you know her name?"

"On the contrary, I know quite a bit about your conniving, ungrateful ass, Ms. Ramona Maria Gillard. I know a great deal about you more than you know. And how I got my info on you is not your concern, not what is, or what happens next. And if you run to anyone with this, everyone you love or care for will be in danger." I then dropped and smashed the burner phone before she could respond. This would be my first cautious decision of getting rid of a problem, but not life."

I asked Mr. B. to handle her, but I also had to remind him that he was only to frighten her, not to make her ass disappear.

After dealing with Ramona, I called Cynthia to make sure everything else was in order. I needed the same reports as before by the end of the work week. She guaranteed that I would have them.

"I had a conversation with hotel reservations and they informed me that they would be sold out with the medical convention taking place on Thursday morning. There are four hundred reservations that were booked, guaranteeing a full house." She sounded like she was on top of her game. "Averie, I assure you that it would be taken care of."

And for some reason, I believed her. Cynthia was sincere and loyal to the project; her hard work would pay off.

42

Days later, I came across a guy named Jay whom I met through a female friend of mine, right here in Atlanta. He was an expert in the fraudulent flight business and would later help me perfect my game. As with all things, even the best, there were always flaws. At times, Jay would get sloppy with his dealings and have run-ins with airport security. This never deterred him from handling business though.

Jay was a native of New York, Harlem to be exact. From my experience, some of the slickest people lived there. Whether male or female, those I've meet from the Big-Apple have been scammers. Jay was no exception. He had more game than Madden Football. He was seriously connected with some of the majors. He had inside sources with hotels as well since he knew that air travel and hotels went hand in hand.

People used air travel as frequently as they used cars. Business people, especially, flew from coast to coast to various cities and didn't mind searching to get a cheaper rate. Soon, people began to contact me 24 hours a day trying to make reservations. I would guarantee that I could get them on last minute flights. If the ticket cost $700 from the airlines, I would give them my quote for half or three-quarters the price and it didn't cost me a penny.

That was the game I was in; flights, hotel, and car rental reservations. Celebrities, sports figures, just about anyone who had the need, spent money with Travel for Cheap. It wasn't all peaches and cream in the travel business. I knew my associate, Jay had the connections yet he still had some major slip ups in his operation. In one of my experiences, he had booked two seats for Mr. B. and me on North Airlines. This was one of those last-minute tickets, but I felt secure because it was Jay who had booked them. Mr. B. sensed that something was wrong as we approached the boarding area. He advised that I let him board first, preventing me from taking any risks. As usual, I trusted his instincts.

They scanned our electronic boarding passes, but they didn't go through. A few moments after trying to explain our situation, we heard airport security nearby.

"Gentlemen, follow me," her voice commanded. We walked a couple of paces and then she turned and asked, "Where did you purchase your tickets?"

"We didn't," we answered. "We had our knuckle-headed travel agent make our arrangements. We are concert promoters and our itineraries are made through several agents."

"Okay, follow me please."

As we walked behind her, I remembered that I had five fraudulent I.D.'s on me, plus $5,000 cash in my pockets. Yes, I was nervous, to say the least. I saw opportunity in my path and quickly dropped the I.D.'s in the trash on the way to the airport security office with the intention of coming back to get them. They were valuable and I didn't want to lose them, not to mention the feds, homeland security would get involved if they were discovered.

She asked us to stay put in her small office while she radioed the airport police exiting for a moment. I felt confident that the situation would be temporary. There was nothing to link us to those tickets and of course the credit card used was not associated with us nor was it in our belongings. Just as I figured, they searched us, then began a series of lightweight questions. When they were done, they released us. I went back to pick up the faces I had stashed in the trash and we left the airport without getting to board our flight.

After that close call, I learned a very valuable lesson: never trust sloppy ass workers to take the lead for a quick buck and always listen to the advice of those you trust.

43

I worked the hotel & travel business for over a year and really made a great deal of easy money. Just as easy as it came, it also went. One minute I had cash, and the next minute, I was broke and couldn't believe it. Gambling became my pastime and it soon took me under. I went from one casino to the next, Vegas, Detroit, Indiana, East Chicago, even St. Louis. They all got a chunk of me in some major way. When it got too deep I knew I had to call someone to help me out of my pit. I called Chase.

"What's up Cuz?" he answered cheerfully, obviously glad to hear from me.

"I need to see you."

"I'm on my way to Poppadeaux for dinner. Meet me there in 30 minutes."

"I'll be there."

It had been a while since I had last seen Chase and a lot had changed. Some of the things I learned from him, I put into play and it worked. I made quite a bit of money by staying consistent. My downfall came when I lost sight of the goal and started focusing on the spoils of life. Life revealed the mission at hand and I began to squander money left and right. I was confident I could get it back. I just needed to get a grip.

We were seated at a secluded table in the semi-upscale restaurant. A petite waitress approached our table to take our order. Chase took the liberty of ordering for me which I was perfectly fine with. He had great taste in cars and clothes, so I was sure he could handle something as trivial as a meal. As she finished jotting down what Chase recited, she made sure to mention to my cousin that she was grateful.

"For what, sweetheart?" Chase responded in a charming tone.

"I got the money you wired to me yesterday, thank you so much again."

"Oh that, shoot, it was nothing. We good ma. Hit me up later, we can chat then, I know you're working now."

"I'll be sure to do that. Talk to you when I get off."

Chase diverted his attention back to me before she was even out of our view.

"You got her on lockdown, don't you Cuz?" I said.

"Naw… we cool. What's up with you, though?" he asked

"Man, I did something stupid."

"Let me guess. Another concert and you blew all your cash?"

"Almost…something like that. I picked up a little gambling habit. I guess the fast money wasn't fast enough."

"Anything worth having, requires some work to be put in."

"Believe me, I know now."

"So now you're broke?"

"Well, I have a few bucks left to get me from one day to the next. I certainly couldn't afford a meal like this one here."

"That's too bad because the tab is on you today."

"Huh?"

"Yeah, you called the meeting, you got the bill."

My heart nearly sank deeper into my chest until I saw the smile creep across his face. "Just kidding, family." He let out a hearty laugh. "You should have seen the look on your face, classic." I laughed along with him, just not quite as hard.

"Averie, right now my people have me on hold, but what I can do is put you in touch with my man, Colby in New York. He is the one you need to get with. I was going to wait to put you two together, but the timing is good now. With your hustle and his wisdom, you guys should put in some major work."

"That's what I need to hear." Chase then pulled out one of three cellular phones he carried on him for business and dialed up the number.

"Yo Colby, what up? You remember my cousin, Averie, the one; I was talking to you about? I want to hook him up with you to put some things in motion. I'll give him your number and he'll contact you soon." He hung up and placed his phone on the table.

"Put this number in your phone and call him when we leave here. He'll be expecting you."

"Thanks, Cuz. I really need this."

"No problem. One thing, though, you have to watch Colby. He is shifty and good at what he does. Don't be fooled, he has a good heart, but it's cold and he is as fast as the day in February. Be careful and be safe."

I wondered why he was giving me so many warnings with a man he hooked me up with. The thought passed as quickly as it came. I had bigger things to focus on. Getting back on track was foremost on my mind. This time, things would be different, I told myself. And that it was.

44

After a few conversations with Colby, he got me excited about my New York trip. I believed it would be something that would change my life. The information he was giving me was so detailed and critical that we could no longer talk over the phone, he said. So, my presence was requested the next day. A call came and my travel arrangements were confirmed and secured. I wrote down all the confirmation numbers as well as the room reservations. I vowed to make the best of this trip. I was determined to never look back financially after this.

I couldn't really sleep on the plane ride to the Big Apple. It was my first, and my stomach was tied up in knots. When the plane touched down, I wondered what to expect when we deplaned. People were moving around like ants at a picnic and talking as fast as lightning. I grabbed my cell to contact Colby to alert him that I had arrived. Looking around, it seemed like everyone had a phone to their ear. I fit right in.

"Yo son, glad you made it in safe. I'm about 3 minutes away, come out the front of the terminal; I'll be there shortly to pick you up. I'll be in a navy-blue Excursion."

The three minutes really was more like fifteen in New York time. I was cool, though, I realized that they do things differently everywhere you go.

"What up? How was your trip? You hungry?"

It made me smile to know he was concerned. I was hungry because they didn't feed us anything but peanuts on that flight.

"I know this spot where we can pick up some turkey

sandwiches on the way in. You good with that, son?"

"Cool." Where do they get off calling everybody 'son'? I wondered.

The ride out to the Bronx was an interesting one. The New York culture was something like no other place in the country. Each borough we went through displayed a different environment. The personalities, the swagger, the language all depicted individuality. It was a world inside of a world.

Once we arrived at Colby's condo in an upscale section of the city, he warned that there would be some company already occupying the space inside. I thought to myself, why did it matter? It was his space to have anyone he wanted over. But I soon realized when we went inside that the women he had around were pictures there to keep the place hospitable.

"We will be going over some things a bit later, for now, go and get some rest. Desire will escort you to one of my guest rooms."

After a couple of hours of much-needed slumber, Colby requested my presence in his room, which doubled as his office. There were documents with names and personnel information scribbled on them spread out all over his bed.

"Look at this. Do you know what these are?" he asked.

"Not really."

"Look again, examine them closely."

I took a second look, this time a bit more carefully. I saw personal information from a few of the biggest celebrities in the music industry. Colby could see my wheels turning which made him giggle. I was very curious now. "Man, where in the hell did you get those from?"

"I have sources. You'll be surprised what you come across being in business and close to so many celebrities within the circle." He handed me three more documents which had names of the highest profiled entertainers and moguls in the country.

"This is B. Diddy's info!" I exclaimed like a groupie. "You have Irving Getty and Russell Sampson too. Damn man, this is crazy, how in the world you come across information like this?"

"Easier than you think."

I perused over one a bit more carefully and saw where B. Diddy had a beacon score in the 800s. Everything to know about him was right in front of me. Name, birth date, social security number, student loans, home mortgages, car loans, cell accounts, everything about the mogul was there in black and white. I began to filter through some more of the pages.

"Okay, you have my attention. So how do we make this work and how can it be of benefit?"

"Averie, what we have in front of us can bring us a fortune," he stated.

"Can you break it down for me? I mean, I can see where you're coming from I'm just not putting it all together."

"Look, you've already accomplished a lot in the credit card game, right? Well, this is on a much higher scale. You will almost use the same format, just step it up a notch."

"Okay, okay, I'm getting it. Since all the personal info is being provided like their beacon score, loan info, etc., we can actually live their lifestyle and become them. Am I correct?"

"Come on, Son, I know you didn't fly all the way up here to show me that you're slow in the game." He chuckled at his own joke. "You're from the Chi, from my research, that's where they do all this identity theft."

"True, but I've never known anyone to do it on this level."

"You good, son. Look, take these and study them. In the morning, we'll be taking a flight to California."

"Cali? LAX?"

"Yes, B. My peoples, Big Homie and Lil Man from around the way will be coming with us. We have a connection in L.A."

"I see this thing is deep and it requires a good team."

"You are absolutely correct. We must meet up with our folks on the coast, we have orders to fill. Today you will hang with us and get firsthand knowledge of the operation, so when we arrive in L.A. you'll have it down packed."

Colby was no ordinary man; he had a wealth of knowledge

which in most eyes would make him dangerous. I would keep a close watch on him and his actions. My objective was to analyze all that was going on around me. Meanwhile, I studied the paperwork with the names and information. Each document one by one. I digested them until it became a part of my memory. Soon I would become my work and become "Everybody."

*****

I took a seat right across from him in pure amazement. As the one writing this story, I was totally drawn into every event being told by Averie.

"Okay, this is about to get a bit crazy, so listen well, Mr. Campbell."

"Oh, I'm all ears. Listening to every word, Mr. Everybody." I joked.

I studied intensely to make sure I could put it to use soon. While studying for hours the 5 pieces he provided to me, I began to understand it fully and my mind reeled with the possibilities. Nothing could compare to what I was about to get into. Not the nickel and dime hustling back in Chicago. The only thing that did was school me in the ways of street knowledge. But this, what I had at my fingertips was a dream come true.

"I'm speechless, sir, please continue."

*****

The door at Colby's condo opened and in walked his compatriots. They came in and the noise level increased 30 decibels. Their voices bounced off the walls with the native tongue of New York dialect. I had met Lil Man and Big Homie once before, but they greeted me as if we had been running partners for years.

"Yo Averie, what up son?" Lil Man belted out giving me a dap and then a hug.

"What's going on?" I responded in a more mellow tone. "How's your mom doing?"

"Oh, she's good. Still has to go back and forth to them doctors, kind of wearing on her. Thanks for asking."

"Your mom is a tough cookie."

"No doubt."

Colby came in and interrupted our discourse with today's assignment. "We have to fill these orders before we leave in the morning. Big Homie, you and I will go inside and do the transactions, Lil Man you'll stay outside and watch for the boys in blue."

"Cool."

"Averie, you keep an eye on the blue boys too, just stay in the truck and observe what we're doing."

"Gotcha."

"Everybody know what's up? Good, let's ride."

45

As we drove through the busy streets, I was amazed at what was about to take place. I was a bit nervous knowing that if something went wrong, I was in the middle of it, but these people were pro's, so I felt somewhat safe. We made it our destination, a huge Big Box warehouse store that kept hardware materials and other items. Colby orchestrated the plan. It was his show, he was the man and the other two were to listen and move.

"We should be back in about 30 minutes or so, Averie. Once you see us approaching, open the back door of the truck so we can put all the materials in quickly."

"I got it."

"It's Showtime!" Colby shouted as they exited with confidence.

While I waited in anticipation to see what they would bring back, I decided to call Chicago. I got in contact with Mr. B. and told him my situation. I alerted him that if he didn't hear from me in an hour that something went wrong. He said he would be on standby which I was sure he would.

It took precisely 48 minutes,18 past the allotted time they said they would be back. They came to the truck quickly with smiles on their faces like they had just hit the lottery.

"Here Averie, grab this and push this to the back."

There were 20 slabs of 2x4 plywood, 2 chainsaws, 1 generator, some faucets, boxes of roller shades, flooring, light fixtures, a conventional oven & microwave oven, universal piping and a vacuum cleaner. A lot of household products, which had me curious as to who was into cleaning, certainly not Colby and his crew.

We went to a nearby parking lot to tally up the prices of the items. It totaled about $5,000, maybe over. Colby then contacted their buyer for the merchandise and met them a few moments later. They exchanged the materials for money and then headed to another Big Box to do the process all over again. This time, however, the card they used did not work which raised suspicion. Instead of sticking around to try and figure it out, they got out of there fast.

At the end of the day's experiences, they split $2,400 which made $800 each. Didn't seem like much to take such a risk for. My notion was that I would pack up this part of the game, but wanted to see what was up in California.

46

Before we could head out west, I had to have the right credentials to be effective with our mission. We drove over to meet up with this guy called the "Face man." He's the one who can turn anyone into "everyone." This guy was the most vital person to our plan. Without the Faceman, there was no mission.

Faceman resided in Harlem, the home of the Renaissance. When we pulled up to his block, he was already waiting for us; a man about his business. I liked that. After an introduction and a little small talk, we got down to the purpose of the visit.

"Ok Averie, first, I have to snap your picture a couple of times to match it with the file we're creating."

Fifteen minutes later, he was ready. He worked fast, which was a good thing. What I saw had me amazed. His work was not only fast but good too. I studied the identifications and couldn't believe I was Mr. Benjamin Davis and Morris Henderson at the same time.

Big Homie paid him for his services and we were on our way.

"Yo Averie, you ready?" Colby asked waking me out of my brief slumber. We had to catch a cab to JFK and traffic in New York was like a ball of yarn. On our way, I remembered as a child wondering what it was like to fly above the clouds. Even as an adult, plane trips were still enjoyable and anticipated with kid's excitement.

Colby had booked everyone's flight the night before, so the only thing we had to do was show identification at the ticket counter to receive our boarding passes. Things went smoothly at check in and moments later we were off to the West Coast.

The trip from the East coast to the West took a little over 6 hours. That allowed for enough time to eat a couple times, watch an in-flight movie, as well as read or engage in conversation. Colby and I decided to get a better understanding of our mission, not to mention, a bond between each other.

"So, what made you choose me to work with you, Colby?"

"Honestly, I got word from Chase that, you took some losses with the music business and you needed something a bit more solid. We both agreed that you would be a perfect candidate to learn the game." I was honored to learn that. "That was why, plus your leadership with people is always an asset. From what I heard from Chase, you always had a gift of gab to get people to believe in you. Even though you aren't on the same level as the rest of us, I'm quite sure you'll be there soon."

"Well, I can't wait to eat from my own pot."

"Right now, we just need to get you started by getting you ready for your first transaction. Tomorrow morning it's on and popping. Get some rest, Averie, we will talk later."

We landed safely in Los Angeles and got settled in at our hotel, which was booked under an assumed name. The next morning, we took a ride to Beverly Hills Blvd to get our plan started. It was simple really. I entered the establishment, met a male sales associate, and told him what I came for. He then took it from there. He asked for some documents. I provided my driver's license, proof of income (pay stub), proof of insurance and residence which were all detailed from the information Jamaica Sam worked up the night before.

He ran my credit card and bored me with excessive small talk. It seemed like hours had passed before the accounts returned with my news.

"Congratulations, sir!" Mr. Sawyer, the leading accountant exclaimed. "You are a first-time buyer of a Mercedes-Benz 350ML series SUV."

As I was signing off on the paperwork, I thought to myself how easy it was to obtain this vehicle. I didn't have to put any money down. Deep down inside, I was excited. My first purchase as Mr. Gerald Henderson and I won, worked without a hitch. Problem was that my joy would be short-lived because the new SUV wasn't mine. Jamaican Sam would be reselling the vehicle for $20,000.My take would be half of that.

I wasn't sure I liked the arrangement. I take the risk, then I must trust that this Jamaican Sam would pay me. Colby tried to assure me that Sam was a good man, but that flew in one ear and out the other. Too much money involved to be trusting in the unknown. My gut was telling me right. I didn't receive a dime for my efforts. The truck I had just purchased as well as the cut of the money disappeared, as did Jamaican Sam.

"Averie, we're heading back to New York. Our work out here is done." Colby stated the words I'd wanted to hear. For me, this trip taught me two lessons, one good and one bad. The bad: don't trust what you can't see. The good: as long as you have your paperwork in order, anything can be purchased. My goal was to put my own plan in motion. No need to put in work for someone else if I have the skill to do it myself. All I needed were the tools, and the Faceman was going to be my first stop back in New York.

47

I awoke at 7:30p.m. to see that Colby was gone. I immediately called him.

"Yo! Where you at?"

"I'm on my way back from seeing the Big-Homie."

"You have my joints with you?"

"We're all together."

"Big-Homie and Lil-Man?"

"Yes!"

"Cool."

15 minutes after the brief conversation, I heard the key turning in the lock.

"What's up, Son! You about to be good, Son!"

"Why you say that?"

"Yo Son, word to my mother, we know you're on something B. You too quiet."

"Just ready to see what I'm made of from this."

"I bet Averiegoing to do his thing back home. Am I right, son?"

"Time will tell."

"Here's your joints. He was able to only make you two joints."

"I'm thankful." Now it feels I'm not leaving empty-handed, but with a few new learning experiences."

"Come on, B. Your about to be straight!"

"That you bet your ass," I said to myself.

"You ready to leave?"

"Like last year."

"Your flight leaves in an hour so let's get you to the airport, son."

"Don't tell me, you already booked my flight?"

"No-Doubt son!"

"I'm ready!"

During the ride to the airport, I was very silent. The fellas were acting as if they were on cloud nine. And maybe so. I never knew what transpired while in California with the Mercedes and other transactions, but who gives a damn. I was on my own cloud thirty in the making of an "Empire."

"Yo B," Colby called out to me. "You good?"

"I'm good," I mumbled, as I thought, *these motherfuckers made money and did not even offer me a dime, a cent, and you disrespect me by asking if I was good.*

"Colby jumped from the truck and shook my hand."

"Yo B. hit me up once you touch down."

"I got you."

"Yo Averie, be safe Son," Big-Homie and Little-Man shouted."

I didn't even respond nor look back. My mind was looking forward and getting the hell away from the Big-Apple. Well only for now. The last thing that was said in New York that made any sense was, "*this is the final boarding for Chicago Midway Airport, last call.*"

I arrived back home, but not the same. The name I flew on was a Mr. James Bell.

This trip left a bad taste in my mouth, yet I was still optimistic and didn't let my emotions show too much. Colby was the plug to everything I needed; I just had to watch him a little closer. Chase did try to warn me, I should've been more alert. Oh well, you live and learn.

48

We chose Harold's Chicken as the place to meet for dinner. My best friend Tyrone wanted to know all about what had transpired in New York and California. My travels had been quite eventful but I'd never been one to put my business out there, even to a friend.

"So how was your flight, bro?" he inquired.

"Let's just say, the plane ride allowed me the time to reflect on who I am and the person I'd like to become."

"Sounds like you've been doing some soul-searching. When we last spoke, you mentioned something about materials from the Big Box stores for anyone who needs it, right?"

"You got it!"

"Ok. My brother Larry is in real estate and remodels homes all the time. He's always at Big Box stores shopping for stuff. He may be someone you need to link up with. You want me to call him up?"

"I definitely would!"

"What's his spending limit so I can let him know?"

"Tell him $7,500 and up."

"Hold on bro, he's hitting me up now."

"Make sure you don't say anything over the phone."

"I got this."

"I just don't trust the airwaves,"

"We good bro, I know I'm getting a cut from y'all two?"

"This is what you should do, give him a price a tad higher than what I give you. Tyrone, you know how this game works, everybody eats off the next man."

"What's my price?"

"If I charge half the cost, you turn around and charge him 70% of the cost."

"Man, you know my brother, he cheap as hell. He always wants to make his own prices."

"Well, we both know that don't work with me. Never. Give him your price, if he doesn't like it then tell him to kiss your ass!"

"Bro, I don't want to mess up your business."

"I'm straight no matter what." Thirty minutes passed with some more small talk. Tyrone's brother told us he was on his way to meet us. I was interested in what he would bring to the table. Well, it wouldn't take long to see, because he was walking through the door with a huge grin on his face.

"Hey brothers!" Larry greeted us. I'm asking myself, *when did we become blood relatives?*

"You got the better hand, I'll say," I said.

"I might. It all depends."

"I hear you got a deal on some materials and appliances?"

"I do, and I have a proposition for you."

"I knew it! Talk to me. I want something good."

"I can get you $7,500 worth of materials starting tomorrow. Just provide me with a list of items you will need."

"Wait, so how much are we talking?"

"I'll let you and your brother work out the numbers."

"My brother doesn't call any shots when it comes to spending my money!"

Tyrone didn't appreciate the show of seniority his brother Larry exhibited.

"I'm not trying to tell you how to spend your fucking money, bro," Tyrone shot back at his brother. "I'm not benefiting from this, you are. Averie, you two do the deal, I'm out of it."

"Alright, are you two finished?"

"Yea, we good."

"Cool. Here what it is. I charge seventy percent from the cost on the receipt, taxes included. You pay for the truck rental to hand the materials over, or you can meet me and pick it up yourself."

"Hold on man, you trying to get over by charging me seventy percent while everyone else is charging only half of what the price is? What kind of fool you take me for, Averie?"

Now that money is in the picture, you see how fast we become distant relatives, no more brother talk.

"I'm not trying to get over at all, my price is good."

"Look, man, I don't want us starting our business relationship like this," Larry said. "So, here's what I feel is fair for both parties."

"I'm listening."

"I can pay half the amount, along with the rental expense, but that's it."

"Let's just get this rolling. I want what I requested but I'll take it down to sixty percent, nothing less. Take it or leave it."

"Averie, you're not losing a thing. You win."

"Naw, we win. You'll see."

"You'll have to wait until 2:00pm for the order. I'll have to go to the store and get the numbers and quantity for you."

"That's fine. That would give me time to apply for the card and have it ready for my first venture. Tyrone's brother left with a smile while Tyrone sat there pissed."

"Don't worry, I got you," I said to him.

"Bro, I don't doubt that you got me. It's how my own brother acts, as if he doesn't give a damn about me. Always thinking he's better than me." Tyrone was really into his feelings. This was business and I guess he didn't realize that even the closest ones to you would hurt you when it came to money. For the first time, I actually witnessed Tyrone cry. His brother really hurt him deeply, but as time went on he wouldn't forgive him for it. At that moment though he needed a friend, he needed me.

The next morning, Tyrone's whole spirit had changed. He was in the kitchen doing what he loved to do, cook. While lying on the couch, I was awakened to the smell of eggs, sausage, grits, and pancakes. Tyrone was one of the best cooks on the Southside of Chicago. It was a wonder that he didn't pursue a career in culinary arts. There was nothing the guy couldn't cook.

"Bro, breakfast is in the kitchen, eat all you want."

I did just that. I was starving after the tiresome day before.

"Larry called me and apologized. He also said for you to move forward with the deal. He really needs the materials to close on one of his properties. He has until the end of the month to get it ready."

"We good bro. When I'm done eating I must make a few runs and will be back by the time he's ready. Just make sure he has all he needs on his order."

"Will do, bro."

I knew I had to choose the right location to open an account to start my operation, timing was everything. I looked up the various Big-Box locations online and ran across a few that I felt wouldn't give me any problems. Once on my way to the first location, which was on the outskirts of Chicago, I decided to pull out the profile of my subject, Mr. James Bell. Pulling into the parking lot, I thought about New York and how it took 3 men to do one man's job. What were they thinking? They were some real rookies. I'm glad I had my new plan organized better. My process was smoother. First, I would go inside, stroll around a bit and get comfortable with the players in charge. At the same time, I would keep a sharp eye on the security, watching their movement. I had outstanding warrants on me from 3 different states, so I definitely wasn't going to let a security guard take me in on some humbug bullshit.

My nerves were on full charge. So many things could go wrong, but everything could go fine if I just remained calm and stuck to the script. I walked over to the lumber area but focused my eyes on the contractor's desk. That's where I would have to get my approval from. The walk over there was like the final walk on death row, it was either do it or not. I'd come too far to be scared now.

Luckily for me, there was a female representative at the customer service desk, I had a good rapport with the ladies. I walked up and requested an application for one of their loan accounts.

"Please fill this out, then get my attention and I'll process it for you." She flashed me a smile which eased my nerves.

I quickly glanced at the information I had written on the palm of my hand for Mr. James L. Bell of Memphis, Tennessee. I made 100% sure that I had all the information filled out correctly on the form, especially the social security number, birth date, and the other vitals. I had everything down to a Tee. However, there was a spot where it called for Mr. Bell's mother's maiden name. I had no clue what it was. His credit report made no mention of it so I took a gamble and wrote Marlene Anderson. Hell, it was a common name, who would know? Funny thing is, it worked!

The sales rep got on the computer to process the application and made a call to their home office for the approved amount. To my surprise, it came back lickity split.

"Mr. Bell, you've been approved for $15,000. Your minimum purchase will need to be at least $2,000. Here are the interest and payment information. You can make purchases now if you wish."

"How's that?"

"I'm on the phone with the accounts department getting your approved account number now. Ok, that's all I need, Mr. Bell," she said, handing me my temporary card with the account number and expiration date written on it. "Feel free to grab whatever you need now or you can wait for another time."

I thought to myself that I'd like to recruit her, but that too could wait for another time. Right now, I had to tend to business.

"No, I think I'll shop at a later date. Speaking of a date…" I paused. "Never mind, I won't take up anymore of your time, I can see you have other customers to service."

"They can wait," she said almost too loudly.

"Take care, Ms. Beautiful, and thank you."

"No, thank you. Come back soon. Infact, I hope to see you sooner than later." I walked away smiling knowing sooner it would be.

Now, after breaking the ice, it was time to hear from Larry. This was going to be the beginning of a lucrative relationship.

49

While I waited impatiently, I began to consider a few more ventures, especially now that I had this new identity. I didn't want to be greedy, risking any red flags on the name before I even had a chance to use it. Moving too fast could kill the entire profile, and in the end, we would profit nothing.

"Hello, I wanted to know if you have instant credit and, if approved, would I be able to make purchases onsite?" My calls were toward store credit departments seeing how each spot differed.

"Why yes. Were you thinking of stopping by today to see if you're eligible for a Myers Card, sir?"

"I was, ma'am."

While I was getting acquainted with their service, my line was interrupted by Tyrone telling me that his brother wanted my number. I gave the okay then ended both calls in anticipation of the most important call.

"Averie, this is Larry, Tyrone's brother. I'm ready to go."

"Okay, whatcha got?"

"I went up to the store and got everything I'll need but it came up to a little over $13,000 and didn't know if you were cool with that."

"Oh, I'm cool, as long as we have a clear understanding about what we agreed upon."

"We're good Averie. I know that with the taxes it will be close to the $15,000 mark."

"That's fine. That's what I have. A $15,000 limit is ready to be used immediately."

"I can meet up with you right now." That's what I've been waiting to hear.

"Cool. Let's meet up off 87th Dyan Ryan, in the grocery store parking lot. What are you driving?"

"I'll be in a 4-door blue Cadillac Seville."

"See you in 20 minutes then."

On the way, I thought about how I was going to make it with the two joints. I was going to need more really soon because I could foresee business booming.

I saw the blue caddy as soon as I pulled into the lot.

"Hey, I see you have the order."

"Right here. I will need to be compensated for the deposit of the U-Haul and gas." Without hesitating, I agreed.

He had all types of stuff on his list. Cabinets, Refrigerators, microwaves, light fixtures, washing and drying machines, generator, flooring, tiles, wood, vanities, even a damn chainsaw.

"What are you, some Jason serial killer or something with this chainsaw?"

Larry busted a gut laughing. "Naw man, I have some trees to cut down."

"Oh, ok. Give me a call when you're leaving so I can go to the bank to grab your money. The bank closes at 5:00p.m."

"No problem. It's only 2:00p.m., I should be ready within an hour if they have all your materials."

I got into the U-Haul on my way to the store feeling like a champ. Everything was going well inside the store, I was filling the order according to the numbers and items on his list. When I got to the front of the line and the cashier started tallying up the high-priced items, I became nervous at the inconsistencies on the order. A man in a white long sleeve dress shirt came sashaying his nosey ass to the counter.

"Hello sir, I'm the store manager, Mr. Friendly, I'm trying to figure out why you're purchasing so much material at one time. Are you a contractor, sir?" My mind was thinking of a million smart ass things to say, but I refrained.

"No, I am not! Is there a problem or something?"

"How are you making your purchase today?"

"Excuse me?"

"Sir, we've had a series of fraudulent activities lately and I'm making sure this isn't one."

"Hold on. Out of all the shoppers in this store, you're singling me out as a suspicious figure? Well, to answer your question, I have an account with you guys and I thought I'd be able to make purchases today with it. I mean, that is what I got it for and what it's used for, right?"

"Can I see your account, sir?" At that time, I eyed a six-foot-tall Caucasian male figure with regular clothing standing by the door ready for my attempt for a quick exit.

I handed it to him as another store manager walked over. I was ready for the unexpected. He viewed my card and then contacted the home office credit department. I couldn't believe these people were putting me on blast like this. They were doing their best to make a major scene in front of their other patrons as if to warn all not to come to their store with any attempts to do wrong. They thought embarrassing me would make their day, but I had my shit tight.

"Yes, this is Mr. Friendly, at the Big-Box in Illinois, store number 054321, I have a customer here that has what looks like an account of some temporary card of ours which I've never seen used before. Yes, I will. Sure, here they are."

He read off the numbers on the back of the card to the representative, said a couple more words then handed me the phone.

"Giving his ass a look to kill, I calmly stated "hello?"

"Yes, is this Mr. James Bell?"

"Yes, it is," I responded confidently."

"Sir, I'm with the fraud department and would like to ask you a series of questions, things that you should know."

"Sure, ma'am, ready when you are, but first what is your name?"

"I'll address my name at the completion of my questions. Right now, can you please tell me when was your first school loan and where did you receive it?"

"The loan was issued from the bank of Olympus for me to attend U of M, the University of Memphis."

"Okay… your last car loan and what year and model is the vehicle?"

"Let's see…I believe the loan amount was $25,342 for my black 1999 XLE V-6 Sedan. Matter of fact, my mortgage for my home was $148,545 a month ago, from the bank of Bells Largo, monthly payments of $1,322.00, my Mapy's store card has a limit of $1,500.00, my freaking visa, master cards…" I was ready to go on, but she cut me off.

"Please excuse us. You've proven more than enough information. You sound agitated, Mr. Bell. I am very sorry to put you through this, but this is to protect you and us from any illegal activities of identity theft. It is an epidemic that's running rapid for numerous consumers of ours."

"I understand and I do thank you. The problem is that the manager here has me all out in the open, interrogating me in front of everyone."

"Again, I apologize, Mr. Bell. Could you please give the manager the phone back, please?"

"Phone is for you, Big Man!" I heard him mumbling some replies into the phone and I could see his demeanor changing.

"Ok, I understand. Thank you." Then he ended the call.

"Mr. Bell, I'd like to apologize. Lately, there have been…"

"Wait. Stop trying to explain yourself. The only thing you've done is single me out as a black man making several purchases in your establishment. The last time I checked, that wasn't a crime."

"I do apologize, and you're right to feel that way, sir. Where did you open your account and with whom?"

This butt head just wouldn't leave it alone.

"Does it matter? Why didn't you ask the fraud department?"

"But…but I've never seen anyone from Memphis come way over here to shop with us, that's all."

"You're doing the most! You just won't let it go, will you? If you weren't stereotyping one from the jump, you wouldn't need to know where I'm from or why I'm shopping here." He quickly changed the subject.

"Let's get this sale going, Mary have you rang his order up yet?"

"Yes, and it totaled at $14,798.47."

"Wow. Well, use this account number to ring up the payment. Thank you for your business, Mr. Bell."

All of a sudden, he was part of the cordial committee. I didn't even ask for it, but he arranged for all my materials to be pulled to the U-Haul outside waiting for departure. My guess was that he was trying to expedite the transaction to get me out of his sight.

That first mission was crazy, but it taught me a lot. Mainly to have all my ducks in a row and be ready for the unexpected to beat the surprise attacks. Now I just had to contact Larry.

"Man, I've been waiting on you. You almost missed the bank. What took so long?"

"I had a minor delay but all is well."

"Good to hear. See you soon."

I pulled up on Tyrone's block with a loaded truck of requested materials. I parked, jumped out then went over to Larry's car and handed him the receipt. Without asking any questions, he calculated the money then put it in an envelope.

"Here you go, $8,880.00, keep the change."

"Oh boy, a whopping dollar and some change," I said sarcastically.

"When will the next time be, or was this a one-time thing?"

"I'll be ready when you need me. Just give me a twenty-four-hour window to get what I need in place."

"I'm definitely going to need more, but I can wait a few days after dropping off this load. Hey, what about electronics?"

"I'll be looking into that right away."

"Let me be the first one you contact."

"Will do."

"Thank you, bro."

"Thank you. Until we meet up again, be safe and don't spend it all in one place."

"Hey, what do you think about us putting something together for my brother, for hooking us up?"

"Wasn't a five-hundred discussed already?"

"Naw, I was thinking more like three-hundred."

"That's a legitimate number for a day's work. Make it happen, Larry."

My next spot was to put my money up. After that, the plan was to expand.

50

I knew I had to diversify my business. There was definitely more to home improvement than just building materials. What about the home furnishings and electronics? That's what prompted me to explore other avenues in the credit world. I made a stop at one Electronics "R" Us store and viewed the entire showroom. There were electronics of every kind, as far as the eye could see. Right then I was concocting a plan to return back to Chicago in a major way. A female customer service representative approached me.

"Hello sir, do you see anything you like?" She asked.

"Not sure at this time, but I do have a question for you."

"Well, I'm here to help."

"I noticed the signs posted everywhere that you guys offer some type of instant credit. How does that work?"

"Yes, sir, we do have instant credit for qualified applicants. The good thing is, if approved you can use it today for your purchases. Does that sound like something you'd like to consider?"

"Very much so."

"Ok, if you'll walk over here to the register with me we can see if we can get you qualified."

"How long does that process take?"

"Only minutes, sir. That's why they call it instant credit. We place your information in our database and the automated system at our credit center will quickly determine if you qualify. If so, they will approve you and a credit limit will be provided for what you can spend."

"Just like that?"

"Just like that." She said, casually. All I will need is your driver's license, social security number, phone number, your earnings, and your mother's maiden name." I pondered what she requested. Mr. Bell, how large of a credit line are you looking for today?"

"How much can I have?"

"It all depends on the type of shopper you are. What do you plan to purchase today and will you be making any other purchases in the near future?"

"I'm looking to dress my man-cave up with a new sophisticated look I can be excited to come home to."

"What do you have in mind?"

"Flat screens with a surround sound system and maybe a laptop or PlayStation to take the stress off, or is that too much at one time?"

"Oh no, we have first-timers come in all the time like this every day, get approved and make purchases of everything. So, Mr. Bell, this isn't odd at all." While we were talking, she was running my credit. "Mr. Bell, congratulations, you've been approved for a ten-thousand-dollar line of credit." My mouth dropped. "Now, there is the interest rate and payment due date that will be mailed out to you by the credit center within the first month."

"I understand, sweetheart." She blushed.

"Oh, here's your temporary card with your account number. Your actual card will be mailed and you should receive it in about 10 business days. However, you can make purchases right now of you want."

"Thank you very much."

"I hope we've made you a happy customer today?" *More than you know*, I was thinking to myself. "Do you have any questions, Mr. Bell?"

"Not at all, thank you again, lady Gorgeous."

"Let me know if you need me," smiling as she walked away swinging her fat rump.

It's show time! Within twenty minutes I gathered every

item that caught my attention. Before I knew it, there were several associates assisting me by rolling out the cart with my brand new 50" inch HD Plasma flat screen, Sony Dolby surround system, PlayStation, Laptop, and even the latest Apple Desktop computer with all the extras. I left a little room on the card because I did not want to raise any red flags, but just enough to make a statement that I, Mr. Averie Bod'e made his presence known. $8,939.44 was the ticket. I made sure to fill up Tyrone's flatbed truck to the max.

When I pulled up to his place, he had a huge smile on his face.

"Do you have a buyer for all this stuff?"

"Actually, your brother has acquired some of it, so I'm granting him first pick."

"Have you hollered at him already?"

"He should be here in a minute."

"Man, you're on a roll with this credit card business. I know you couldn't wait to get back to Chicago to run your plan," Tyrone said, obviously impressed.

"You have no idea what I had to go through, but it's all panning out the way I intended it to." And it was. I was impressed with myself.

"Averie, here comes Larry up the hill," Tyrone pointed out a few minutes later.

"Damn, you're not playing! You have everything to dress up a man-cave."

"I told them what I wanted and they pulled it. Even more, I have a fine ass sales person contact for a later plan here in Chicago. But I'll bring her in from another route. I'm thinking Atlanta."

"What's up Averie," Larry said, stepping out of the truck. "So how much you letting all this go for?"

"Here's the receipt, add it up."

"I'll give you…"

"Wait! Just wait, man. Stop the dumb shit and just get your money right for my price! This is the only business I need to hear."

"What is your price?"

"Four-thousand, nothing less."

"I can work with that. You'll have to wait until the morning for your money, banks are closed."

"For you, not a problem. Just remember one thing, you only get one chance to cross me. I need you to remind yourself of this, Brother! See you tomorrow."

Now since I still had one more profile to activate, it was time for me to go in full throttle. With Big Box and Electronics "R" Us under my belt, the future was near. I found the formula for becoming Mr. Any and Everybody. I'm now Mr. Averie Bod`e. People will soon see how I can turn profiles into a revenue with the swipe of a card.

It was 9:22a.m. the next morning at Tyrone's throwing down on some cuisine. His brother came over to drop off my money as agreed. I love it when grown men keep their word, it separates men from boys in business.

"Tyrone, I need you to do two things for me while it's still early."

"What's that, bro?"

"First, put this money up, its thirty-five hundred from your brother."

"I thought it was more than that?"

'It was, but I took out a little."

"Oh, Ok."

"After you put that somewhere safe, I'll need you to swing me over to the Alamo car rental to get me a rental for the period of my stay."

"Sure."

On our way to pick up my car, I got an unexpected call from an unexpected associate.

"Colby, what's up man? What can I do for you?"

"What's up, son?" You've been busy, I see."

"Busy?"

"Come on B. I know you've been doing your thing. You can keep it 100% with me, B. I can tell when motherfuckers at their lowest. They always find a way to contact you in need, helping dumb ass's in survival mood."

"Ok, I have made a few transactions." Remembering that the Big-Box accounts kept records of all transactions on the names he provided me with. Every transaction made by Mr. Bell could simply be tracked by just calling the automated line to recall the activity. "But not any other accounts opened."

"C'mon B., I need mines. I need to eat too. Just like them deceitful New Yorkers always eating from another."

"Get to the point, dude. What's your cut?"

"How about you wiring me half of what you made." I offered his ass $1,000 and that's all I was willing to give in good spirits. Any other spirit he wished he never called me

"I'm good with that. Oh, Big-Homie and Lil Man are asking for something too. Before his thirsty ass could utter another word, I ended his call with the push of a button, Click Mother Fucker!"

"You okay, bro?" Tyrone asked, always listening to my conversations and other things he keeps his nose in.

"Yea, I'm good. Just pissed at myself that's all."

"Why?"

"It's nothing. Don't concern yourself with my business, bro, got me!"

"Gotcha, with a kill Bill look on his face."

51

I rented my vehicle then went on my own to see a few people that I knew would love to hear what I had going on. Chicago was a big city with plenty to get into. You had to keep your eyes open because things moved fast. If you didn't have a plan in Chicago, the streets did their own planning.

I come from these streets, the wild 100's on Chicago's far Southside; where there's a homicide every day and the drug trade is heavy. I turned onto 116th and Michigan Avenue and saw one of my old acquaintances. I call him Homer Simpson because of the enormous head on his shoulders.

"What's up, Averie?" he greeted me in his signature whisper.

"Why are you always whispering, man?"

"You never know who might be wearing a wire? Now a day anybody is a suspect." This was one paranoid fella I ever met.

"I hear you, man. Look, you still in the real estate game?"

"It's my bread and butter, why what you got up these days?" Every time we run into one another, you got a hustle going on. And what happen with promoting concerts and parties? Last time we came together you had Pelle-Pelle designer jackets for $400 and flights and hotels for the low-low, now what, cars?"

"Oh, you have jokes, right. Mr. Hustle man of all trades as well."

"I'm not knocking you, you always got your money one hustle to the next, never waited on a handout, Averie, but I know you and it's about making money, my money."

"Big-head, check this out. I have a friend that can get materials for half the price."

"With a grin on his face, he whispers, I'm guessing at the Big-Box store, right."

"That's right."

"How much can he get me?"

"Hopefully, all you need. Not to mention he can get his hands-on electronics like flat screens, computers, and more."

"I sure could use a few of them flat screens right now. How soon can he be ready?"

"I'll hit him up and give you an answer within the next hour. What about materials?"

"I need that too. I'm ready now. Tell your friend I'm going to need at least $50,000 of building materials and whatever he can get on the electronics. Let him know that I'll take everything off his hands. Averie, you know I'm about business and I got the money, so whenever he's ready to deal let's do it."

"He'll come through, you just make sure you come through. He's no one to be fucked with, I'll say this now, Homer."

"Let him know I won't pay anymore than half from the total."

"We know how this works, Homer!"

"Hey Mother Fucker, I don't know where you get this Homer shit from."

"Oh, you do know, like Homer Simpson, the cartoon?"

"I got your Homer, dude." We both shared a laugh.

Tayzon was one of my right-hand men. At times, you wanted to keep your distance from him because of his activities. He was a very dangerous man you didn't want to cross. I'd heard stories about him having bodies in a lake near Kankakee, Illinois. Right now, I needed his money and nothing else.

"You know the Big-Box store where we go to the show? Everybody hitting that spot up. You may want to let your guy know this."

"Is it real hot over there?

“Dude, everything getting a piece of that place. You can try the one out in the suburbs, maybe Oak Park or something.”

“I’ll call him shortly then contact you.”

“Tell him the money is in hand.”

Those words were the most beautiful words to hear. The location in the city will be better for me since I know the area. However, a safer location with a friendlier staff seems to be my ideal place. I had a choice to make and the outcome would be determined by what I decide.

“Hello and welcome to Big-Box! That’s what the slender built associate said to every patron who entered.”

Out front, I noticed the Chicago Police vehicles parked near the building that alone told me that this city locale had more activity than the others.

“Yes, I’d like to fill out an application for a credit loan.”

“Ok, take one of these and fill it out then give it back to me when you’re finished and we’ll get you processed. I quickly ran through the application, knowing the format.”

“Here you go, ma’am. I got this down to a science.”

“Can I see your driver’s license please?”

“Sure can.”

“Wow, you’re from New York?”

“No doubt, Ma!” I put the accent on a little heavier to sell her.

“I’ve never been there but my sisters and I want to go for New Year’s when they drop the ball. They say it’s fast up there, faster here or there?”

“They say it’s fast there, but I don’t see the difference, Ma.”

“Well, hopefully, I can find out for myself. Okay it went through and they’re approving you for $22,000.00, you won’t receive your hard copy for another week or so, but here’s your account number and you are free to make purchases with us around the store today with this temporary card. I just need your signature, Mr. Johnson.”

“Please call me Justin.”

“Ok Justin, is there anything else I can do for you today?”

I left without even looking back. I just loaded $22,000 on the temp card and it was time I got up with Tayzon to relay the message. After a quick conversation, we agreed to meet up, eat, and talk business.

"My guy has $22,000 on a card, ready to shop with at Big-Box he should be straight with the electronics in a few hours."

"What will be the numbers on the electronics?"

"He said should be $10,000.00. He only needs you to get the order ready and give it to me. Also, he gets paid on delivery and I'll be the one who delivers the merchandise, so you will have to compensate me for the U-Haul and gas charges."

"Man, how much is that?"

"U-Haul is about…"

"Hold up, I got my own truck, so we just need to focus on getting the stuff. Give me a few hours to come up with my order."

"I'll be in touch. One hour, that is."

"I'm on it as we speak because I know your ass don't have patience and won't wait around for nobody when it comes to getting your money, even though you say it's a friend of yours."

"Okay, Mr. Know It All, just be ready within the hour agreed."

"While grinning, you can tell this friend of yours, if he can produce, he'll make a lot of money from me. Averie, you do know I still have the city on lock with flipping houses."

"If that's your belief then that's fine with me, but maybe a few others who can contest to that." I know a few and I will be in their territories as soon as my business has concluded with that big head fucker.

"I do."

"I know you do. Let's get this done then worry about all that later."

We parted ways, which gave me time to handle my next order of business. Time was of the essence, so I had to make the most of every tick of the clock. It seemed like the more I was in motion, the more people I was meeting and the better the network.

The call from Tayzon came a half hour sooner than expected. He must've been putting in work.

"Yes, sir."

"Meet me in front of mom's crib in twenty minutes."

"I'll be there in ten."

I saw Tyrone's name flash across my phone screen.

"What's up, bro?"

"Just checking on you, bro, everything good?"

"So far, everything's going fine. Let me hit you back, I'm trying to find an address."

"Alright bro, be safe man."

I totaled out at $19,000 worth of merchandise and to my surprise, there were no hang ups, absolutely none. On my way back to the city, I hit Tayzon up and arranged to meet at a mutual spot. I saw him standing on the side of the building motioning me in.

"Pull the truck over here," he signaled. You got everything?"

"Receipt speak for itself."

"Cool, let's go in here and talk." I got out and walked with Tayzon to a side room. The problem was, I wasn't feeling too comfortable with the situation.

"Everything cool on your end?" He sensed my apprehension.

"Man, I aint on nothing, if that's what you're thinking."

"Just making sure."

"Sit here, I'll be back." I sat there, wondering if this motherfucker was out the back door along with the truck with my merchandise, or was he setting me up for a robbery or something.

He walked in smiling.

"My guys just did the inventory to make sure everything was good from the receipt, that's all. Looking out for myself, Averie. Damn your guy is really doing it."

"Yes, he's well connected."

"$19,873.08 in half is $9,936.54."

"That's right. We're not talking about nickel and dimes."

"Here," he tossed over a stack of money wrapped in a rubber band. "Count it so you don't think I'm trying to short you."

"You already know I'm counting every dollar and every penny. Business is business."

"All in hundreds, fifty's, and few twenty's, my man. You still have some money on the card?"

"Like $2,100 and change."

"When is the next time he's going out?" Tayzon was anxious to spend the remainder for some reason.

"You need more now?"

"If he can just max out the card by getting a jet spa, I'll be good. It can be any model that's covered by the balance."

"Do you want it tonight or tomorrow morning?"

"If he can get it by tonight, I'll grab it."

"I'll see what I can do." I ended up grabbing the spa and delivering it, leaving a balance on the card at $41.56. That's as close as I could come to maxing it out, I could've bought a snorkel or some rubber flippers to go with his spa. Maybe a year's supply of bubble bath, but he would've felt a certain way so I kept it safe.

I met back up with him to get the business handled.

"Hey man, whatever happened to your right-hand man, the big mean dude, with the name B something?"

"He's actually not far from me now. Been with us throughout our entire transaction."

"His smile raced off so fast as if he'd ran to a wall."

"I'm out of here, and keep him far away from me."

I then jumped in the rental to see Tyrone about my money. It was time to move it and me to a safer place. Not that I didn't trust him, my gut was just telling me it was time.

"You want that now?" Tyrone said after greeting me at the door. His place smelt delectable as always which meant he recently made one of his dishes.

"Yea bro. I'm about to see a friend for the night."

"We'll be safe and hit me when you reach your destination."

"Will do."

52

The only thing I was concerned with was comfort. When I checked into the McCormick Place off MLK Drive, relaxing on the king-sized mattress and a hot shower were the first things on my agenda, besides putting my money up in a hidden area of the room. I remembered a time when using the fraudulent cards wasn't always a benefit.

There was this situation we had when we were at the Jacobs Hotel in St Louis and things didn't go according to plan. After we checked in, we got comfortable in the rooms we booked on one of the cards. Evidently, the original card holder got wind of what was happening with his account and called the fraud department. We got the heads up from Chase and Colby who witnessed security approaching the elevator and phoned me from the lobby phone. I flew ass naked out the room so fast you would've thought I was at the butt necked Olympic trials. We all ran down the emergency stairs to our rental cars which too were under the name for the rooms and hightailed it out of there. And when I say out of there, I mean out of the state in a hurry the very next hour. With cards at your disposal, you can do and get things done swiftly. We boarded a flight, yes you guess it, to Chicago. Those were some fun cowboy days.

That's when I knew I would make a serious impact on the world of F.I.F.

"Mr. Averie, are you okay?" I was drifting into my past.

"Yes, Mr. Campbell, just reminiscing." Maybe we should break for a while.

"That sounds good, I need to stretch and use the bathroom. I'd also like to check on Angela if that's ok, sir?"

"She's downstairs in the steam room. She has been alerted that you're on break and to be awaiting you. See you back in about 30 minutes, Mr. Campbell."

Mr. Frank escorted William to the pool area and led him to the room in the back where steam filled the windows.

"William, I'm in here," Angela yelled through the thick air. "Come in this one beside me."

"How long you been down here?" William whispered.

"Baby, why are you whispering?"

"Because you never know who Mr. Averie has in here with us?"

"I think you're paranoid, sweetie."

"If you've been through the things that I have…wait you have too, so you should know, he could be anywhere at any time."

"Well, we only have a short time together, so let's enjoy it."

They stayed in there relaxed and talked about multiple things. Mainly they just wanted to enjoy each other's company.

"It's time, Mr. Campbell, the loud voice bellowed from what seemed like out of nowhere."

"See, that's why I was whispering. We don't have peace in any part of this facility.

"I'm so sorry William. You better get back, sweetheart. Please cool down before you get back."

"I'll be cool. Mr. Frank popped back up to escort him back to the conference room. Do you even rest?"

"I grab about 5 to 6 hours a day, whichis good for me. Too much rest and I'll be sluggish, we wouldn't want that?"

"I guess not."

"I'm glad you had a chance to calm yourself before returning to the story. Mr. Averie has high expectations for this book and you. Now go in and knock that thing out so you and Angela can get back to your lives."

William sat back and settled in to write the story that would service America's consumers and everyone who was trying to protect their identity.

"Let's get back to work, shall we?"

I'm an early bird when business is on the line, so when I grabbed my watch and saw it was already 10:24a.m., I cursed myself for being late to rise. My time was valuable not only to me but to others, I can't be slipping. I began making calls, unfortunately, my first call would be to Colby, in New York. After three rings, he came on the line irate.

"Yo B, I didn't get the money from Western Union."

"I know, that's why I'm calling. What name you want me to send it in?"

"Use Terry Thomas, but I won't have I.D. on him, so send a test question for pickup."

"The test question will be, who's your daddy?"

"You're stupid. Man, use the same question you had the last time here in New York."

"Ok. It'll be done shortly."

"Good looking out. So, what you got going on?"

"I'm good. Maxed out the two joints. Waiting to get the rest of my eggs from the first nest."

"Don't you hate it when these roosters slow up on the road after feeding them?"

"Two minutes and he was still rambling. I just let him go for it on his penny machine transactions. I would never tell all my business on what I really had accomplished. My business is just that, my business. I decided to change the subject after 3 more minutes of laughter from him and small talk operations he and the other two stooges were into."

"Your money will be there within the hour."

"No doubt. Good looking, again."

"Hey, I have a situation here. I need to come there tomorrow and see oleboy. Got to get some of that soap to re-clean my face." I kept everything coded over the airwaves not knowing 100% what they were into and with who.

"What time?"

"It's supposed to rain at about noon, in and out."

"I'll have Big-Homie hit him up. How many times are you

taking a shower while here?"

"As long as it makes big bubbles, something I can wash up with at least 5 times."

"Man, you're doing the washing up more than you said. He was catching onto my moves, but couldn't do a damn thing to figure out how."

"Holla at you around noontime. I'm out."

I had to make full use of my day. My first task was to go to a different Electronics "R" Us location and open another credit line to finish Tayzon'sorder. Walking in with confidence, I knew all the steps to process Mr. Kevin Johnson's application.

"Hello, may I assist you?" the gentleman asked.

Glancing at his name tag, I made it personal. "Hello Mr. Atkins, I'd like to open up a line of credit today and hopefully make purchases of a couple things I need. Now can you help me with my request?"

"Well let's see if we can accomplish that for you, sir. If you would follow me to the register, we can get started. It will only take a few minutes; instant credit is faster these days."

"Yes, I think I've heard that before."

"I'll need to see you driver's license, contact number, mother's maiden name, sir. Oh, do you know your social security number?"

"I do. 050-11-5144."

"What type of social security number does that come from?"

"Up top New York."

"You stay here now?"

"That I do."

"That's what's up. Have you ever met or do you know people like L.L. Cool J, Puffy, R. Kelly, Mary J. Blige, Jermaine Dupre, Nelly, Luda, Too Short, Jay-Z, Nas, J-Lo, or anyone on the video channels?"

"In fact, I have met quite a bit of your list and have done business with almost every name except J-Lo, but I've seen her face to face, my eyes to her booty."

"Man, that's what's up. How much credit you need today?"

"What's the range you can grant me?"

"Depending on your credit, I've seen as low as only a $1,000 all the way up to $15,000. He went on to submit K. Johnson's information, but it was taking longer than it did the day before."

"Is there a problem?" My patience was long gone after listening to this young boy groupie talk about celebrities.

"It's asking me again for your mother's maiden name, sir."

At first, I thought it was a diversion, but just as the first store the register kicked out a receipt for approval and a credit line was birthed.

"I won't need it, Mr. Johnson, you have been approved for $4,500.00. Here's your account information. You can now begin making purchases today."

As you should now know, I maxed out the small line of credit then met Tayzon over at the Lincoln Mall to exchange gifts. His items and my money. While there, I ran inside briefly for a few things for my trip back to Atlanta. Prada, Gucci, Fendi, Mauri, all were at my fingertips as I shopped to the fullest, making my style known to every sales associate in my path. Watches were my fetish as were shoes. I saw a Sapphire Movado I had to have. Went in and headed to the counter to check on their credit plan.

"Could I interest you in that watch, sir?"

"Why yes. How does your options for financing work?"

"We have instant credit, if approved you wouldn't have to make a payment the first 60 days and you have 12 months to pay it off." Is that something that might interest you today, sir?"

"Sounds like music to my ears and my name is Kevin Johnson."

"Well Mr. Johnson, the Movado watch you interested in original cost is $3,895.00 but is one of our sale items and today it goes for $3,395.00."

"$500 off huh?"

"Would you like to see if you qualify? Did you plan on

putting money down today and finance the balance or straight out finance, sir?"

"Let's see what the creditors think first, shall we. I have a good credit history."

I went through the formalities of providing the necessary information and I was approved in no time. My watch was bagged as fast as lightening. From the looks of it, I would be using Mr. Kevin Johnson's booming credit for a while. I know you're probably saying to yourself if Mr. Kevin Johnson had booming credit, why was he only approved for $4,500 at the Electronics "R" Us store?

Well, you were in the closet of his past account with them two years' prior which he recently closed his account for unauthorized activities prior to what I've done. The young sales rep. did question me and submitted into the computer which he too did a little persuading with home office to allow me a credit line.

One thing I've learned is that once I'm on a roll, I'm just that, rolling like a bowling ball with no striking in distance. Everything else from the Gucci to Fendi and all other items was purchased by cash. One thing I knew in my lifetime, money will always be made. You spend a thousand, you make fifty thousand back. That has always been my motto.

Back at the McCormick hotel, after putting my items up, I sat back and thought about my son and wondered how he was doing. His mom couldn't get on the same sheet of music, that didn't mean he should change his tune. All I did and still do, I do it for his future. Hopefully, he won't have to go through the struggles of life like I have.

A quick trip to New York is just what I needed. My plan was to dip in and out, but somehow, I didn't see that happening. Colby sent lil man to pick me up. He tried to squeeze information out of me about my dealings in Chicago, but I wasn't feeding into his attempts. I gave him $300 bucks and told him to have a nice day.

"Yo B, what's the deal. See you been shopping? Colby yelled as I exited the car with designer bags from my shopping sprees."

"You already know. Are we straight for departure?"

"Got everything, just need to pay him and me."

"Here's $750 for the five faces. Big Homie said this should be enough for him and $100 for the 2 profiles."

"C'mon B, you know he charges more than this."

"We'll take me to him and I'll negotiate my own price." He didn't want to hear that.

"Naw, I'll take this to him." He paused, me and Big Homie are moving to Norcross Georgia you should get at me.

Hit me up when you touch down. Tell Colby thanks for the business I'm out.

Placing the demos inside my wallet, I headed back to LaGuardia airport without a care in the world. I wasn't worried about airport security or anything else for that matter. You see, I do my homework and I know red flags are thrown at passengers who come in and out in the same day if they're not a frequent flier on business. I, however, am a business man, well connected, well known across the nation from airport to airport because of the relationships I made with different flight crews. Even on the ground, I was as fly as they come. Nobody questioned that.

53

After matching all my faces to the profiles from Cynthia in Chicago, and the two from Colby back in New York, and studying each one thoroughly, I knew there had to be a better way to have my credit loans approved. The Big Box stores were getting risky and I didn't want to chance them calling the fraud department again. This meant I had to involve Colby to make the operation run smoother; this also meant I had to do some kissing up, something I didn't want to do. But to get to where I needed to be I had to bring him back, at least for a brief moment.

A full month being in Atlanta made me realize that this was where I needed to be. Business-wise, Atlanta would be the new headquarters for me. There were a lot of movers and shakers looking for a buck, so opening accounts should be easier. My mission was to gain the trust of the store associates and inside traders.

It seemed like everyone was relocating to the south to get their grind on. Colby and his crew were in a suburban area north of Atlanta. I met up with him at his new place in Gwinnett, Georgia. We agreed that I would temporarily reside with him, Lil man, and Mr. Jay, the new kid on the block. I moved in with a light load knowing my stay wouldn't be long but hoping to milk this cow this time with Colby and make it beneficial. Colby would be the one to teach me the art of Social Engineering in the phone world of credit.

He broke it down and showed how you can call toll free numbers to the credit departments and get approved in minutes depending on how the representative was feeling at the time. He wasn't anticipating that I would master it overnight. The key was to contact the reps late in the evening before midnight closing when they were quick to process credit applications wanting to get off. This way you would be approved quicker.

I ended up getting approved by several customer service representatives. My theory worked. Because it was later, they paid less attention to the details and ran them through. I got the first loan approved for $25,000, the second, the same amount as the first, then the next one for $22,500, and the last two were $20,000 and $15,000. The only differences between the two processes were that in the store, instant credit would allow you to shop immediately onsite, over the phone you had to wait a few days for the card to be delivered by mail.

Now that made me have to change my strategy on how I would get the cards to me. Before I made contact with the Big Box reps, I had to walk through the entire subdivision and write down addresses for the cards to be sent to. I felt as though I was literally stalking the mail carriers, but found this to be risky to the operation of F.I.F. The U.S. postal Service is nothing to play with.

I had everything in order for my next order of business. Next thing was to rent a truck to haul everything, then it was off to the races. But this time, it was time to change the game up. Each of my clients would have to meet me at the designated stores, go in and do their own orders while I sat outside and watched all movement. My call would come when they grabbed their last item, then I would step in and take control. Walking in with an earpiece, I would survey the scene before approaching the counter for payment. Everything went like clockwork, after sometime doing it this way. Soon I was making history in Georgia, Illinois, Ohio, and other locations in the United States.

My schedule became more hectic. Any given day was payday for me. While other identity thieves were resting, I would still be on the clock. Remember this was a first come, first serve basis. If I was slow, I might as well give up and work a 9 to 5. I wasn't in the game to fall short but to win and progress. Anything else I considered uncivilized. The only thing that could slow me up would be an unexpected hitch in the game. After carrying out my last job, I ran into a problem, there were no more profiles. Colby didn't have any either, and all other sources were dry. I needed my own direct contact right here in Atlanta. This way I could stay away from the most watched airport in the country and keep from being red-flagged. Ever since September 11, and the terror attacks, traveling in and out of New York was dangerous for someone like me. Every agency was on high alert for anything, anyone who looked suspicious.

I cracked my brain to come up with a resource, and that's when I remembered one of my associates mentioning to me that there was a place that produced fake I.D.'s in Georgia, a novelty store inside a strip mall. I was so excited, I immediately traveled there to see it for myself. As soon as I entered, there were all sorts of merchandise. Clothing, electronics, furniture, hairweave shops, African braiding salons, barbershops. This place had everything. The only thing that interested me were the *faces*.

Going from aisle to aisle, I came across a section of the shop called "Heaven." There were fake I.D.s from every state in America pinned on the wall to choose from. Out of all the states, there were five that I saw that would make my operation invincible. New York, Ohio, Georgia, Tennessee, and South Carolina. I marveled at the texture and the authenticity of each one.

A soft-spoken African queen came from the back office and spoke. "Hello to you, sir." When I turned around she looked like she had wings and floated down from heaven. In this moment, she was a gift from God sent to help me in my time of need. Her beauty was breathtaking, and she had a body to rival most strippers making the dollars rain.

"Um...are you just going to stare or can I help you with something?"

Her voice was so soft and sweet, I had to snap out of my trance.

"How long does it take to make the I.D.'s?"

"I'll need to take your picture and get the information to place on the card then wait to put it together. It'll take 20 minutes tops."

"That's all?"

"That's it. So how many you trying to get done?"

"None today. I came to see aboutthe process and ask a few questions."

"Well, what questions do you still have?"

"Do you have a business card or can I get your number?"

"Kind of bold, aren't you? Asking me for my name would be a better start. After seeing you stare at me, I thought you were one of those creepy types. Is that you?"

"No, not at all. Just taken by your booty… I meant beauty." Damn!

"Um huh… I bet you were," she said, looking back at her own backside.

"This is starting out all wrong. What is your name so I can properly address you?"

"Natasha. Here, my cell number is on there," she said smiling.

"Don't just use it for the hook up either; call me to take me to lunch or dinner or something."

"I'm Averie. How about I call you later this evening or before the week is out?"

"Yea, we'll see."

All I could think about after exiting that place was the transformation of my business. I was going to have the whole Financial Identity Fraud game at my feet. Before this could happen though, I had to make contact with one man who could confirm my presence is this game and give me no limitations on the beacon scores that I'd need to complete the profiles. Covering all my bases would make for a flawless business. Leaving my new facemaker gave me a renewed confidence going forward. This connection with the Face-Lady was just what I needed, the right price for the faces. The price for each was only $75.00 which would give me a 10,000% profit, definitely a win-win situation. This would depend on the negotiations with a man called Chris.

54

I walked into a nearby cellular store in Atlanta that I'd researched from time to time. There were several customers being assisted while I sat back and observed. I saw how each processed the personal information of one customer to another. I listened intently to see how their process worked.

There he was, working with his customers, making sure everyone was being serviced. Then it was my turn.

"I'm in the market for one of your top of the line cell phones."

"Ok, sir, let me get my assistant to help you with that. Just one a minute."

What this man didn't know was that he was the one I needed to talk to.

"Hello, welcome to Fast Telecom, my name is Shundra, how can I help you?"

I saw an in route to my source to the information. She couldn't provide the numbers but she could get me close to the man.

"Hello, Shundra, my name is Pete."

"Pete, what are you looking for today?"

I didn't waste any time. I pointed out the phone, had her run the credit. Wouldn't you know it, the name was a no-go, and Pete was on the bad credit list. Any other time I would've been tripping on Cynthia from the hotel in Chicago for feeding me bad data, instead, I took it as an opportunity.

"Shundra, I do apologize for wasting your time."

"You didn't. It's my job and we have many customers come in and get denied for various reasons."

"Are you married or have a boyfriend?"

"That's a bit personal don't you think?"

"You're right. It's just that I have an opportunity for you. What about kids? Any little ones?"

"No husband. No boyfriend, but I do have kids."

"I bet it's hard raising them on your own, not to mention how the expenses mount up."

"They sure do. Now, what's this opportunity you're talking about? Does it involve making money, because I could use some extras right about now."

"Sure does. I really would like to discuss it elsewhere if you don't mind. Can I call you?"

"I don't normally give my number out to customers, bad relations."

"Well, just say it. Can't help what I remember."

"Clever." She voiced it in conversation and I put it to memory.

"I got you. I'll hit you later. When do you get off?"

"A few more hours, then I have to pick up the kids."

"Do you think you can get a sitter for a few hours while I take you to dinner?"

"Is this a dinner date or a personal date?"

"Depends on how you feel during the dinner. Here's my number, call me when you leave here."

"I will."

Like clockwork, Shundra called. She could get a babysitter but needed $30 bucks, I figured that was well worth it, hell I'd pay $1,000 just to lock her into the operation.

"Ok, where are we meeting?" She asked excitedly.

"I'm not too far from the Cheesecake Factory off Peachtree Street, how about there?"

"Sounds good."

We ate and talked, explaining what I needed from her. She told me about her previous relationship and the falling out with her baby daddy. I really felt bad for her the way it ended. She deserved better, she deserved a chance.

Shundra loosened up after the dinner drinks and became vulnerable. After we ate, we went back to my truck where she let me know just how much she appreciated me. Before I knew it, my tinted windows were fogged out with the heat of our bodies colliding, doing a dance to the slow jam pulsating through the speakers. I could tell she hadn't been with a man in awhile the way she let me take advantage of her wanting body.

We retired to my hotel room to finish the evening off. Four hours later, we woke up in full sweats. I had her in the pocket and she was ready to work. I dropped her off at her apartment and returned to my hotel room for some much-needed rest.

I thought I'd just close my eyes when I heard the phone ringing. It was Shundra, and she was calling me with questions about what we talked about over dinner.

"Averie, are you free for lunch?"

"What's wrong?" I thought she may be reneging on me.

"Nothing bad. I have something to show you, meet me at the Chic Fila at 12:30p.m."

"Ok beautiful." I had a good vibe from her. Glad she was on board.

12:30p.m. on the nose, I showed up. She was already waiting for me. I greeted her with a hug and a kiss on the cheek.

"What's all that for?"

"What you think?"

"Last night?"

"Yes, baby-girl." She perked up, face full of smiles. "Ok, so what's so important?"

"Don't you at least want to order something to eat?"

"Ok sure thing." I put in an order for 2 number ones with 2 lemonades.

"Now what's up?"

"Look, I have 5 approved apps here with scores of 700+. They're men in the range of 27-40. The only thing I ask is to use them out of this area, I don't want it to come back on me and get me in trouble. I've never done anything like this even when others have asked me. The reason why I'm doing it for you is because I feel it would help you do whatever it is you're doing. I want to see you succeed. Plus, I know you got my back, right?"

"Of course, I do," I said peeling off two $100 bills and sliding it to her under the table where her hand was waiting.

"Shundra, as long as you do your part, we are going to work very well together. We already have chemistry, now let's see if we can have symmetry. Success will make our bond long lasting."

55

Back at my hotel room in Buckhead, I knew I was ready to prepare myself for the next phase in my plan. The first thing on my agenda was to go back and arrange a meeting with the face lady, as I called her. The next afternoon I made the trip back to make things happen. I traveled from highway 85 around 285 East with my mind focused. Before I knew it, I was reaching speeds well over 80 mph. If I wasn't careful, the boys-on-bikes would be on my tail, and that would be trouble.

I arrived at the mall with expedience and moved swiftly to the back of the mall where "Ms. Face" was stationed.

"Well hello Natasha", I greeted. "How's everything with you?" She returned my grin with a smirk.

"I see you haven't called me. Why is that?" she asked, obviously not as pleased to see me.

"I've been crazy busy, sweetheart."

"Umm-hmm. Whatever." She gave me her attitude to chew on.

"Look, I haven't forgotten about you or our date. Just timing is bad right now. You understand, don't you?" Her emotions were riding strong.

"So how can I help you today, Averie?"

"I need a few of them things you do so well."

"Oh, don't try to butter me up. What I look like toast to you? How many?"

"Five please."

"You have the names?"

"Right here." I handed her the piece of paper with the information on it.

"Okay step over here so I can snap a few shots."

"You're so professional, Natasha."

"Whatever, Mr. Busy. Look, it's going to take me about a half an hour to finish. You may want to walk through the mall or get something to eat."

I thought for a minute about something I could take care of in the mall but then decided to stick around not knowing whether she was trying to investigate me or if the cops were lurking. In this line of business, paranoia runs wild and you learn quickly not to trust anyone.

Twenty-five minutes passed and she had completed the process; I had to admit, I was pleased with what she had done.

"So how do you like my work?"

"Amazing!" I kept staring at the new ID's I had in my head.

"Words are not enough. Thank you gorgeous."

"You're very welcome, now where's my money?"

"You are a bully in your spare time? How much do I owe you?"

"$75 times five so what is that?"

"Should be $375, right?"

"Correct. Cash only, please."

I pulled four crisp one hundred dollar bills out and handed them to her.

"Keep the change and buy yourself something with it, my dear."

"So, I guess this is a parting until I see you again?"

"Not at all. I'll call you before the week is out."

"I hope you keep your word this time."

"Always do," I said with a wink as I exited the shop and some patrons entered.

I walked briskly through the mall traffic hoping not to get stopped by the authorities. I kept the FD's in hand just in case I had to discard them quickly. Once I made it back to my hotel, I could breathe easy.

Now it was time to put the plan into action. I would make a

list of companies that I would forget in the major cities of Georgia, Ohio, and New York for starters. Next would be the studying process of each potential candidate and their personal history. I understood that the mission was bigger than one so if I were to become them I would need a helping hand.

Finding liaisons was key, they had to have the exact attitude and ambition as I did in order to make the operation steady. My contacts in Cleveland, Shaker, Cleveland Heights all would be powerful pieces and would open doors for everyone in my circle. New York was a bit different because of the bad relationships. However, there were a few good apples in the batch of the rotten. Georgia, I could handle privately. I lived here and knew the people I needed to connect with. The problem here was that you took a chance of either being set up or robbed. Atlanta was the headquarters for all identity thieves, young and old, of all cultures. You could go to a night club or eating establishment and watch just how many fraudulent credit cards were being used. My eyes were wide open, so I didn't become the hunted instead of the hunter.

56

Georgia would be a pivotal point of the operation. This southern Mecca of sorts was home base to some of the largest corporations in America. By being a resident I'd had the opportunity to study the business environment and figure the game out to the fullest.

As I saw it, each profile would bring me in close to $50,000 plus. It all depended on me and how far I was willing to go. During my stay, I'd encountered a few good clients looking to save a bunch or two. I first began channeling through my sources in real estate and often consumers who had many to play with to upgrade their homes. I began my client list with on-demand customers. Soon they made me their go-to man for supplies, appliances, electronics and more. At the end of a good week, I made purchases of over$150,000 to $200,000 here in Georgia alone. Once I got into the other states on my agenda, I would take flight. I was mastering my craft. This was a job for me, my job.

I was handling my own business and my destiny was in my own control. I made sure that what had happened in New York would not happen again. The more transactions I made, the more faces I obtained, that turned to more profiles needed, but at the end of the day I was prospering and that was my reward. White collar crimes across America have existed long before me, as a black man, I at least wanted to be credited for recreating the Game.

"Sir, if I may? I want to stop the tape for a minute and share something with you."

"Sure, Mr. Campbell. I'm always interested in hearing your insight."

"This story you have here is going to change lives. You will be doing the world a grand favor and you very well may not get the full credit you deserve."

"I realize that, my friend. I still have a responsibility to the bad and make good with it. Hopefully, this information will keep others out of harm's way. Mr. Campbell, later you will know the one who inspired the story. He was an inspiration from the beginning; he wanted me to change my life."

I sat there watching the pain and anguish on this torn man. Averie was indeed torn between the past and a world he was deeply rooted in. An evil world he worked hard to create to destroy the lives of others. At their expense, he had obtained a great deal of wealth. Now he is trying to right the wrong and show the world he had a heart. The question was, would people be willing to overlook his mistakes and forgive his past while embracing his efforts in the present. Only the future remained. We Americans can be the cruelest when it comes to forgiveness. It's easy for us to judge, but are we as strong when the judgment falls upon us.

"Mr. Averie, please continue when you're ready. The details of the story need to be told still. The hour is at hand."

"I agree, Mr. Campbell." He proceeded.

57

The flight to Ohio was very comfortable, which allowed me a chance to think. First class was a luxury I afforded by booking my ticket in advance. I realized that travel was an essential part of my business so why not do it in style. Besides, if I aspired to be a multimillionaire and beyond I had to start living like one.

Cleveland was a dark, gloomy city in the Midwest. It was equally as dangerous as any other major city in the country, just not with all the notoriety. Murders were recorded continuously and the news reported numerous senseless killings. Knowing all of this did not deter me from making Cleveland my safe place to lay my head. I got my Intel on my potential clients from my very reliable sources. They provided me with information that would make the connection solid. She knew she had to be accurate with the Intel because our first encounter would determine how well we would work together. She set up a meet and greet to line up the business arrangement.

When we met, there were two very distinct associates that were present. The first I saw was a short, portly fellow standing about 5'1" who appeared to be of a round nature. The other was the total opposite, tall and slender was his makeup. Prince and shortly were Jocelyn's people and they got right down to business.

"Look, we're not going to keep you on hold for your money. We're ready to take care of business, Jocelyn told you we don't play."

"Oh, and she told me plenty about both of you, but it will be my judgment as to where we go from here. No disrespect but I don't know you, however; Jocelyn speaks highly of you guys. I am 100% about business and this, my new friends, will take us to a new level. My job is to provide the orders yours is to provide the cash caprice?"

"We agree."

"So, do you have an order ready for payment?"

"Bro, we know how this works. Business is business."

"But not how I do business."

"Ok, you can sit in the car until we get our order pulled then we'll call to make the purchase."

"About how long?"

"30 minutes tops."

"We talked about $30,000 of material, right?"

"We got this. You need to see how they act on the order we have. Hopefully, we can get over half then finish at the next spot."

Apparently, thirty-nine minutes went by before I got the call I've been waiting for. I walked in as a contractor, Thomas Jefferson and in less than an hour, it was done. These guys were on it. They already had everything scanned and was waiting on me. The total tab was over $19,000 and the card was ready for payment. We loaded the materials in their truck and they were off.

I reunited with them later after they unloaded and got paid. A full payment of $9,500 plus airfare and hotel was given to me. Within the next few hours, we traveled to another location to do it again and made the balance complete. $5,500 was paid and they wanted more. They were addicted now.

"How much more can you get?" Shorty asked.

"How much you need?"

"We can make all and get all of them and have them gone before you leave. That way you don't have to take any back. The only thing you have to worry about is getting all that money back to the plane."

"Oh, don't worry, I have my method."

They made some calls like they said and connected me with their associate. This fella paid me $10,000 and owed another $6,500. He got his materials and promised to pay me the next day which meant I had to stay overnight with no guarantees that I would make it home. So I decided to make the best of it.

Shorty and Prince picked me up the next morning to do another job. Only $8,000 was the payout, half of that went to expenses. Then trouble hit.

“Bro, we been calling dude up about your money and he won’t pick up. We even went to his place but his car wasn’t there. “I don’t know what’s up.” I was infuriated.

“Take me to his place.”

They took me there and every hang out he frequented. I had no luck. I ended up leaving town with money in the sheets, not something I wanted to do. I was fed up with the losses. I planned to get my money on the next trip there.

It was time to re-establish myself. When I got home I knew I had to do things myself. Hiding money here and there had me paranoid. Problem was, I had trust issues. The only man I could trust was my main guy, my right-hand compadre, Mr. B. I was traveling this road alone for too long, it was necessary that I used the help of my team.

58

After the hour and forty-fiveminute flight back to Chicago, I felt a little more at ease. Of course, traveling in first class always helps matters. I made it in at about 9:00a.m. and everything was in order with my car rental which was always a plus. Nothing better than having your plan come together.

My day began with making rounds. First, I had a meeting with a man named Kentucky. He had a listing of the store I should target to get my money lined up. From one Big Box to another I worked. By the end of the day, I had hacked up a bit over $60,000 in merchandise and another $15,000 from electronic retail stores. My take was a cool $40,000. I made a little extra from a new client who just so happened to be a Chicago police officer.

The evening ended early enough for me to get some rest from running all day. I had arranged a meeting with a friend of mine from way back, heard he was doing good business in the real estate game which would be a powerful connection. Hopefully, he had what I needed to add to the pie.

The people in Chicago called him money because of his ability to generate capital but I knew him as Mr. White. I gave him a call to pick his brain.

"Is this Averie?" he answered, amazingly recognizing my voice.

"Yes, Sir."

"Hey man, it's good to hear from you. Where you been?"

"I haven't heard from you in what? About 3 years?"

"Something like that. I've been making big moves. I'm coming through, do you have company?"

"Nah, man. I'm good."

"Cool. I'm right up the block, just circled once or twice to make sure the stickup kids weren't, scoping me out."

"Go ahead and pull up behind my truck."

"10-4."

I saw his cherry red Hummer parked and smiled. My friend was really doing well for himself and the monster machine was a token of his success. He came out and greeted me while nothing me checking out his ride.

"That's alright, right there, white." I acknowledged.

"Yeah, she gets me around," he answered modestly.

"I'll say."

"The real estate game is booming."

"I can see that. That's what I wanted to converse with you about."

"What's on your mind?"

"You probably have an inside connect at all the Big Box stores, right?" I got straight to the point

"A few that knows about getting money. We've been getting our material for half the cost. Why? Do you have a hookup?"

"More than a hookup. I am the plug and pocket."

"So, what's the move?"

"Depends on how much ya'll buying."

"Averie, we buy a whole lot of material almost every day. There's ten of us flipping houses like crazy, man, I can get all you need." I loved the way he was talking.

"Good. Perfect."

"You have cards?" he asked and I smiled.

"I'm strapped, white, and ready to work."

"You for real, aren't you? If you really go the cards, man I can make you plenty of money while you're here."

"I'm ready now!"

"You got some on you?" I pulled out with a line of credit for $25,000 and he nearly jumped on my back with excitement. "Man, I can move all that and whatever else you got tomorrow."

He was interrupted by a call from one of his associates that just so happened to be in the real estate business looking to deal. I heard him explain that he had me standing there ready to shop in the morning. I listened to white as he put things in motion. He sounded like a real boss and that was ok, I knew he wouldn't get things confused: This was still my operation. The true reason we had distance in the past he seemed to always try to control things. We'll see how long this last.

"Between Frankie and me, we'll max out all you have." He stated matter of fact. "I have plenty of guys who have money that would fight to get to you."

"You're going to give mine for half the price, I'll raise theirs for little that way I can make some extra cash. Everyone I bring to you, I'll give them a price, you just agree with it."

"I'm cool with that, just don't go crazy over changing them, you may run them away."

"Averie, I got this. Nobody has what you have."

That was music to my ears. I still had to keep my eyes on him. My main focus was the meeting with this guy he was talking to. Evidently, he was the one with the money.

The next day we met. He had a resemblance to the character Frank Lucas, guess it was ironic that his name too was Frankie. A real laid-back gentleman with an abundance of money. He was a man with many businesses which allowed him to be a millionaire, real estate just happened to be the most lucrative. Frankie was someone I needed to get close to.

"Averie, this is Frankie, the one I told you about." We greeted each other with a handshake.

"Nice to meet you, Averie. So, what's been up with you?"

"Just trying to make it, bro."

White watched is exchange pleasantries then interrupted.

"Let's get down to business, shall we?"

"So, White said you can get us all we need at the Big Box stores?"

"I can," He looked at White and smiled.

"So, all you'll need from us is an order list?"

"Hold up, I don't go into the stores, doing the leg work. I used to shop in the beginning."

"Damn, why you just saying this now?"

"Everything is about timing; I don't make moves without thinking things out."

Mr. Frankie quickly saw how I like things organized and appreciated how I moved.

"White, I can get a guy to go in and do the shopping. Averie, how you do it? Get the stuff then you come in and make the payment?"

"That's all I do."

"I got you then. We should be ready for you in 2 hours and have your paper on delivery."

"I'm good with that."

59

It was 10:28a.m. and still no call from Mr. White or Frankie. I fed my son, showered and got ready to hit the sheets. I had to drop him at his grandparents which I knew he would not like. My son wanted to be with me. My folks were cool with him coming over so that relieved me of some stress, I had a long day ahead and didn't need anything extra.

11:44a.m. and the call finally came in.

"Averie, we're ready."

"You already pulled what you need?"

"By the time you get here, we'll be good."

"Alright, cool, which way am I going?"

"The Big Box in the city."

"Give me 30 minutes. Make sure everything is in order, I want to be in and out."

"We got you."

"How much is the ticket?"

"It should be $20,000 but we good. These are our people at this location and they know we spend big money so no need to be leery." I still had my doubts. Until the deal is done, that's when I'll be comfortable.

"We'll see. I'm on my way."

When I pulled up at the store I stayed in the parking lot and watched the scene from the outside. After my mind eased a bit, I made my way inside. I moved around inconspicuously for a while then made my presence. Frankie saw me first.

"Averie, we're just getting the last of the material pulled, everything else is up at the counter." It was time for me to become Mr. Jake Dawson and make this purchase.

"Sir, will you be making the payment?" the lovely salesclerk asked.

"Yes, I will ma'am."

"Ok. The total came up to $22,491.71. Are you a contractor, sir?"

"Indeed not. I'm actually taking my vacation time to refurbish my home. Is there a problem?"

"Not at all. Just with this being such a large order, I had to ask."

"Is that normal procedure to ask customers about their purchases?"

"Well, I just needed to be careful with so much material at one location. We've had a lot of fraudulent activity here at this store recently and I'm just trying to cover my own ass you know what I mean."

"Certainly, and I don't blame you. I thought you might have been singling me out. I'm legit with my own money and excellent credit. Run it if you don't believe me."

"Oh no, sir, I believe you. I do apologize, Mr.?"

"Dawson, Jake if you prefer my first name." She smiled.

"Ok, Jake, how did you wish to make payment?"

"I do have a new account with you guys and wanted to use my line of credit if that's alright?" she batted her eyes and smiled again.

"Why yes, sir. Can I have your card, please?"

As I handed her my card, I noticed the shadows moving behind a tinted glass window. I thought I may have to make a getaway, but I played it cool for a second, careful not to panic. She gave me my card back.

"Ok, Mr. Dawson please swipe your card for me, sir." I did as she requested and watched the amount of $22,491.71 display then register on my receipt.

"Do you guys need help pulling all this or do you have it from here?"

"Oh, we have enough hands to pull ourselves, thank you. We hope to shop with you again in the future." Frankie said.

We began loading and they sent four of their guys to assist anyway: our guess was that they were trying to be nosey. It was cool. With the extra help, we were done in 15 minutes.

"I could've sworn you said they were your peoples," I said as we exited the parking lot. Looked to be the opposite, the way I was questioned. I never had that happen. She was tripping like the Feds."

"All I can say is damn, you're good! When she started in, you took control like a veteran."

"She has never met Mr. Averie Bode'."

"What was with Mr. Buttons who was there when we arrived?" White was full of questions.

"Buttons was always a leery fella. I had to find a position for him in the operation. So, I placed him at the location to do the preorder. He was to deal with the store manager and I would play the part of the contractor who sent him to pick up the order."

"You sent him to get the order?"

"Yes, but that was just a play. However, after Buttons called me panicking, I quickly sprang into action, asking him to follow my lead. Just say yes or no to the questions I ask. Things like: Was he still in front of you? Is security around? Was the order confirmed or canceled? Simple YES or NO. I told him to put the manager on the line and we conversed. He asked me some personal question then I provided the necessary information: Name, social, address, and business contract. I had it all recorded on my phone which I made a habit of when doing profiles. I gained the confidence of the store manager and cleared Buttons of any more responsibility. This is part of the business set up. A lot of others don't take the time to study the system and make it work for them. It comes back to haunt them every time."

The moment we arrived at the Less-A-lot Builders store, Frankie and his crew were already there to help unload the materials. We then went into one of Frank's offices to handle our business. $11,250 was handed over to me, which I recounted to make sure. My goal was to reach $250,000 and I planned on keeping this pace up. Hopefully, with these guys, I could surpass that amount.

My trip to Chicago was successful but it was time to return to Atlanta and set up my foundation. I targeted Buckhead before I left for Chicago and had high hopes to make that my new dwelling. Now with enough cash to get started all I needed now was to expand my team. I had a few players in mind.

60

"The Paper Maker"

For the next phase of my operation, I had to put together something with traces. I needed an expert to make me into somebody who wasn't real at all. There was only one person I knew that was capable of making this possible. He was the best of the best when it came to creating a new existence. He produced the best documents money can buy.

Mr. Suave, as they called him in the business, was another native New Yorker. It appears these guys were always placed in my path along my journey. Maybe it was the high speed in which the people in the Big Apple move or it could just be that New York was home to a large number of criminals. He ended up migrating to Atlanta, as I did to expand his criminal enterprise.

"What up, baby boy? Where have you been man? I see you been eating well, Son!"

"I've been doing alright," I responded humbly.

"Alright, my ass, look at you. You look and smell like money."

"If you say so."

"What up, though? You got your operation together, your

living good, what can I do for you?"

"I need your magic touch, Suave. Something very important to my growth, something I know you can keep confidential. It's imperative this stays closed door."

"You know I got you on that. What you need me to do? Some socials, birth certificates, faces, what, Son?" This man had it all covered, a regular jack of all trades.

"Man, you don't play. I need two of what you said."

"What, the socials and birth certificates?"

"Naw, just socials and faces to match," I confirmed.

"Cool. I can have them joints done by today, in fact, in about an hour for the right price." Here comes the hustle I was waiting for.

"How many of each?"

"One and one."

"Normally, I would charge one of these jokers out here that I don't know, $250 a whop but for you, Averie, just give me $300 for both." I pulled out the cash quickly and peeled off 3 crispy bills, knowing how vital this was for me. You have to pay for what you need in this business.

"Averie, if you don't mind me asking, what are you using these for.?" Right then and there, the ice rose in my blood. That's something I don't do, that's not part of good business. The look on my face said what I was thinking.

"Actually, I do mind you asking. My business is my fucking business. Now I can take it somewhere else if __"

"Wait, B, I didn't mean no disrespect, I asked because I could put you on to where and when to use these. What I'm about to give you can really establish yourself. You can create a credit report, bank account, new driver's licenses, utilities, even obtain a house or apartment all with a new name."

"You know what? I like how you think, Suave. I may get into all those things, right now I want the identity."

"Once I'm done, a new man will exist."

My mind opened up to the endless possibilities of new identities I could become. Maybe I could be the cousin of the famous Roc-A-Fella, CEO and entertainment marketer, Dame Dash. That would be the coolest not to mention the massive list of networks I could come across.

"What's on your mind, Averie?"

"I was thinking about using the name William Dash, the long-lost cousin of Dame Dash, entertainment mogul."

"No, what's hot is me getting next to his sexy, fine ass cousin, Stacey. I'd love to ease into her." My lust ran wild for the moment.

"Ahh, excuse me, isn't that considered incest?"

"Well, technically, incest is brother and sister or first cousin, some shit like that. However, in this case, she wouldn't know her cousin, joke or real, was tapping that ass until the Dash family reunion which I don't plan on attending."

We both cracked up laughing at my twisted humor.

"So, what you think?"

"I think you nasty as hell for wanting to fuck your cousin."

"No, stupid, about the name. Can you make it happen?"

"No doubt. That's a done dada."

Suave resided out in Alpharetta, Georgia, an upscale area right outside of the Atlanta metropolitan area. There was nothing but private communities where people could literally hide away. Most of the money makers in Atlanta made their home in this area in spaces like this.

While I waited to see what he created, I tried to make contact with Shundra, the woman who handled my credit information. I tried a few times but I couldn't get an answer. My money quickly dissipated when Suave appeared coming down the stairs from his office.

"Check these out, Averie." I looked them over thoroughly and couldn't find any flaws.

"Damn, this is just what I need. Hold on, I need one more thing."

"And what's that?"

"I need a picture taken."

"Oh, I didn't know we were doing that too."

"How else could I become the new William Dash?"

"Got a point. Ok, I need you to step over here, while I set the blue sheet up for the background. Now, look straight ahead, Son." Click… Click. I heard the shutter on the digital camera activate. "Let me take one more. Cool. Give me a minute to put all this together."

"I'm on your time."

"Hey, I got something you might need for your business that you may like. He hollered back down the stairs."

"Alright."

10 minutes later he came back down with a plastic card with the new identity of William Dash, a new start to re-establish myself as a model citizen.

"Look B, since you have these joints, go up to the DMV today while it's still open and apply for a state ID and driver's license. They will look at you funny, but people go there all the time."

"My mind opened up to the time, renewing their cards. With these joints I made you, it won't produce a red flag on the DMV database at all, these will go straight through, promise. William Dash won't register in their system. Now if you had a license in another state then you would have to be on top of things because they now have a facial recognition system that matches your face statewide. They take months to track though, you need to go ahead and make it official in their system so you can start to establish things with the new identity."

I owed Suave big time, way more than what he charged me. His work was unmatched and he handled business like a fine professional. In fact, we had unfinished business to square up.

"Averie", he stopped me as I began to exit. The face is another $150 and I still have something to show you."

Now I know I had to pay him for the face but why didn't he include that in the original quote? I only like to pay out once. The look on my face must've said it all.

"I'm just saying, Suave, I wasn't thinking about the

additional fee. Thought it was all in the price you gave me."

"Yo, Son, this shit don't come for free. My fees are my fees. Damn, you're making all this money from everywhere and you tripping about another $150?"

"I have my money in other places, not on me," I explained.

"What you mean other places? You don't have your money in a bank?"

"You are way out of line for even questioning me like that. That's my business where I keep my money."

"My bad, son, I wasn't thinking. It just had me wondering how you doing all this business and don't have the money secured. That's part of the reason you need to see what I have."

"What is it you wanted to show me?"

He pulled out a black portfolio and turned it towards me.

"Check these joints out, they can elevate what you're doing to another level. You see, what you're doing, I used to do years ago."

"What you mean?"

"I never told anyone this but I used to tear the stores up. The same way you hit 'em, I was doing them major. So, when they told me about you, I already knew what you needed." He had me really working my brain now. Coming here gave me way more than what I paid for.

"Here, look at these and tell me which one is real and which isn't."

Check # 1

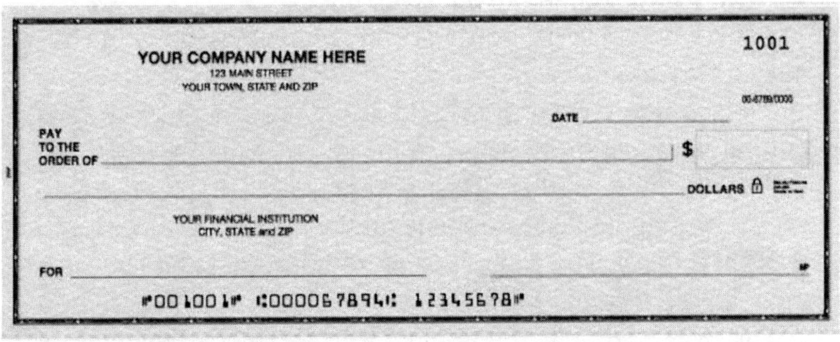
1001

YOUR COMPANY NAME HERE
123 MAIN STREET
YOUR TOWN, STATE AND ZIP

00-6789/0000

DATE

PAY
TO THE
ORDER OF $

DOLLARS

YOUR FINANCIAL INSTITUTION
CITY, STATE and ZIP

FOR

⑈001001⑈ ⑆000067894⑆ 12345678⑈

Check # 2

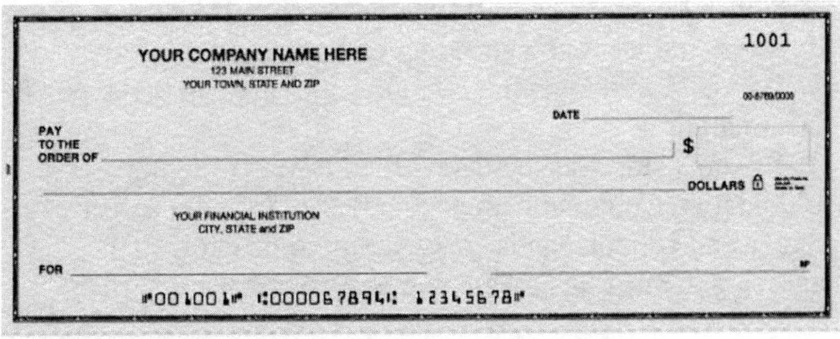
1001

YOUR COMPANY NAME HERE
123 MAIN STREET
YOUR TOWN, STATE AND ZIP

00-6789/0000

DATE

PAY
TO THE
ORDER OF $

DOLLARS

YOUR FINANCIAL INSTITUTION
CITY, STATE and ZIP

FOR

⑈001001⑈ ⑆000067894⑆ 12345678⑈

I rubbed the surface of both then examined the two carefully. I couldn't see the difference.

"Can't tell, can you?"

"Man, they seem the same."

"You sure? Rub them."

"I really don't know."

"Exactly and no one else will either."

"Suave, I'm really not trying to get into checks."

"And you won't be. Having a few around will come in handy in the long run, trust me."

"I'm still not getting you. How will these help me?"

"Look, man, as you're working these businesses you can utilize the checks as payments to your accounts."

"Ok, I'm beginning to feel you, but __?"

"But what? Averie, you've come a long way but you still have a way to go."

"Ok, where you going with all this?" Seemed like he was talking in loops.

"Look, dude, William Dash, every time…

Everything he just said made all the sense in the world. I was speechless. The game is to be sold not told and he just hit me with the formula for nothing in return. A few hundred dollars was a comparison to what I just learned. "Suave, I can't thank you enough for the info. You have my mind going, wondering what I'll do with the checks you make up."

"Oh, now I'm back in the production big?"

"How fast can you get me some of these?"

"Just say how many and I'll get right on it."

"Once I come in contact with my people, I'd like to see the outcome and what you generate from them."

"Cool," I said knowing I would never give up that type of information.

My next stop was the DMV, then it was off to the Liquidation Communications to pay Ms. Shundra a visit. Suave and I shook hands concluding our business both agreeing to meet up again in the near future.

61

"The Birth of William Dash"

As I looked at the sign out front that read "DMV open until 6p.m.," I felt crazy for even considering it. I went in anyway knowing it was what I had to do. The number B012 was printed on the card putting me on a list to be seen. I sat and waited to be called, eager to get my new Georgia driver's license.

After about 5 minutes or so, I stepped in front of a young, medium brown skinned woman with a lot of weave and even more attitude.

"Let me get this straight, you've applying for your first driver's license?"

"Yes ma'am," I remained calm despite her inquiry.

What was it to her? Her job was to wait on me not dig for answers. She looked at me like, "Boy please, I know there's more to this."

"Ok, I need to see two pieces of identification, please."

Now, this is where Mr. Suave gets tested. Either I fail and get put in handcuffs for falsifying documents or things go through and praises to Mr. Suave, the miracle maker. While I waited for my fate, I decided to work what I know I could control, my ability to charm the ladies.

"So, I was just wondering how a young, attractive woman could get stuck working in a place like this."

"It's alright. Nothing to brag about."

"Yeah, but a face like yours needs to be seen. Exposure is what's going to get you to the top." To the top of what, I didn't know I was in the moment, pouring it on thick.

"You really think so?" she batted her eyes and blushed as if no one had ever told her such a thing. Well, thank you. I was considering doing some modeling. I wanna save some money first."

"I completely understand." She handed me an envelope.

"Here are your documents, Mr. Dash. Fill out this questionnaire for the driver's test then wait for them to call you."

"What about you? You won't be calling me?" I said now in full flirt mode.

"Ah, no, that's not in my area. You're done with me."

"Am I?" I smiled. She smiled too.

"Well, you don't have to be." She scanned the room then slipped me her number. "Now just wait for the call… and I'll wait for yours."

"And you do the same."

In less than an hour, I had my Georgia ID and license, proof that I was now William Dash.

62

"Inside Buckhead"

I made it to Buckhead in record time, pulling up in front of Liquidation Communications, the store where Shundra played as assistant manager. I didn't see her car anywhere which was a concern for me. She was a prime piece to this ever-growing puzzle. I waited around for close to ten minutes wondering why I was even going through this. Relying on incapable people was the most disturbing thing, and frankly had me pissed. The time I visited last should've shown me she wasn't the one I needed. There was another one there that could make my vision come alive. Once I had the chance I would make him an offer that I knew he'd accept.

My eyes scanned the store and I found my man.

"Hey, I've seen you before when you were shopping."

"That is correct."

"I do remember you. You hooked me and my girl up last year with a Vegas trip, right?"

"Yes, I did," I said smiling, knowing we would be doing business together soon. "But when I came in here a few weeks ago, you put me off on Shundra."

"My bad bro, not my intention. So, what's up with you

these days? Still in accommodations?"

"Nah bro, I've moved on to bigger and better things."

"I know what you mean, bro." I gave him an incredulous look.

"Check this out, let me cut to the chase. What's up with you and my staff member Shundra? You hitting that, buddy?" I took a second. "Wait… you don't have to answer that. Your expression says it all. Plus, I can tell by how she's been acting lately."

"And how is that?"

"Well, I remember when she used to be lively, smiling all the time, now it seems as if she's lost it, not really the same. I've noticed her cutting her hours and having an absent mind while she's at work. What you do to her, man?"

"Me? Nothing… nothing at all. I've seen a difference in her too, don't know quite what it is."

"I'm sure she will come around. Look, what time do you get off, I need to talk with you about something away from the workplace."

"I'm good in about 10 minutes."

"And…I'm sorry…what's your name again? I didn't catch it."

"It's Chris."

"Alright, I'll be out front."

"Cool, let me wrap things up in here then I'll be ready."

"Have you eaten? Maybe we can grab a bit."

"That'll work."

As I was saying, I realized how I must've sounded. If I were on the other end it would've appeared as if I was coming on to him. In the gay community that would've probably been considered an aggressive approach. However, this was not my intent at all. I do realize that I could be sending the wrong signals.

Chris was leaving out of the door, strolling through the parking lot. I had to get him hooked on my plan.

"Follow me, I know the perfect place."

We headed to a spot called Fellini's. It was quiet and

familiar, a good place to discuss business. The waitress put us in a section in the back.

"I come here at least once a week since locating here in Georgia."

Damn dude, I don't even know your name."

"It's Averie Bode'."

"Everybody? What kind of name is that?"

"No Chris, not everybody, Averie Bod`e, with an accent. AVERIE BOD`E"

"Oh ok… it sounds like you're saying Everybody!" Little did he know, I was EVERYBODY! "I get that all the time, it's cool."

"You said you have a proposal for me."

"Oh, I do, and I think you will like it."

"You have my attention."

Since my first visit to the Liquidation Communication store, I knew Chris would be the key to opening up my Financial Identity Fraud operation. I got his gears turning by picking his brain on his views about finances. I had to know whether his mind was on the money like mine was. What I liked was that Chris wasn't scared to take risks, and he knew that I was someone he could trust. Our preliminary conversation led me to introduce him to my new venture. At first, I was apprehensive about revealing my plan to him, but in this business, you have to trust someone. I gave him a day or so to marinate on everything I had dropped on him. All he had to do was give me the green light and we could start working together.

63

Chris, I'll get right to the point. You told me that you have access to all accounts, for all the people that apply got credit, correct?

"That's correct."

"That's the resource I need," I affirmed.

"Just tell me what you need and I'll see if I can pull it off."

"For starters, a large number of credit applications."

"How many?"

"No less than 50, all with a rating of 700 and above. If you can grab all men of ages 25-55, preferably Caucasian or African American, that will work. Other nationalities tend to score lower. Look at the names of the apps that should make it easier to port out."

"Wow that sounds very specific. You're talking about some major searching to find exact matches."

"Believe me, you will be well paid for your services. Just think about all the bills you'll be able to pay off in full. All that you told me about your girlfriend worrying you about money? Those days will disappear instantly." I could see his wheels turning.

"I'll tell you what I'll do and it makes a lot of sense. I'll pull a few boxes of apps I have, both approved and non-approved, that way some that are in there can still be used for what you need. That will make it well over fifty. Now let's talk money, shall we?"

"I actually see a price in my head."

"I hope it matches the one in mine." We both chuckled.

"And how much would that be?"

"I'll allow you to throw a number at me. Your product, your service."

"I'm thinking for the 50 plus…how about thousand cash on delivery?" Smiling at him, I paused before I answered his offer. "We're not seeing the same picture. I was thinking more like half of that, but with a contingency."

"Man, are you serious? I'm taking a huge risk, could lose my job or go to jail and you're talking about a thousand dollars while you stand to make hundreds of thousands from what I provide you. Remember, you might want to keep me happy if you want me to stay on board. Shundra already bailed on you."

"Oh, so you bringing up our business dealings huh? And how do you know that?"

"It wasn't hard to figure out after the meeting we had yesterday. I started thinking about why you were so concerned about her whereabouts." He had me pondering now.

"I see, Mr. Chris. Maybe I can pull five hundred cash. The things I'm trying to do will require finances so I can't really afford to go any higher. Next year, however, I'll more than makeup for it."

"I'm cool with that."

"And don't forget my contingencies." He looked at me suspiciously.

"What will that be, Mr. Averie Bode'?"

"Whichever ones don't get approved I'll bring back to get replaced without question."

"That shouldn't be a problem. There are more at the store than I can handle."

"Let me ask you a question? What do ya'll do with all the credit apps just sitting around in boxes?"

"Honestly, we're supposed to shed them but since no one

really wants to stay after work so we just box them up, then stack them in a corner."

"Man, if my credit were to leak out because of your lazy staff, I'd be more than a little ticked off."

"Lucky for us. Tomorrow, say 11:15am? Is that a good time to meet back up?"

"Sounds good."

"Oh, and don't ever park in front where the video cameras are."

"I Gotcha. I'll see you tomorrow, cash in hand."

Everything was falling into place. That was the break I needed. Information like that in volumes, with those specs, could go for one hundred dollars per name easily. But thanks to Mr. Chris we were going to be able to put in motion one of the greatest criminal enterprises ever. My plan was almost complete. I was just missing two key components to make the pie whole. First, I'd need to contact my lady friend to run the names of each person's credit app and gain full knowledge of their personal information. The transformation must go without a hitch. Next, I had to meet with Natasha, the face lady.

64

"My Banker"

Now that all my paperwork was in order, I was ready for business. Opening an account was the first thing on my agenda. Mr. William Dash was about to spring to life in the world of financial institutions.

"Good morning and welcome to Madison Mutual Bank, my name is Towanda Parker, how can I be of assistance to you today?" Her line was so scripted, but it was okay, I just enjoyed watching the words leap from her sexy lips. Ms. Towanda was a looker, however, I needed to stay focused on the mission at hand. Beautiful women had a tendency to mix business with emotions and it was up to us men to keep things in the right perspective. As soon as we lost the angle, we'd lost the game.

"Yes, I'm William and I'd like to open an account with you today."

"Have you done business with us before, sir?"

"No, I haven't," I replied sincerely. "Okay, what would you like to open with us, checking, savings, or business, Mr. William?" She was being so formal with all the mister this, mister that stuff.

"Look, Ms. Parker," I said looking at her name tag again. "If we're going to do business we've got to lose all the formalities. So, let's try this again, my name is William Dash, you can call me William or Will. Your name is Towanda parker." She smiled when I said her full name. So, I choose to call you Towanda or lady "T" like the legendary Teena Marie, because you're my fire and desire! I sang out, obviously embarrassing her. She looked around then shushed me, blushing at the same time.

"Okay, okay, William, please don't sing again. You are no Rick James."

"How you know? You've never seen me *super freak* before." She turned a different shade of brown at my remark. "Just kidding. Back to business, ok!"

"It'll just take a few moments to run you through our systems," she said, after receiving the two pieces of identification I wholeheartedly volunteered.

"Well, William Dash looks like we'll be seeing each other quite often, hopefully. You have been accepted for an account here. I'm almost finished with the preliminaries. How much were you thinking of opening with us today? We have a policy that at least $50.00 has to be deposited, is that something you can handle today?"

"Yes, I can handle that."

"What is the amount so I can log it in?"

"Around $10,000."

"What! She exclaimed probably louder than she wanted to. She leaned in close to me and whispered.

"William, you don't want to deposit such a large amount starting out. The I.R.S. and the feds will be investigating your ass before the week is out. Not to mention, having me answer questions too. Just put in anything under $10,000. I'm assuming you're holding cash, right?"

"Pretty much."

"Look, after today, have someone write you a company check from an established business, then deposit that amount. This keeps you and your money safe, understood?"

"Thanks," I whispered back. "And for the record, I'm not a drug dealer."

"I never said you were. But I know you're into something, walking around with large sums of cash in your pocket. Not my business. What is my business, is how it's handled here? So, give me $9,500 and that will make it look a little better on the books, but don't come down here like that again putting the heat down on you and me. If I'm going to be your banker, you must legitimize yourself. If you don't know howI'll show you."

I had to admit, she was 100% on point. I needed to keep her around. From that day forward, Towanda would be my personal banker. I knew she would school me on being a legit business man. In one month, I would make my way back to the entertainment business. My new company name would be Millionaire Entertainment. You must think big in order to grow big. I had a vision and I would soon make it my reality.

65

I really needed to pay Chris another visit. The fact that I had his cell phone that he left at our meeting the other day, gave me a reason to pick his brain some more. I could never understand how one could lose a phone, especially given how important it was for business. Yet they're people misplacing them every day, Chris was one of those guys.

I drove the rented SUV over to the store and pulled around back like he had instructed the last time. Avoiding suspicion, I quickly let down the window and slipped him an envelope with cash in it. He exchanged with a huge white box full of credit applications. I could tell from the weight, that he had doubled both boxes in one. Smiling, I knew I was on my way to success. With the applications, I'd be able to create an unlimited amount of new identities or profile as I call them. With the profiles, my plan could go into action.

My first mission, and the one I dreaded the most was having to meet up with the face lady. Her services were necessary, but the bullshit I had to go through with her was definitely something I didn't need in my life. If we hadn't had previous dealings, maybe doing business wouldn't be so difficult these days, but the past is what it was and that's why mixing business with pleasure isn't good.

"Hello stranger," she greeted me with a half-smile and a body full of sex appeal. Walking like I was the most powerful man in the world, I approached her with extreme confidence.

"Everything is as smooth as peaches and cream, you missed me?"

"Like you miss a summer cold on a visit to the dentist." Wow, so cold? I knew she was lying by the unmistakable gleam in her eyes.

"I'll tell you what, maybe another late-night hookup would help you warm up."

"No deal. We are not going down that road again. Now, what is it I can do for you today?"

"You already know. I need some faces."

"Where's your info? What you got for me?" I condensed the big box into smaller packets and presented it to her.

"Wow, you've been on your game!" I looked around.

"Looks like you're having a slow day" I started noticing the lack of normal traffic she had.

"At times, it can be so busy and other times just as slow as you see now. Ok, you know I have to set things up for the pictures."

"You don't have any picture on file from before?"

"No sweetheart, we delete everyone's pictures after the I.D. is made."

"That makes sense."

"You better not leave me in the crossfire's messing with this shit. All these I. D.'s you have me making, do these names even exist?"

"Nope. I make my money on the side doing odd jobs like getting people's cable on with these I.Ds. It works." She gave me this crazy look. "My friends didn't believe me at first either until I proved it by getting them their cable while it was disconnected." She looked more at ease. "How long before you're done?"

"Just sit down and call somebody on your phone, I'm trying to hurry up." An hour went by and she finally brought them guys to me.

"Here's all ten, Averie. You owe me big time."

"Since I'm grabbing a bundle I should get a few bucks off,

right?"

"Well, how about I take $15 off each one as that'll leave you with $600 and a small tip."

"I pulled out seven crisp $100 bills and a $50 to show her gratitude. Having the ten demos made me feel like my day was a success. It was money well spent."

With all this money on my mind lately, I was seriously considering returning to Cleveland to pay that dude, Steve, a visit. He owed me money, and I wasn't trying to miss a dime. However, I chose to cut my losses and head back to St. Louis instead. There was a lot of money to be made there, as I remembered from the first trip. Although, this time, I was better equipped to make my mark in the Show Me state.

66

"Understanding The Plan"

Mr. Bod`e, I'm getting it now. I finally realize why each person that you met was so vital to your operation. There were a lot of moving parts and every piece had its intended purpose."

"William, I'm proud of you. Not only because of your attentiveness but because you are the only one who truly understands the plan. That is why you were chosen. Your intuitiveness is unmatched by no other. Indeed, you are correct, there area lot of pieces to this complex puzzle, however, once they're all put together, it's a beautiful masterpiece."

"So, in your travels, were there any moves made unnecessarily?"

"Actually, I was kind of skeptical of heading to St. Louis. I didn't really know how things would pan out. The "Lou" as they called it, has some very peculiar people, yet there was a great deal of money to be made there. I had to at least see what it had to offer."

"Well, tell me more."

St. Louis was a place like no other. Missouri was called the "Show Me" state for a reason, maybe because the people were more about action than a bunch of talk. That's how I like to operate anyway, don't talk about it, be about it! My contacts who directed me there knew that I would flourish in that environment. Everything just had to be connected and I would play my part. I did just that.

I stepped out the first day off the plane, commanding attention. I had on my Gucci framed eye glasses, beard trimmed to perfection, and even though I wore some ordinary looking workman Levi jeans and a crispy white Tee, the diamond encrusted Movado told everybody that I meant business.

My first stop, as always, would be Alamo car rental. I had reserved a vehicle under my new alias, William Dash, and from this day forth everyone here would know me as such. Exiting the airport garage, I took the twenty-minute ride towards the south side onto highway 170 to 70, exiting 244 and making a left towards 212 Kings Highway at the Chase Park Plaza. After a good night's rest, I would be ready to take on my targeted interest, Big Box, Less-A-Lots, Electronics *R* Us stores and a few more.

It seemed like time was on pause trying to go to sleep. My thoughts were dancing with figures and whom I was going to put on my list. I had a few names and in the morning, I was determined to put all my efforts into phase nine, here in St. Louis.

I got up early the next morning, studying the eight profiles, demos, matching each to its proper owner face by face. After an hour or so, I knew everything there was to know about Isaiah Denzel Washington, Rashid Lyondell Lynn, Michael Jones Jordon, John Singleton Davis, Greg David Stern, Willie L. James, Aaron Jimmy Kimble, Mitch Lee Daniels, and George Lucas Davis. These chosen ten were real professionals who not only sold, remodeled and flipped real-estate, but they kept all their business in order. There's always a lead man out of any crew, Leroy Brown was this man. He gave orders and they were followed.

My man Leroy, had everything in order when I arrived at the first place of business. When I arrived, I was only inside maybe 7 minutes. It took longer for the bank tellers to compliment me on how good I smelled and to engage in some small talk then it took to look over the amount, make the transaction, and grab my receipt. I was out the door and the wind with LeRoy waiting for rounds 2, 3, 4, 5, and 6. Hopefully, those go just as smooth as the first.

Like clockwork, we not only completed the tasks but in record time. We had, swift run all the other locations on my list located throughout city and metro areas. From how things were turning out in St. Louis, I knew my dealings would be short here. LeRoy and I decided to contact the rest of the team and go straight to the locations and fill the orders. LeRoy impressed me on how he ran his operation, allowing me not to feel any insecurity in his business practice.

Money always is a touchy subject, so after our long day's work, the inevitable was before us: the payoff. I made contact to arrange a meeting for later in the evening. My main request was for us to be alone at that time with no friends, no business associates. That way the exchange can go down with no hitches.

After I arrived at his office and entered around back as I was instructed.

"Here you go, my friend, $70,000 from the $100,000 in materials as we discussed. No bull crap, all your cash." LeRoy had his game face on and was sincere in his generosity. It's hard to trust dudes in this game, every emotion is questioned. LeRoy put me at ease. That didn't mean I put all my trust in him just was good to be on the level on this one.

As the days went on, I continued in my successful ways. It was the right place and the most lucrative I've been throughout all the capers. They say "Show Me," well I showed them. So, with all the Big Box's, Less and A lot, and Electronics "R" Us stores I now had in play, I was about ready to formalize my team. I wanted 30 good qualified men for my future project.

With more orders to fill, I knew staying in the same place too long was way too risky. In this line of business, you had to be smarter than the game itself. Greed could distract you;

speed could get you caught up in the worst way. So I gathered my things to make my exit out of St. Louis, just temporarily, I would return when the time was right.

Just as I figured, LeRoy began calling me about his other 90,000 order grossing $60,000 plus another side order which he'd play the middle man to make some easy side money on the hookup. I didn't blame him, I'd do the same.

I checked the message LeRoy left on my way out of the city limits heading passed the famous Arch towards the expressway. I called him back on the throwaway phone we both agreed to conduct business on. No traces mean no problems.

"When and how many seats?"

"Tomorrow and he needs around 55, it's a good concert."

"Let your friend know there are only 9 seats left."

"I already told him that."

"Oh, okay, well, let him know that only one can get in free."

"Alright, what time can we get together?"

"I'll call you."

"Bet."

After our brief conversation, I quickly deduced the breakdown. Nine meant $9,000 and one get in free meant to take off $1,000, which went to LeRoy for the hookup. It was cool, my mission was to get back to Atlanta and regroup. There was a certain young lady I needed to see to get her on board. I also had to holler at Mr. Suave. It was time to put his paper checks into play for my next visit. The money would move some things for me, I just had to get my operations in order.

For the next 8 ½ hours, I cruised the highways in the new rented Black GMC S.U.V. The entire time crunching on Pringles and sipping on ocean spray cranapple juice. I chased it all down with a Five Hour Energy drink. My destination, the Gala-Suites, this is where I would stash my earnings. I would be resting at the Buckhead Estates a few miles away, never laying my head where my business was, just a precaution.

It felt good to be me, felt even better being back safe and sound in one piece. Everything was coming together, too good for just one man, I needed to put an elite team together, a team of identity theft bandits whom I could train. This would take some masterminding, but success always requires hard work.

I quickly made two deposits at the Gala-Hotel, one with the sum of $70,000 and the other $64,000, all in one-hundred dollar bills. I had a sudden urge to look at all my money together, I really wanted to see what a half a million looked like. With my brand-new money counter, I ran some water into the bathroom, sat down by the tub and put stacks of money in the machine, and watching the $100 bills flutter.

My count would total, $294,594.00.

67

"Money Moves"

At 6:45 a.m., I was up early feeling like a champ, Floyd Mayweather style. The new money from the intake had my nose wide open with the scent of fresh bills. Next on the agenda was to grab a quick bite to eat then focus on the execution of phase 10.

After taking in a little room service, I had to get a jump on the things I had to do that day. I climbed into the truck and drove over to the Estates, a couple miles from where I was. My mind was on upgrading to a loft. Mr. William Dash had standards and I wanted to be the best man I could be.

"Hi, welcome to The Estates, how can I help you?" I was staring at the image of the Estates development portrayed in a painting. If I didn't know any better, I would've sworn a female was yearning for my attention, but it was a man with a feminine sounding voice.

"Yes, I'm interested in a 2-bedroom loft."

"And when are you looking to move in, sir?"

"I was hoping today, if possible?"

"Well, let's see. What's your price range?"

"Maybe in the $1,500.00 per month range."

"Only, here's what I have in that range and here's what we have available now." He showed me some pictures in a brochure.

"Are any of these available now?" I really wanted to move in as soon as possible.

"Not for $1,500.00 per month, but for $1,898.00 the

Tuxedo will be available within a week!" Would you like to go see our demo unit?

"I would be delighted."

"This is the tuxedo?"

Yes, it's a very spacious two-bedroom loft, over 1,500 sq. ft., with a balcony, spacious walk-in closets, hot tub, standup glass enclosed shower, double sinks, and a view overlooking the city.

He gave me a tour of the tuxedo and we returned to the office where I put down a healthy deposit. Of course, I had to hear the normal blah, blah, blah, work history, credit history, you know the routine. I provided all the necessary documents then waited for him to run my background check. When you have nothing to worry about, you just sit back comfortably for the process.

"Mr. Dash, will you be able to put up the first and last month's rent plus deposit?" I almost laughed but kept my composure, "Next week is as soon as I can have the place ready for you, sir."

I wanted to sign those papers today, but I had to be patient. "I gave him my business card, call me and we can close this deal."

While waiting, I moved money over to Riverdale, Georgia, with a female associate of mine. It was a risky move for me, but I needed a discreet place, not too busy.

Before leaving my hotel room, I rolled up my money in $25,000 bundles then took it over to the makeshift stash spot. It took a total of thirteen days before I finally got the call that my new home was ready. I went to the office to receive my keys, my remote key card, parking number, and key remote code, then routed over to my new king's headquarters.

Now, there was the order of business of making this place a home. I headed to my office to setup first. At the same time, there was the matter of home furnishings; food, cleaning supplies, hygiene, dishes, bath essentials, you know the necessities. I went to Wal-Mart and seemed to buy everything in sight. The crazy part about it, buying so much I forgot all about the food I purchased left back in the cart. My bill was $1,145.77. Credit is such a wonderful thing, but paying with cash this go around was no problem at all. I will say, I've always respected the Big "W." They help in the community, plus returning to recover my food, my food cart was put up awaiting me.

Next on my agenda was to gather some electronics. My favorite place was Electronics R' Us because they would have everything I needed. I came out of there with a laptop, computer, fax machine, shredder, monitor, entertainment system with the surround sound system, video cams, 4-LCD screens of every size for all rooms and, last but not least, two 60-inch plasma televisions. I had everything brought to the front for purchase and the store associates came together to start loading them into the rented U-Haul truck. Going out was always a guarantee. I vowed to never come back empty-handed from the experience in the trials with Colby in Los Angeles. When it came to me professing, it always had been done correctly the first time. Next stop and final destination for the day would be for furniture.

It was time that I put the finishing touches in play. Designs Furniture was an upscale exquisite furniture store for the rich and wealthy located in the Atlanta-Buckhead area. I needed an MTV Cribs kind of look for comfort and a homely feel. Contemporary, yet sexy in all the right places, just like I like my women.

After making a cash payment, I confirmed and scheduled the delivery date to be last delivery of closing hours. Actually, making this possible, I briefly spoke to the delivery fella with a $100 hand trade. Making a king's palace is hard work but well worth the time and effort. I wanted everything to be the way I wanted it.

Traveling back to my loft, I thought about the amount of work I'd been putting in and how it was all beginning to bear fruit right before my eyes. How I see it, I've been blessed beyond measure. Even if others don't agree, my work is to make change for others and give back.

On my way off Hwy 85, I got a call from Chris asking me to come see him, he said it was urgent. We ended up meeting in the back of his store. He jumped in my truck and began explaining that he was relocating back home and this would be out last time doing business.

"Averie, I'm going to keep this brief, here's three boxes of approved applications that should hold you down for a good while."

"I'm not tripping on the money because I know you got me."

Now my antennas were up. Why would Chris call me out the blue and offer me over 200 credit apps without asking for a dime up front? Was he trying to set me up or something?"

"Get out!"

"What?"

"You heard me, get out my fucking truck, now!" I made my words loud and clear. And he slowly climbed out. I, too got out and went around to his side of the truck, whispered in his ear then turned him around for a pat down.

"Man, I ain't wired! You think I'm working with the fed's now, man?" Chris exclaimed.

"Don't know, but I'm damn sure not trying to find out the hard way."

After I did a mild search, we both got back in to talk.

"I'm no snitch, bro, and I sure as hell wouldn't try and set you up. I know you crazy."

"Crazy!"

"Man, I know you are crazy just being from Chicago. It seems all ya'll have something going on in the head that aint right." Little did he know, he would beg for the crazy side of me if he had it in his mind to set me up. I leaned in to whisper in his ear, "Chris, once I drive off, I want you to quickly go to your car, get in and let the driver's side window down. Now, go quickly!" I ordered him. He exited and did as I instructed.

By the time he got in, I drove to exit the parking lot, grabbed the thousand-dollar bundle I had in the armrest. I stayed alert, watching for any sudden movements or jump outs by the boys in blue. I put the truck in reverse and sped backward before coming to a screeching halt right at Chris' jet black Caddy. His eyes were big as the moon as I opened my door sliding the bundle of money in his direction, under his car. Without any traces of a transaction from one hand to the next, I pulled off just as quickly as I had arrived.

I took an extra half an hour to make this trip home to be absolutely sure I wasn't being followed. After I was sure I was not being followed, I made a trip to my favorite eating spot. The spot was the Diner off Piedmont and Roswell Road. I could see everything and everyone within a one block radius. I ordered chicken and shrimp alfredo and waited for my paranoia to settle.

I let another twentyminutes pass before I decided to head on home. I thought, maybe Chris was telling the truth, I couldn't tell, time would reveal. I dumped all the contents of each box, skimming through one credit app after another looking for the one that would fit my needs. Finally, one jumped out amongst the others, it was a profile like no other. A middle-aged male from a part of New York, single with no children, perfect for the cause.

Putting his to the side, I continued perusing through each application one by one until I came across one that raised an eyebrow. It was a credit that showed one Pastor Freddie Long. This was one I would not peruse. One of my golden rules is to never victimize churches or the elders. "That Kelvin Donald Thump I wouldn't give a hoots ass!"

After two hours of studying and matching profiles, I decided to give it a rest. My mind was settled on the one I put to the side and wondered why it tweaked my interest so much. It was as if it was a woman coming onto me strong, wanting me to take hold and become one with her. Well, I guess I will oblige her every wish and make this particular profile personal. In the morning, I would contact my source within the credit world and find out everything there was to know about this man.

68

"Team Players"

My thoughts consumed me as I sat back on my king size, sleep number bed, letting my mind race. I put the setting on 32 then sank deeper into the mattress wondering who was truly qualified to become members of my famed team. Before I began gathering Intel on Mr. David Samuels, the new profile I acquired from Chris' batch of apps, the team had to be secured.

Orchestrating a criminal enterprise was no short order. I felt like I was mastering my craft, but could only go so far without solidifying the people around me. Making this operation work on a grand scale would take work. Through my travels and local business connections, I was able to compile a network of potential associates.

First on my list was a woman by the name of Victoria. She was a former employee at Point Choice, which meant she had a vast knowledge of credit. She did a small stint in the banking industry working accounts, and then she switched gears and became a freelance consultant on money management. When I saw her at my cousin's party, a glow from her radiant smile is what caught my eye. It was as if the whole room stopped to gaze at her beauty, but she didn't carry herself as some sort of diva or debutant. She was more of a working professional in the disguise of a fashion model. Her speech was eloquent yet tactful, particular with her words and strategic with her motives. Definitely a thinker, which I liked and respected.

It took a while before I could put my trust in her. I wanted to make sure that what I was forming would fit what she had to offer.

In actuality, she didn't even know I was targeting her for a position in this organized, white-collar world of financial fraud. That alone could scare the average everyday 9 to 5 business person. However, she didn't appear to be the type to scare easy.

I needed her to help in the operation of this enterprise; she, in turn, was willing to take on the challenge of being the first lady of F.I.F. Because I've learned that beside every successful and powerful man is an equally powerful and supportive woman to complement.

After bringing Victoria aboard, others began to fall in by way of references and networks. Tom, Frank, Steve, Alex, Matt, Claude, and the other sub-level players became vital pieces to a team forming up to rival the Chicago Bulls of the 90's. Of course, I was in the role of Phil Jackson, so with that being the case, my childhood friend, Mr. B., would be considered my Michael Jordan.

We meshed instantly and had an unwanted working relationship for years which others would normally envy. However, that wasn't the case; there was nothing but mutual respect amongst this newly bonded unit. Mr. B. came highly recommended; his experience in different levels of business made him a valuable commodity and soon a loyal comrade. Anything asked of him, he delivered.

The next order of business was to get these new apps checked out. My home girl, Porsha was always reliable and always on point in her business. Sure, she had an attraction to me and didn't hesitate to show it by being overly affectionate. I played along but it was obvious that the cat and mouse would prove to be more harm than good.

"Averie, I ran all the credit apps and printed each one." I scanned the documents and then highlighted the things I needed to know. "Now, understand this, you cannot under any circumstances, show up here with your mess," she chided me in a way that I thought was cute.

"When you called my cell, I knew you wanted something."

"And I did. You mad Porsha?"

"Let's just say I agreed because I knew you needed this information immediately," her attitude was evident. "I just don't want them to start investigating me at my job."

"Then I'll bring you on to work for me."

"Ha-ha, Averíe, very funny. You know I need the benefits for my Asia, health insurance ain't cheap."

"I got you, Porsha," I said sliding her some money" for you and Asia of course. Leaning in to give her a soft kiss, she accepted and returned my gesture with a warm hug. I took her for a quick bite to eat then dropped her back off at her job.

Back to business, I called the Big Box and Less & A lot store locations, getting their credit centers to run the ten applications I chose for approvals. For the next hour, I went down the list of names and made contact with the representatives. To my surprise each of the ten were approved in the order of $30,000, $27,500, $25,000, $25,000, $25,000 $22,500, $22,500, $20,000, $15,000, and $12,500. I was pleased with the amount given; now I want to see how much I can pull together with these profiles in St. Louis.

Just to test my ability to change into this person, from the intel I had on him, I went on a fishing exhibition, contacting each relative until he had surfaced. After dialing a few times with dad, sister, and a cousin I finally made contact with the man that would make me famous. The greatest reward was that he was right here in town only miles away from me. I was more excited than a gay guy having balls in his mouth or a lesbian sucking on a fat ass tiddy. Using a non-traceable burner phone, I made the call to Mr. Samuels. "Hello… my I please speak with Mr. Samuels."

"He's in a meeting but I'll take a message and once he

comes out from his meeting I can pass the message over to him."

"Thanks, but I'll just call back, click!" That was my introduction to get closer to this man."

Within 20 minutes from the rush in my body, I traveled over to his office. Before leaving my Buckhead, office I had already run a check on this guy with full knowledge of his appearance. I now only needed to meet him face to face. As soon as I parked my car which was 3 blocks from his office I saw a man who fit the description of what I knew as Mr. Samuels. I quickly strolled across the street from a busy lunch, period of hungry business people; I fit right in without a trace that the enemy was walking into the life of Mr. Samuels.

There I was, standing 5 feet away in the shadows from my newly appointed identity. As he walked across the street I could only smile knowing this man was beneficial to my cause. Staring from a distance, I had to give him his respect by allowing him to live his last peaceful day. I continued to just marvel at how we had so much in common. But the one thing we did not, I would be a half million dollars richer and he would be the opposite in the hole from this day. Mr. Samuels, I am Mr. Averie Bod`e.

The following Wednesday, I had to pay a visit to Natasha, my face-lady. She had exactly what I needed; getting her to work on short notice was another story.

"Boy, what is it that you need now?" she said, acting like she wasn't glad to see me. "Averie, we haven't seen each other in a month and now you show up here unannounced like you with the I.R.S."

"Well in my defense, I am with the I.R.S. the Iron Rod Society, I am not only a member but the president." That made her burst out laughing.

"I hate you! What do you need?"

"Your very best work on these rights here."

"Hmm…all ten?"

"Yes, but especially this one."

"Why is this one so important? Wait, never mind, how fast do you need them?"

"I can sit and wait."

"In other words, right away."

"Yes please, sweetheart."

"I'm on it, Averie."

I decided to take my mind off things by making a few calls. I also kept a watchful eye for the ever-lurking authorities preying on business owners like Natasha. Minutes passed from contacting some people when my last call was placed to Leroy back in St. Louis, Missouri.

"Leroy, my friend, I'll be heading your way soon."

"That's the best news I've heard all week, hit me when you're on your way."

We kept it brief. We know the business that needed to be handled so there was no need for small talk.

Natasha walked up looking indifferent.

"Averie, I have good and bad news."

"Give me the bad first."

"My computer crashed, but I was able to finish 7 of the ten, the other three you'll have to get tomorrow."

"Tomorrow?"

"Yes. It's almost closing time and the system won't be up till tomorrow. The least I can do is bring them to you since you did get my car fixed last month."

"I can roll with that. Appreciate it, Tasha."

One by one I skimmed through my new faces. The last one I examined was my new benefactor, Mr. Samuels himself. I couldn't help staring at the details and authenticity. Natasha did an outstanding job with them. Now I just had to put them to work. What better place than St. Louis, Missouri. I booked a flight and got ready to introduce them to the American Identity Bandit.

I met up with Natasha before heading to the airport. She gave me the last three faces as she had promised. I paid her handsomely and got on my way. I had a date with first-class under the name of Mr. Davis Samuels, my main man.

69

"The Lou"

Mr. Campbell, would you like to take a break? I know this whole process has been grueling for you. For the record, I want you to know that your work has been appreciated.

"Well, thank you, sir. The experience, I can honestly say, has shown me another side of white collar crime. You, sir, are an example of a consummate professional. Just hearing and witnessing your story gave me real observation of the work put in to organize an enterprise.

"That's a very genuine compliment. And I am grateful to be in a position where I can make the world aware of what's going on right in their faces."

"Oh, I'm sure after reading this, they will be much appreciative."

"I agree, son, I agree. Mr. Campbell, we've developed quite a bond over a short time span. Is there anything that I can do for you at this juncture? We're almost at the end, and your life, your new life will be beginning soon. Let me know and I'll have Mr. B have it taken care of."

"Sir…"

"Please, call me Averie"

"Ok, Mr. Averie. But out of respect, I'll add the "Mr." You have been generous beyond measure. You and your team are embarking on something epic and I'm just honored to be a part of the process."

"Oh, you are more than part of the process, your involvement makes you a key catalyst to putting the nation on alert."

"You mention your times in St. Louis often. What made that city open to opportunities? In other words, it's flowing with money just has to be tapped into."

"Is that what made you return?"

"Once I had recognized that St. Louis was my sugar cane, it was just a matter of time before I knew I would go back."

Throwing my luggage on the bed, I pulled out my cell and gave Leroy a call informing him that I was in town. My mind was already set on staying a bit longer this time due to a few other things I had to do to fully legalize my trade. Leroy got his team together and within 30 minutes of my arrival, we were ready to work.

The scenario was basically the same, filling orders and making tens of thousands of dollars in a few hours. The only difference was the change of identities and the clients. Me posing as a hardworking contractor made everything believable. Everyone wants to deal with the common man.

In one of the Big Box stores, while making my transaction for payment, I met an attractive young lady working the register. As always, I saw this as an opportunity to turn on the charm and see where it goes. I struck up a general conversation on various subjects and she seemed interested in my stories about my travels and money made contracting. She had no idea the type of income contractors made. What she didn't know was that I was no ordinary laborer.

After about 10 minutes of waiting for my order to be pulled, it was finally delivered to the service area. My total was rung up at 17.874.09 instantly; the young clerk was amazed at the amount showing on the screen. I handed her my card, identification, and any other credentials needed to complete the transaction. She was still in awe, trying to figure out how someone of my status could afford such a will. Young guys, such as myself weren't doing it like this at least not seen by her.

"What's your name?" I asked, pretending not to see her name tag.

"Jessica," she volunteered.

"Beautiful name for a beautiful young lady. Can I come back and talk with you after your shift?"

"What makes you think I'm available to talk? Besides, you probably got other things to do than to make false plans."

"False plans?" I chuckled.

"Yeah. People like you don't generally make time for someone like me who work a job like this."

"I resent that. You can meet some of the most genuine people in the most common places. Now, what time do you get off?" She still seemed skeptical of my motives."

"I'll tell you what, if I don't show back here when it's time for you to leave, I'll come in tomorrow and hand you $1,000 cash." Her eyes nearly bucked out of her face, thinking she was about to get some free money. Little did she know that the whole situation was a win-win. My word was my bond.

"I get off at 9:00p.m."

"I'll be here at 9:00p.m sharp."

The rest of the day went smoothly. All the other locations ran like the first with the accounts totaling over $75,000. Business would pick up again tomorrow, hopefully with the same results. For now, I needed to rest for a few hours; 9 o'clock would be here before I knew it and I couldn't miss that by any circumstances.

Back at the hotel, I chilled in the lobby just watching people. In this business observing the way people move, how they interact, what they spend money on is important to know. You never know who could be a potential profile. I heard some loud talking and snickering between a couple of guys in an area near where I was sitting. They sounded a little bugged by the way they were joking and carrying on. Then one noticed me sitting there.

"Hey man, what's good?"

"Nothing too much. Just staying busy."

"How long you in town this time?"

"Maybe a week or so, why?" I really wasn't feeling all this buddy-buddy stuff. I don't do the drunk thing.

I was focused on my mission.

"We need to go and kick it before you get out of here, man."

"Cool, find out the spot that's jumping, then we'll hit them up." I just shot him a curve ball to send him on his way. I had no intention of partying with him or anyone else. I looked at my watch and saw it was going on 8:30p.m. Still having to wash and change clothes, I excused myself.

"Uh, man, I have to be going. I'll catch you in traffic."

"Alright, I'll meet up with you one of these nights."

No, he wouldn't because I would be giving him the slip for the rest of my time here. By the time I got myself together, it was nearing 9:00p.m. The Big Box wasn't far, so I was in good shape.

Pulling into the lot, there were way fewer cars than were there earlier. I managed to spot Jessica walking to her car, a new model Nissan Maxima. I didn't want to startle her, so I flashed my headlights a couple of times to get her attention. Smiling, she responded with a wave.

"Is there somewhere we can go to talk?" I said pulling in a spot next to her.

"Sure, there's a spot not too far from here, we can get a bite to eat."

"It's not too crowded, is it? I'm not in the mood for crowds."

"How about we can go to my place? It's about the same distance."

"OK, but can we just sit in the car when we get there? I don't' want you to think I'm one of those weirdo guys trying to take advantage of you."

"That's fair."

When we got to her complex I got in with her. We kicked some getting-to-know-you talk, then I decide to get to the point.

"Look, Jessica, I think we can help each other."

"What do you mean?"

"Do you work over at the desk all the time?"

"Yes, most of the time. Either there or at one of the cashier's stations, why? I went for the gusto and pulled out $5,000 to convince her of what I had in mind. Her eyes were glued to the knot in the rubber band."

"Oh, my God! That's a lot of money."

"Indeed. Jessica, I deal with more than this, probably way more than you've seen the average man have. At times, I help those in need."

"And how exactly?"

"By paying you cash for your services."

"Wait a minute! I aint no hoe if that's what you're implying."

I couldn't help but laugh hysterically.

"No. No. What I'm saying, Jessica, is this, everything that you do at work, do it naturally, no differently. All I need from you is you waiting on me when I come into the store. I'll have a series of gift cards, I want you to scan them with the amounts that will be placed on them. "Her mind was working. I could see the wheels turning."

"I suppose you have accounts and funds in place for this to work?"

"Jessica, I have already shown you the process works. Remember earlier? Those transactions were made for me by you. I have several accounts, way more than you can imagine. We can make this happen."

She was really thinking, recollecting how much she tallied my account to be earlier. "So, Jessica, before you respond, I'd like to know if you have any children or any outstanding loans that need to be paid off?"

"I do. I have two littleones, my baby girl is 4 and I have a 2-year-old son. Of course, I have this car note and other bills, you know the everyday usual. I could definitely use some extras but I need this job for insurance, plus I can't afford to get in any trouble being a single mother."

"If you don't mind, but is the father, or fathers, involved financially or involved at all?"

"I have two sperm donors who both aint shit!" Haven't seen nor heard from either over a year, so I'm mommy and daddy to my kids." I know this story way to well dealing with the moms at the registers from my journeys.

"Jessica, I'll pay you $800 each time you do the transactions, how's that sound?"

"Cash money?"

"Yes Jessica, cash in hand."

"And how long would we be doing this?"

"Only briefly."

"Briefly!" Why not as long as we can get away with it?" This totally surprised me. She was thirstier than I thought.

"We'll see how things go at first. We don't want you to be compromised. You already know not to tell anyone and if you see anyone watching or doing something different or suspicious I need to be called immediately. In fact, here's my phone, put your number in. you see mine, put it in yours."

"So, when do we start?"

"Your ass ready, huh?"

"I need some quick cash like yesterday. I've been trying to figure out how I was going to pay all my bills from the paycheck Big Box pays. Then this fell in my lap. Big Box don't pay us shit, and they average over 10 million dollars from each region per month.

"Okay, we can begin tomorrow. What's your schedule?"

"I work the morning shifts, so if you show up maybe between 12:00 noon and 12:30p.m., things will be slow. I can quickly scan all the gift cards to whatever amounts. Matter of fact, I'll text you when it's a good time and you just show up. Be on time."

"I'm always on time with my business."

"Thank you so much for this opportunity, I sure need it bad."

“Just don’t let yourself and those little kids of yours down, meaning don’t do anything stupid. I’ll know if you do.”

“Me, no sir. I’m very loyal and smart.”

“Well, just thank me after the cards are processed. We have to make sure they go through without static. Here, take this as a token of our success.” I slid her a crisp50 dollar bill. She gave me a big hug as she teared up before departing.

When I got back to the hotel, I had a hard time getting to sleep. My mind was in full motion. So much was riding on this one move. How fortunate was I. There’s a girl, a plain Jane who was in need. I didn’t even know if I could put my trust in her. Something in my gut told me to continue on with the mission and give her a shot. I wanted to make her dreams come true, making her debt free. I couldn’t wait to put this plan in action. It would prove to be beneficial for all parties involved. To Jessica Julie Frances was about to change her life and the long distance of Mr. David Samuels who I waited for this moment to become you and for the next thirty days, we became one.

70

"The Rise"

Today was going to be history in the making, well I was hoping anyway. I was up early, 7:35a.m., ready to fuel my body with a hearty meal from the breakfast buffet downstairs. By the time I got to the lobby, there was a line filing out of the restaurant adjacent to the front desk. With my bold self, I strolled up the front of the line and got in where I fit in. Pulling a tray, I gathered some fruit, a couple waffles, eggs, and a glass of orange juice. While I ate, I decided to do some studying of the profiles I had recently acquired. I started to have doubts, wondering if Ms. Jessica would even call. She could've developed a case of cold feet over night. It was still a few hours before she was due to call and I was anxious to start the transactions. I had an extensive list of client's ready to be ran.

My eyes were beginning to get heavy back in my room, a nap was in the very near future. A call interrupted me drifting off.

"Hey W.D, what's up man?"

"Who is this?"

"This is Buck over at Cristal Event Center."

"Oh… What's going on, Buck?"

"I wanted to know if you had any shows coming up, I'm looking to put something together."

"Not at this time bro, not at the time."

"Well if you come up with something, please let me know."

"I got you."

I hated to have to lie to Buck, but I had to blow him off. He knew good and well that our business hadn't been good in the past. Doing the music thing with him was almost always a lose/lose situation. The only time I profited was when I did the thong contest with the girls shaking their asses; we made a nice piece of change. But then I turned around and lost with the Bad Boy show featuring Black Rob, Mark Curry, G-Dep, and others, they weren't that hot in the south. Ginuwine and his wife Sole' had mixed reviews and ended up diving. There was no way I would take a risk dealing with the Cristal Event Center again.

It was mid-morning and I needed to occupy my time somehow. So, I jumped in the Tahoe I rented and headed out to the mall. My guy Zac the jeweler was there with one of the most successful jewelry shops in the city. He was responsible for many of Nelly's pieces and one of two for St. Louis artist Chingy. Soon, he will be designing for me. He was young, cool, creative, and ready to be big time in the game.

My mall expedition bought me some time and a few packages. When I returned to my room, I sat my purchases down in the corner then took a load off. Was Jessica really going to call? Noon was upon me so I made a move to put some pressure on her. Right when I entered the elevator, I saw her name pop up on my phone.

"Is this Joe?" for a second I almost forgot who Joe was.

"Hey Jess, are we ok?"

"Sure, why you ask?"

"Just making sure before I got on the road."

"Everything is fine, in fact, I'm the only one working the service desk today so once you get here, come straight over to me so we can do our thing."

"Wonderful."

"See you in a bit, bye."

I hung up feeling dated. A new era of doing business was at my fingertips.

"So, Mr. Averie, I'm curious, what made you choose Big Box stores as opposed to others?"

"Well, Mr. Campbell, I did my research and found out that there were contractors looking for the best place for their materials. Big Box is the best store to cover big budgeted projects. This is where I found my niche."

"I have to admit, you took the buying and selling game to another level."

"Not quite where I needed to be, but I definitely put in work planning the process."

"I understand."

"Do you, Mr. Campbell?"

"Yes, after viewing my credit report, the one in which you invaded, I see where there are benefits for someone in your field."

"This is just the beginning. My intelligence will be revealed by operating my plan."

I had a confident stride as I walked across the parking lot. I didn't know what to expect on the inside but I believed in Jessica working her side of the deal. So much could go wrong. There very well could be suits inside waiting to ambush me. Once, inside, to avoid suspicion, I called her from the opposite side of the store. I could see her from where I stood, so I could see her reaction.

"Yes, sir, where are you?"

"I'm right outside, about to come in."

"Um… please, hurry it up."

When she hung up and I saw that the coast was clear, I strolled over to her. Pulling out several gift cards which needed to be activated I stepped up to the counter. Going into covert mode, I disguised myself well, with braids, a beard, and a slick New York accent just in case there were cameras watching and listening.

When she looked up I was in her face. "Yo ma, I need

these joints activated."

"Excuse me sir?" She had an annoyed look on her face.

"Jess, it's me woman! Joe, I must keep these folks thrown off. Can you do two transactions from the gift cards and I'll put whatever you want on each."

"Boy you're crazy. Give me the gift cards and I'll out whatever you want on each."

"Ok, there's $30,000 on this card, $25,000 on this one. So first put $10,000 a piece on these three, then on these two $12,500, this one has $15,000 split $7,500 on these two cards, on this, it has $12,000 so place $6,500 on this and $6,000 on this one. This will max out all accounts." As I instructed her she worked meticulously on the register. Jessica was a pro, following directions without any questions.

Transferring the last amount by scanning the original loan card over the gift card. Jessica reminded me that she gets off at 3:00 pm.

"Where can we meet up?"

"How about dinner at the Olive Garden? I'll take care of dinner and pay you double of what we've agreed on."

"Sounds good," she said while handing me the gift cards and receipts.

Without looking back, I was out of there. Someone was about to receive $82,000 in materials and me $55,000 in my pocket. Everything was smooth as butter. The first thing I needed to do was contact the buyers and alert them of the new process. Finally, everyone could just go in by themselves and make purchases at any given time. Only thing they had to do was swipe the card and their balance would show from each transaction.

This would be the new way of organizing white collar crime; however, for this all to work it would have to be accomplished by putting the checks in play. My genius associate, Mr. Suave back in Alpharetta Ga., would need to be contacted. Once I finished here, I planned to take my show on the road, city by city, state by state.

"Mr. Campbell, I seen two years going back and forth

making a lot of bad choices from the meeting with Mr. Chase to the infamous phone call to Mr. Colby, to the insider of Big-Homie in New York. Remember that?"

"That I do, sir."

"To the credit apps, I.D makers, face-makers and inside traders of Ms. Shundra, Ms. Porsha, Mr. Chris, Ms. Jessica, Ms. Cynthia, Ms. Jocelyn, and Natasha to the inventions of Mr. Suave the paperboy. The birth of William Dash by the sexy DMV agent to the banking Ms. Tawana, hideouts, and money stash spots and countless hotel stays, all that played a role in this intricate process. Every person had a purpose like Ms. Nina, the flight agent, car rental agent, even the unpaid job from Mr. Steve had significance in this operation. And now a half million is in arms reach, the start of the multimillion dollar gift card scam will put me on the map or the radar, which ever you choose."

"Either way, Mr. Averie, everyone will take notice."

"America, this is the takeover!"

71

"The Take Over"

The word was out in several states about the gift cards and how to operate them at various stores. They were better than golden eggs. Calls were coming in from clients in droves. These gift cards were like the crack epidemic from the 80s.

After the first few weeks traveling from one city to another by air and ground filling orders, the gift cards started to come in by the bundles.

My elite team of I.T.B was born, Identity Theft Bandits. There was another mission in motion; the money being compiled. My banker, Ms. Parker, had inspired and advised me to build an establishment by banking my money and investing it. Doing music, the right way had always been on my mind. It took a while, but I was finally able to finish my dream.

One thing still loomed, though. In the months to come, after millions have read my story, there will be those who will do their best to condemn me. The shock will be on them. I'm the only one who knows the truth of my intentions. It can't be revealed at this point because there's too much at stake; too much work has been put in to make this mission successful. Keeping my identity safe from the public until the end of this journey is of the upmost importance. You just remember this;

I could very well be watching you or even worse, in the process of becoming you.

"William, this is where you and Angela come in."

"How so?"

"I knew I had to put something together for you two for all the hard work that has been put in to get this project to work the way it has. Money, as in most things, is a motivator. So, I had to come up with a way to generate the two-million-dollar purse I offered you to write this story."

"With all the money, you've made, I don't see where that would be a problem."

I didn't want to come out of my own pocket if I didn't have to. So, I called the team together for a meeting which was focused on fundraising. The remaining credit applications I had in boxes from Chris, I used to produce cards. I personally took the time to sort through 200 plus applications then divided them up so that each team member got twenty a piece. Their job was to apply for the cards. One goal was to get 200 cards, all Big Box stores with credit limits ranging from $20,000-$35,000. The limit wasn't my priority concern because there was another purpose in mind.

Once the cards started coming in, I began putting the faces together to match each card. I worked out a flat fee of $10,000 that I paid out of my own pocket to ensure that we had what we needed. When we reached the 200 mark, that's when our networking skills kicked in. The team was responsible for selling their allotment of 20 cards and faces for $11,000 each.

Within a month's period, we were able to achieve our goal. The team diligently worked to meet their quota. For efficient communication, I set them up on a corporate plan with Mayweather Mobile Telecommunications so we could all be on the same network, able to handle business nationwide"

"So, William, this is how you were able to become an instant millionaire. You can thank this team for their efforts. Angela, since you're here, for your editing services, I personally put up one hundred thousand so that you would know that your time was valuable to us. Half of each of your purses was automatically wired into an account, which Mr. Campbell already knows. At the completion of the story, the remainder will be transferred to a banking institution of your choice.

"Sir."

"Please, call me Averie, enough with the formalities."

"Averie, you have a brilliant mind. They would need to know the compassionate side of you without getting clouded by the negativity that surrounds the stolen identity crisis."

"You are so right William. This story should enlighten not only those who have been victimized and look at me as a heartless villain but also those of this generation that will need to understand how important credit is and the effect it has if targeted. I admit my faults. The human side of me knows that I have an obligation to change the views of the public. In regards to identity theft, I am the disease and cure all in one. My hope is to show the people that wrong can turn into right with a change of heart and the stroke of a pen.

"William Campbell, you have the knowledge to help make this possible and for that I am grateful and the American people will be grateful also. Hopefully, by the end of this trial, all eyes will be opened. With all the dangers that lie within the confines our trusted country, I am at peace knowing that I made sincere effort assist in the healing process. Those who have been subjected to this growing crisis, remorse consumers my being. This story should to help those who need to know the "how's" and "whys." William, I want you to make sure this makes the news."

"I plan to pull my resources together in order to publicize this. The same media that wants to bring you down will be the same ones to raise you up."

"That's the spirit! I also have to applaud Equitax and their work to ensure the safety of the American people against identity theft. I hope to one day shake the hand of the Vice President of Public Relations, Mr. Stevens, I've watched how he shakes things up within his organization, I plan to pull him in real soon. I wish him the best keeping things in order over at Equitax, they're blessed to have him."

"Averie I believe you have their attention. Now that everyone is on alert and open to the possibilities what are you going to do with this platform?" "How about change?"

"Yes, William. We can… all change our ways. Don't tell me you haven't heard that beautiful song by the kids on YouTube?"

"I have," Angela blurted out, the kids at the school were singing it one day, "We Can Change Our Ways" it's on Youtube.com

"I was thinking how good the message could be as my inspiration to a new path.

We Can Change

Change Our Ways

Giving Us Hope

For Brighter Days

We Can Change

Change Our Ways

Let's Make a Stand

Starting Today

Then I can come in and speak to the people, America, take charge. Be more responsible. Get a credit report. Protect your good name. Place a fraud alert on your credit. There are numerous protection agencies. You do not want to become the next target. It's like losing your life. Get protected today.

"If Not!"
Averie Bod`e might become you!

72

"The Closer"

I sat at the conference table reviewing my notes for the conclusion of the part one of the story. Angela was across from me plucking away at her laptop, working the edits for the beginning of the book that had already been written. I could see Averie's face filling with pride as he watched us working together on his masterpiece. To see his life's experiences transposed on paper had to be a dream come true. Now, it was up to us to make sure this page was a must-read.

Honestly, this book has the potential to have a lasting effect on the public; maybe more impact than any other project I've worked on. The content alone makes it relevant to the needs of many. Awareness, sometimes, is all people want. They want to be made knowledgeable that there is a crisis present so they can act accordingly. Most people become victim's due to lack of information. After receiving the intricate details about identity theft, I now see the importance of this project.

Ms. Victoria entered the room looking radiant as ever. It seemed as if everyone had major stress relief knowing this stage of their lives was coming to a close.

"Sir, there's a Mawuli Davis on the line waiting to speak with you."

"Thank you, Victoria, I'll take it in a moment." Averie gathered some notes in preparation for his call. One thing I've noticed over the time with Averie is that he is very selective when it comes to those whom he allows into his private life. Usually, it's the relationship that makes him comfortable. The bond he forged with his attorney, Mawuli Davis, was instant and long lasting. A type of bond he knew he had to have, facing a situation like this one. He had done his research to find Mr. Davis.

His research began in Atlanta where he knew legal representation thrived. Mawuli Davis was a true Georgia native who fought for the "little man." In his 10 plus years litigating, Mawuli had amassed a flawless record defending his clients. In Averie's eyes, Mr. Davis had the total package and that was his basis for choosing him. Being a senior partner at Davis / Bozeman, Attorney at law, his credentials were exemplary, making those who opposed him cringe, and those who worked with him revere him for his ethical procedures.

Averie saw him as a stand out guy amongst the list of attorneys he had to choose to defend his life. He would put his livelihood in no other hands.

"Mr. Davis, how are you, my friend? How's everything looking with the case?"

"Averie, I have things in order, but I need you to return soon so we can prepare for this trial. This is no small thing we're dealing with here. These people up here are trying to bury you."

"The question is will they succeed? Hell no. You know why? Because you're the best attorney I could have handling this. How long have we known each other, Mawuli?"

"Averie, you know how long."

"Exactly, and I haven't seen you lose, have I?"

"None that I can recall."

"So why should this situation be any different? Listen, Mawuli, I want to do something that will impact the world."

"Oh Lord, Averie every time you start talking "BIG," you always have something up your sleeves. What now? Relax, this is going to be epic. I want you to set up a press conference."

"A press conference, Averie? I don't about that."

"Let me address the public, Mawuli, let them see me for who I really am. Besides, this whole thing is about the public, right?"

"Yeah…but…"

"So, let's make this a public setting, an open conversation."

"You know I'll have to get some major clearance to pull this off. This trial is so big; there will be a roll of red tape to cut through. Just come back this way and we'll discuss the particulars."

"I'll be on my way shortly, I just have one stop to make first. I'll contact you when I get there."

"Be safe, Averie."

"I will, and you be blessed, my friend."

After that lengthy interview with William Campbell, I felt mentally, physically and most of all, spiritually drained. I had mixed feelings about the trip back to Atlanta. This was the place that now held the fate of my future. What the public didn't realize was that my heart cried out for understanding. Only God knows the sincerity of my heart and He's the only one I trusted to be my intercessor. Throughout my travels and escapades, I did manage to attend church service from time to time. I'll admit that it wasn't as regular as I wanted it to be. Of course, my parents' voices always seemed to loom in my head.

"Averie, in life there are going to be ups and downs, good and bad times, the only thing that remains consistent is God's undying love for you and you should always take time out to thank him."

Hearing my parents talk about God's love and their commitment to reading his word gave me a sincere appreciation of just how much God loves me and I love God. So, I took their advice and went by the Word of Faith Cathedral to see Bishop Dale C. Bronner. My heart had been tugging at me and there were some things I needed to get off my chest. Bishop Bronner was one of God's chosen messengers. He listened intently before responding then gave advice only when necessary. When I sat down with him I immediately felt comfortable.

"I want to thank you for agreeing to meet with me, Bishop. Back in 2009, we talked briefly over the phone and had one face to face encounter, but never a meaningful session.

"Oh, it's really no problem. I'm glad you came in, now what's troubling you, Averie?"

"I've done a lot of wrong, Bishop," I confessed.

"Haven't we all."

"Yes, but it seems like my wrongs outweigh those of others."

"In the father's eyes, no sin is any greater than the other.

"I've taken from innocent people with no remorse."

"How do you feel now Averie?" That was a loaded question.

"Terrible, I want to make a change, make a difference."

"Well, with the things you're doing, you'll have a chance to help a lot of people, that's a start." I looked at him strangely. How did he know? "The spirit tells me that you are on your way to achieving great deeds that will impact the lives of many people, so much that it will overshadow the bad."

"I've been blessed with so many talents and haven't used them."

"I understand you have something big facing you, am I right"?

"Yes, I do."

"What do you see coming out of this?"

"I'm usually confident about the events that take place in my life but honestly, I don't know how this trial is going to turn out."

"Trials, trials are more than judgmental procedures, they are tests that come about in our lives testing the strength of our faith. God orders our steps and already knows the outcome before we even encounter a trial. So, it's up to us to rely on our faith to get us through. My question to you is where is your strength? Do you believe you've already won the battle or do you feel that the battle is yet to be won?"

"That's something I have to think about, sir."

"Well, Averie don't ponder too long because the day is near and your judgment awaits."

"Bishop Bronner, I know I'm not as strong spiritually as I should be but in time I'm hoping that will change. I just want another chance to show the positive that I can do."

"Be careful what you ask for Averie."

"What I really wish for is redemption. No matter what the outcome of the trial, I want the people to see the change in me. When I look in the eyes of the public, I don't want to see hurt, but hope. I know it's going to be hard for them, but it's worth the prayers. My actions are the only thing that matter from here on out. I'm searching for that peace, that place where the love that's inside all of us shows on the outside for all to see."

"That's something special, some people go a lifetime without that feeling. It's not impossible, nothing is impossible with God, but you'll have to put in some work."

"Bishop, I'm willing to do it if it means that lives will change."

"First things first, you will have to change."

"I believe I have, Bishop. I believe for the better."

"Averie lets pray. Bow your head son."

"Father God, we come to you with open arms, an open spirit, and most importantly an open heart. We sincerely ask for your guidance through life's trails. Even though you already know the outcome, we ask for the strength to endure the journey. For our wrongs, we ask for forgiveness, and for our future we look for the strengthening of our faith. Allow your will to be done in our lives. In your son, Jesus' name, amen."

Bishop Bronner continued counseling for another three minutes while tears streamed down my face. The presence of the Holy Spirit was strong in that place. I didn't want to leave. The visit to Word of Faith was a spiritual cleansing. After speaking with the honorable Bishop Bronner, I felt like

I could fight any battle and win; go up against any obstacle and overcome it. No longer did the threat of man's punishment put fear in me. My sights were set higher. I am now on a mission to uplift, using my life's experiences as a learning tool to teach others what not to do.

I still wanted to address the public but my attorney advised me against it. Due to the high public nature of the case, he said it would do more harm than good ultimately making his defense more difficult. We agreed to disagree and I had to heed his call because he had never steered me wrong. Before meeting with Mawuli to go over pretrial strategy with me; I felt confident that whatever he was preparing was adequate. Also after talking to Bishop, I realized that there was a higher power in control. Hopefully, my stay would put me in a position to help others so that one day someone would say that life had a purpose.

There was one piece of unfinished business I had to tend to.

"Ms. Victoria, did you overnight that package to Equifax Credit Bureau, like I asked you?"

"Yes, Averie just like you asked. Attention to Jim Stevens, Right?"

"Right. Could you get them on the line and confirm its arrival?"

"Sure, is there anything else?"

"Let me know what they say so I can do a follow up. Oh, and tell Claude I'd like to see him."

Victoria scurried off. Ever since Frank tipped me that special agent Taylor from the F.B.I had been stumbling up on our whereabouts, I became suspicious of some foul play coming from inside our twisted camp. Disloyalty was rearing its ugly head and I couldn't believe it. I even went as far as faking that I knew who it was in an attempt to flush out any infiltrators, but they disguised themselves well. That was until they got comfortable in their ways. The surveillance system Frank installed told the tale when I tapped in and heard the conversations between agent Taylor and one of our team members.

I changed our locale a couple times and we were still being watched, that's how I know it was from inside. The enemy was laying his head right next to mine. Too close for comfort if you ask me, but I had to remain calm, careful not to give the slightest hint that I was on to him. Now that the trial was about to commence, everything would come to the surface, my traitor and I would meet face to face.

"Excuse me, Averie but Claude is gone." Victoria reported.

"Gone! Gone where?"

"I don't know, but there's something else wrong. What now?"

"Frank is missing too!" Now that didn't add up. Something wasn't making sense.

"Sir?"

"What is it Victoria?" I was still angered by her last news.

"Why are you shouting at me?"

"I am sorry," I said, calming my tone.

"I have Dana Jeffries on the line from Equifax, you want me to call them back?"

"No, I'll take it, thank you." I composed myself and refocused on my purpose. This was the opportunity I'd been waiting for, and I couldn't approach him emotionally. I got my thoughts together then picked up the phone.

"This is Averie Bode for Jim Stevens," I said to the Equifax senior director of public relations, Dana Jeffries. "Well, did you receive a package today marked urgent?"

"Yes, yes, we did. We were wondering who was putting us on alert."

"It was sent to the attention of Jim Stevens, did he get it?"

"That's what he's meeting about now, sir."

"Tell Mr. Stevens, your boss, that you have Averie Bod`e on the line. I'm sure he'll want to speak with me."

I heard shuffling through papers nervously.

"I want to make sure I'm saying the name correctly; did you say everybody is calling?"

"No, it's Averie Bod`e."

"Please hold for a moment, sir." The hold music came on and was burning my ears up. Finally, he picked up.

"Yes, this is Jim Stevens Is this Mr. Bode?"

He didn't have a clue that I was watching his every move on my camera I had Frank put in. Over the weekend, he got in there while their so-called air-tight security was off their mark. The camera was minuscule, so it would never be detached. Mr. Jim Stevens was trying to lure me into a taped conversation for the secret service agents who were probably listening in. Right plan but the wrong man.

Click! Hanging up the phone was my next move. He would pay for trying to set me up. Here I am trying to help them. Equifax, I really was trying to be on your side, but now they will be back on the list of targets along with Life Lock and a number of other protection agencies, big and small, financial institutions and celebrities. I might as well consider the champ, Money Mayweather's finances as well, he sure wouldn't miss a couple million or so out of his pot. But the man who just jumped to the top of the list is Mr. Jim Stevens.

Averie Bode' never made it to the meeting with his attorney, Mawuli Davis. He felt the need to beat the heat and leave town without a trace. His residence, the executive, as it was called, was located in Buckhead. Somehow it was discovered and raided. Although he left nothing there that linked to him. His place still appeared as if he were living there. His well-designed office space was complete with 60-inch plasma televisions, computers, laptops, four LCD monitors and all the equipment, and cameras. Even the money vault was present. Yet Averie wasn't. Averie Bod`e's last sighting was somewhere in Seattle, Washington, but that was subject to change at a moment's notice. Those who spoke to him afterwards said he urged them to do what was right.

"Turn all this bad into good," he said. He also warned those who thought that they could capture him to remember that he could become anyone he wanted to. "Good luck in your attempts, you are going to need it", he often told them.

Epilogue

I had every intention of turning things around in my life. My confessions to the Honorable Bishop Bronner did stir some things up inside of me and my heart. The objection I had with the way this whole ordeal had turned out was the blatant disloyalty that was shown to me by one or maybe more of my so-called team members. We were embarking on a ground-breaking event in history and for whatever reason, someone had chosen to turn traitor. It happens but I never thought it would happen to me. From the infiltrator within to those on the outside, like Mr. Jim Stevens at Equifax, it was painfully obvious that even though you try to help make someone's life better, there will always be a hidden agenda. That alone could make a person feel underappreciated. The fact that a certain person or persons (I won't mention names because I have my eye on them) would go to lengths to learn about your organization and gain a measure of trust all in an effort to gather information on you. The act of treason leaves a lasting scar on your psyche.

So that's why I've decided to disappear, regroup, and figure out how I am going to attack this situation. Literally, I wanted to address the public about the dangers of identity theft and some of the ways to remedy it. My hopes now are that William Campbell can get the necessary press and promotion on this controversial story to raise the awareness. For me, there's still work to be done, not only on myself, but for other people. Some just don't get it. It's up to me and only me to make sure the light is shone brightly.

They need to know that the message is clear: they must understand that I mean business.

The fact that my life is at stake only means that your life could be considered expendable …

Only when it's… "Into The Wrong Hands"
but soon "Into The Right Hands."
AVERIE OUT!

Resources

New this year, the ***2017 Identity Fraud Study*** identifies and analyzes four consumer personas, Offline Consumers, Social Networkers, e-Commerce Shoppers and Digitally Connected, based on attributes and fraud risks. Significant finding are:

- **Offline Consumers** have little online presence, either social networking or shopping, are exposed to less fraud risk than digitally connected consumers, but their minimal digital life brings other risks. With a distrust of both online and mobile banking, these consumers take more than 40 days to detect fraud and incur higher fraud amounts than other fraud victims.
- **Social Networkers** share their social life in digital platforms (like Facebook, Instagram, Snapchat and other networks, but do very little e- or m-commerce, face the risks associated with having their personal information widely available to fraudsters who can use it to overcome security measures or socially engineer victims. This manifests in a 46 percent higher risk of account takeover fraud.
- **E-commerce Shoppers** (including m-commerce) expose their financial information to potential compromise and experience an elevated risk of existing card fraud. Sixty-two percent of these ecommerce shoppers made an online purchase within the past week. While this customer segment experienced the highest prevalence of fraud of any of the four segments, they also tended to catch it very quickly, minimizing the impact. Seventy-eight percent of fraud victims in this segment detected fraud within one week of it beginning.
- **Digitally Connected Consumers** have extensive social network activity, frequently shop online or with

> mobile devices, and are quick to adopt new digital technologies. Twenty-five percent of these consumers used a P2P payment service in the past week. Digitally connected consumers have a presence on an average of 4.9 social networks, are predominantly female... This also exposes them to greater risks, a 30 percent higher risk of fraud.

"After five years of relatively small growth or even decreases in fraud, this year's findings drives home that fraudsters never rest and when one areas is closed, they adapt and find new approaches," said Al Pascual, senior vice president, research director and head of fraud & security, Javelin Strategy & Research. "The rise of information available via data breaches is particularly troublesome for the industry and a boon for fraudsters. To successfully fight fraudsters, the industry needs to close security gaps and continue to improve and consumers must be proactive too."

Methodology

Identity fraud is defined as the unauthorized use of another person's personal information to achieve illicit financial gain. Identity fraud can range from simply using a stolen payment card account, to making a fraudulent purchase, to taking control of existing accounts or opening new accounts.

In 2016, Javelin conducted an address-based survey of 5,028 U.S. consumers to assess the impact of fraud, uncover where fraudsters are making progress, explore consumers' actions and behaviors and how it relates to fraud risk levels, and identify segments of consumers most affected by fraud.

Seven Safety Tips to Protect Consumers

Javelin recommends that consumers work in partnership with institutions to help minimize their risk and impact of identity fraud. The following are seven recommendations for consumers to follow:

- **Be smart on social media** – Social media can help you keep up-to-date on your friends lives, but can also help fraudsters stay up-to-date too. Reviewing your social media security settings to make sure that your profile is only visible to friends and connections is a good place to start in securing social media from fraudsters. Do not accept friend requests from people you do not know.

- **Protect online shopping accounts** – With fraud moving online, accounts with online shopping sites are valuable targets. Enabling two-factor authentication on sites that have that capability, such as Amazon, can make it significantly more difficult for fraudsters to take over your accounts. For sites without two-factor authentication, use strong passwords or a password manager to secure accounts.

- **Exercise good password habits** – Passwords have remained the de facto first line of defense for most online accounts, which has motivated criminals to compromise them whenever possible. Using strong, unique, regularly updated passwords helps reduce the value to fraudsters of passwords stolen in a data breach or through malware. Password managers can provide a convenient way to manage good password hygiene without resorting to writing them down, which could also place them at risk of physical compromise.

- **Place a security freeze** – If you are not planning on opening new accounts soon, a freeze on your credit report can prevent anyone else from opening one in your name. Credit freezes must be placed with all three credit bureaus and prevents everyone except for existing creditors and certain government agencies from accessing your credit report. While costs vary per state, typically each bureau costs below $20. Should you need to open an account requiring a credit check, the freeze can be lifted through the credit bureaus.

- **Sign up for account alerts** – A variety of financial service providers, including depository institutions, credit card issuers and brokerages, provide their customers with the option to receive notifications of suspicious activity. These notifications can often be received through email or text message, making some notifications immediate, and some go so far as to allow their customers to specify the scenarios under which they want to be notified, so as to reduce false alarms. Consumers should also consider signing up for identity protection services which can provide security that is difficult for them to obtain on your own, such as regularly monitoring credit reports for suspicious new accounts and screening for sale of personal information on the dark web.

- **Be alert for online transactions** – As EMV makes fraud at physical stores more challenging, fraudsters are moving to target online merchants. Some financial institutions offer alerts for online transactions. These can help quickly detect fraud. Since online fraud enables fraudsters to make many transactions in a very short period of time, quickly detecting fraud is essential to preventing greater losses.

- **Seek help as soon as fraud is detected** – The quicker a financial institution, credit card issuer, wireless carrier or other service provider is notified that fraud has occurred on an account, the sooner these organizations can act to limit the damage. Early notification can also help limit the liability of a victim in some cases, as well as allow more time for law enforcement to catch the fraudsters in the act.

Additional Consumer Resources

For a free, easy-to-use identity fraud risk assessment, visit Identity Risk Calculator.

To learn more about how consumers can protect themselves, visit LifeLock's blogs.

To report incidents of suspected fraud or identity theft, visit the FTC online.

About Javelin Strategy & Research

Javelin Strategy & Research (@JavelinStrategy), a Greenwich Associates LLC company is a research-based advisory firm that advises its clients to make smarter business decisions in a digital financial world. Our analysts offer unbiased, actionable insights and unearth opportunities that help financial institutions, government entities, payment companies, merchants, and other technology providers sustainably increase profits.